SECOND TO NONE

Further Titles by Stella Cameron from Severn House

ALL SMILES
NO STRANGER
SECOND TO NONE
SHADOWS

SECOND TO NONE

Stella Cameron

severn
House

This first world hardcover edition published 2012
in Great Britain and in the USA by
SEVERN HOUSE PUBLISHERS LTD of
9–15 High Street, Sutton, Surrey, England, SM1 1DF,
by arrangement with Harlequin Books.
First published 1987 in the USA in mass market format only.

Copyright © 1987 by Stella Cameron.

British Library Cataloguing in Publication Data

Cameron, Stella.
  Second to none.
  1. Nannies--Fiction. 2. Love stories.
  I. Title
  813.5'4-dc22

ISBN-13: 978-0-7278-8114-4 (cased)

To our son, Matthew Cameron

All Severn House titles are printed on acid-free paper.

Severn House Publishers support The Forest Stewardship Council [FSC],
the leading international forest certification organisation. All our titles that
are printed on Greenpeace-approved FSC-certified paper carry the FSC logo.

Printed and bound in Great Britain by
MPG Books Ltd., Bodmin, Cornwall.

Prologue

He wasn't blond. Maybe that's what kept her from the expected response to his famous charm. From the look on her face every time Redford came on the screen, this was a lady who preferred blondes. Not that he was averse to Redford getting her in the mood, if that's what it took. Anything for the desired effect. He'd certainly struck out with every line of approach he'd made in the last four months—until today. Today they were finally alone, if sitting in a movie theater with a couple of hundred people could be called being alone.

Nuts. What was his problem? A man who used to need a forklift to move his little black book had to be nuts to ask the same woman out—and be turned down—repeatedly for four months.

The seats were the pits. No room for the long legs and athlete's body that caused at least a flicker of interest in the eyes of every woman he met, except Sophie Peters. He shifted to a position where he could watch her. The movie stunk, but he wasn't here to see the movie.

Sophie was blond, too. A little woman with long, pale blond hair, always tied back, and brown eyes and small pointed features, and a boyish figure. Not his type. He propped his chin on a fist. She leaned forward, eating popcorn, deeply engrossed in good old Redford batting his baby

blues. If she wasn't his type, why couldn't he keep his eyes—
or his mind—off her? The only things he did keep off her
were his hands, and that wasn't his idea.

"Popcorn?"

He didn't react quickly enough. She'd turned in time to
find him staring at her. "Er...no, thanks." He shook his
head, but she'd already returned her attention to the screen.

Could he be a man who couldn't resist challenge? He
shoved out his lower lip, considering. No, she was definitely appealing, and he was getting older, more mature,
ready to want a woman for her mind. He put a hand over his
grin. Who was he fooling? He might be thirty-four, but he
was as capable as ever of playing the field. So, he'd better
get on with the game.

Caution was the key in approaching Sophie. She was
skittish, shy despite her almost coquettish manner; her instant shrinking away from any physical contact proved that.
Slowly, carefully, his eyes firmly fixed on the movie, he
dropped his hand to her arm, stroked the backs of his fingers along her wrist and reached to hold her hand.

Popcorn, rained against his face, cascading into his lap,
brought him upright.

"What the—"

She'd twisted toward him, stiff, glaring, first at his eyes,
then his hand—which firmly grasped her thigh.

Chapter One

Western Washington wasn't supposed to be hot in June—not this hot. Sophie pushed at damp wisps of hair with the back of her forearm. A child's fretful cry sounded from an upstairs bedroom. As usual, Maren Dorset, two years old, was protesting her afternoon nap. Sophie twirled a glass chimney from the dining room chandelier through soapy water in the kitchen sink. As soon as Maren's four-year-old brother, Justin, woke up, too, she'd take both children to the lake.

Behind her, Abby Dorset sighed yet again. "I can't make anything of this balance. Sophie, do you understand why a man would ask a mathematical disaster to help with his books?"

Keeping her hands over the sink, Sophie looked at Abby. "Because he likes to share everything that matters to him with you?" She smiled fondly. In the year she'd worked as live-in nanny to Nick and Abby Dorset's two children, she'd come to care very much for the couple. They had their troubles, but they also had the kind of marriage Sophie admired, one based on friendship as well as love.

Abby scraped back her chair and stood. An exceptionally tall, slender woman with short black curls and great gray eyes, she made Sophie feel insignificant. The only vital statistic they had in common was their age. Abby was also thirty-one.

Abby came to stand beside her. Instantly, Sophie felt short and graceless. "Michael's coming over this afternoon," Abby said, leaning a hip on the counter, and Sophie knew that, as usual, she was being watched for some reaction to Michael Harris's name. These people were tenacious, she'd give them that. For months and months Nick and Abby had been trying to match her up with Abby's too handsome, too self-assured brother. Even a disastrous first and only date, eight months ago now, hadn't deterred the Dorsets' efforts.

"He really likes you, you know, Sophie," Abby said persuasively. "I don't know what happened between you that time—"

"Please, Abby—" Would she ever be free of the questions about her mini-encounter with the amorous Michael?

"And I don't want you to tell me," Abby continued, and Sophie knew she lied. She very much wanted to know what had happened. Perhaps if more had happened to put Sophie off, explaining would have been simpler. Dumping popcorn in a man's lap and fleeing a movie theater with him chasing after her, simply because he'd put a hand on her leg sounded juvenile, ridiculous.

"Sophie," Abby began tentatively, "has someone been talking to you about Michael?"

Sophie paused in the middle of rinsing the chimney. "Talking to me about him? What do you mean? What would they say?"

"Oh, nothing." Abby colored slightly. "I wondered, that's all. He did have a bit of a reputation as a womanizer when he was younger, but he's changed, really he has."

If he had reformed, he certainly camouflaged the improvement well, Sophie thought, hiding a smile. "I'm sure he's a perfect gentleman," she said. "Anyway, who would talk to me about him? Apart from you and Nick, I don't know anyone here.''

"Well..."

"Don't worry about me, Abby." Sophie inclined her head toward the jumbled papers on the kitchen table. "Nick's in his study, isn't he? Maybe he could help you with those."

Abby's eyes crinkled at the corners. "And maybe you want to get rid of me and my interference?"

"I didn't say that." But Sophie laughed as Abby picked up a ledger and left the room.

When she was alone, Sophie dried the chimney and her hands, clamped her Walkman headset firmly over her ears and hurried to finish cleaning up the kitchen. She wanted to be ready to take the children to the park the minute they were both awake. They could paddle in the shallow edge of the lake and cool off... and, at the same time, she could hope to miss running into Michael Harris. She paused in the middle of wiping gummy fingerprints from the refrigerator. He'd been apologetic after their movie date, had begged her to go out with him again, and begged, and begged, in vain. She didn't need another man obsessed with his sexual prowess. One had been enough, the one she'd loved and married and eventually lost. The next man in her life would be someone interested in her mind more than her body.

Sophie laughed aloud and dropped to her knees. She didn't have much to worry about. As her husband had so often pointed out, most men wouldn't be interested in a female body permanently arrested in adolescence.

She sat back on her heels, hands on her hips, and made a face at her wavery reflection in the front panel of the refrigerator. For several seconds she bounced in time to the music blasting her ears. The sound was too loud for safe listening, but she liked it that way. Turning sideways, she made an elaborate pout and expanded her chest, then let the breath out in a hiss. "It's quality that counts, baby, not quantity," she remarked and attacked the smudges with fresh ardor.

A light tap on her shoulder, followed by muffled words, froze her in place. *Oh, God.* Slowly, on her hands and knees now, she looked up. Michael Harris smiled benignly down at her, and his moving lips let her know he was trying to communicate.

"What did you say?" Sophie ignored his proffered hand and scrambled to her feet, praying he'd just arrived.

She cringed when he lifted one earpiece away from her head. "I said, I couldn't agree with you more."

He had heard. She blushed, crossed her arms over her chest, and couldn't think of a thing to say.

"About quality," he shouted, his face set in a serious pattern, although his deep blue eyes glinted. "It's much more important than . . . than quantity."

Sophie felt murderous. Drawing a deep breath, she removed the headset. Achieving more than external composure around this arresting dark-haired man had taken months after their infamous date. Dignity was hard to accomplish with a male who dwarfed you, who always found a way to stand too close, and who managed to make you feel like a bug on a slide. The kind of ammunition she'd just given him could return her to square one in the game of cat and mouse he seemed determined to play with her.

"How are you, Sophie?" His disarming smile had its usual unsettling affect. "Wilting like the rest of us?"

In other words, she looked as crummy as she felt. "I won't be sorry if the weather cools off a bit," she said offhandedly. "Nick's in his study. Abby's with him."

If she hoped to dismiss him, she'd have to be more inventive. Michael didn't budge. "What are you doing tonight?" he asked.

Trust him not to miss a chance to annoy her, Sophie thought. He'd stopped asking her out several weeks ago.

Now he was launching a new campaign. "I'm going to bed early—" She blushed again.

Michael regarded her very solemnly, his black brows arched. "Are you tired?" he asked. His ruffled hair gave him an almost innocent look—almost. "Have you been working too hard? I'll talk to Nick and Abby—"

"No," Sophie interrupted. "That won't be necessary. Saturday's my early night, that's all. I like to go to bed with a good book." She closed her mouth firmly. Michael was in what Abby termed "one of his moods," which meant he was impossible, determined to bait any convenient victim with his infuriating brand of humor. His broad grin suggested he was about to make another of his suggestive comebacks.

He spread his hands on narrow hips. Sophie followed the motion. His hands were broad, the fingers long—and she already knew how strong they were. Silence became painful as she waited for him to say something. Finally, he shook his head and backed away.

"I guess I'll go find Nick and Abby. See you later, maybe?"

"Maybe." Not if she could help it. He unnerved her too much.

After he'd left the kitchen, she still felt his presence—big, vibrant and too sexually powerful. His interest in her puzzled Sophie, unless he was one of those men who regarded any female holdout as a challenge. She dragged her baggy cotton T-shirt farther down over faded, too large jeans. Who was she kidding? Michael Harris was the kind of man who could have any woman he wanted. She'd guessed he was used to women swooning in his path long before Abby's comment. Sophie wasn't his type. He went for women like the one he'd brought to dinner one night, a glamorous, voluptuous, dark-haired siren guaranteed to reduce any man to putty. Michael's movie date with Sophie had probably been to please Nick and Abby, who seemed determined to worry about her social life—or lack of it. And now he couldn't resist teasing her.... But he had kept asking her out for four months before the movie thing.... And he had asked her again afterwards, many times.... And then, just now...

The kitchen door swung open again. "Back to the drawing board," Abby grumbled, tossing the ledger on top of the heap of papers and dropping into a chair. "I thought I wouldn't have to do any of this once we got the computer. Figures aren't my strong suit." Abby headed the display design team for a major store in Seattle. This elegant house at Leshi on Lake Washington reflected her artistic talent, her eye for the beautiful. She was a woman who disliked routine and logic.

Sophie made a sympathetic noise. With Michael Harris, Nick Dorset ran Islands Unlimited, a seaplane charter service between Seattle and the San Juan Islands to the north. Much of the paperwork for the firm was done here at home, in Nick's study, and Sophie also wondered why the expensive computer system they'd installed wasn't being fully used.

"Well," Abby said, pushing the papers and books from one side of the table to the other and back, "Nick wasn't any help, and I can't make these look right. From what I can tell, we're either a million or so in the black, or in the red. Hopeless. Nick and Michael are going to have to give the time their finances need, or hire a bookkeeper."

"Yes," Sophie said. Figures *were* her thing, and computers, but she wasn't going back to that—ever.

"Did you see Michael?" Abby asked, her eyes firmly fixed on a sheet of paper in her hand.

"I saw him." What would it take to deflect Abby from her Cupid mission? "Shouldn't he be flying today?" Sophie put her Walkman on a counter. Her composure suffered every time she saw Michael Harris, and he popped in and out of the Dorset home as if he lived there.

Abby threaded and unthreaded her fingers for several seconds before she replied. "The charter was canceled," she commented abruptly.

And Nick Dorset was also spending Saturday, usually the busiest flight day for Islands Unlimited, holed up in the house. Sophie had seen him early this morning when he'd come silently into the kitchen for coffee and left without a word, even to Justin and Maren. Justin had offered his usual stream of questions to his father. Nick absently ruffled the boy's reddish curly hair, patted Maren's pudgy hand on top of her high chair tray, and drifted out with a faraway expression in his eyes.

"Is...are..." Sophie stopped. It wasn't her place to ask if Nick and Michael's business was in trouble. But she knew the signs, and some of them were beginning to show up in the slight edginess she felt in the household. The years she'd spent running a travel agency with her husband before his death had given her plenty of exposure to small operations that failed. She decided to change the subject. "Will your mother be coming by this afternoon?" Wilma Harris was another subject Sophie preferred not to think about, but she worked hard at hiding her feelings about the older woman from Abby.

Abby looked up sharply. "Is Mother a nuisance to you, Sophie?"

"No, no," Sophie said quickly. With her husband dead, Wilma had little to occupy her mind but her children and grandchildren. Sophie understood emptiness only too well, and the need to fill vacated spaces in a life. "She's crazy about Justin and Maren, that's all. She likes to be with them, and I can't blame her for that." Her smile was genuine. She'd come to love the children as if they were her own. One day she might be lucky enough to have her own.... The thought dwindled away. Other people's children were just as good as her own for now.

Abby's skeptical "Hmm" made Sophie glance up. The other woman was watching her thoughtfully. "If Mother does become a problem you will tell me, won't you?"

"She's not a problem," Sophie insisted, avoiding Abby's eyes. There was enough potential strain around here without adding more.

Any further thought on the subject was cut off by the front doorbell. Sophie took delivery of an Airborne Express pack and stood in the hallway, considering the unwelcome prospect of facing Michael again in Nick's study. Unless she wanted to look idiotic by asking Abby to take the package to Nick, she didn't have a choice.

She walked reluctantly, her tennis shoes squeaking on the parquet tiles, past the living room with its striking Oriental decor and into the corridor leading to the study.

Outside Nick's door, she hesitated. His normally pleasant voice was raised, punctuated by Michael's softer, conciliatory tones.

Sophie lifted a knuckle to knock, then drew back once more. The door stood slightly open and Nick's next comments came to her clearly. "We'll just have to cut corners, find places to pare down. Any frills will have to be trimmed for a while. The business is out there, and we'll get it eventually if we can outlast the competition. These things take time, and we have to make sure we stay in the running."

Her warm skin turned clammy. Cut corners? She'd been right. There were financial difficulties with Islands Unlimited. Was she a frill they'd consider cutting back? Now of all times Abby wouldn't give up her job, and someone reliable had to look after the children. But Wilma Harris had made it clear she'd be happy to fill Sophie's shoes free of charge. "So much better for children to be with someone of their own," she'd said more than once when they were alone.

"Nick." Michael sounded exasperated. "We can't cut back any more. We're running on air as it is. Cash flow is our problem. We need an infusion of capital, and to get it we'd better be able to lay out a pretty concrete picture of how we intend to pick the operation up by the bootstraps and make it profitable.''

"Great," Nick responded. "All very logical. And how exactly *are* we going to become profitable?''

Michael's answer was too muffled to hear.

Nick's laugh made Sophie wince. "Neither do I," he said. "But we've got two damned expensive planes to pay for. They're what I always wanted, and I'm not giving them up even if I have to quit eating to keep them in gas. I owe that to you, too, Mike. I know that. You gave up a successful career and threw in a lot of money. I owe you...." His voice trailed off.

"Successful career?" Michael said. "I was washed-up as a flier, Nick. You saved me from the scrap heap."

"Bull," Nick said sharply. "You know what I think about that, so drop it. We've been through a lot together and we're finally on our way. This business is what we dreamed of for a long time and we're not bowing out without a fight. Now, what are we going to do? And by the way, I don't want Abby dragged any deeper into this. She's already strung out."

Sophie wiped first one, then the other palm on her jeans. She'd heard all she wanted to hear—more than she wanted to hear. She rapped on the door.

Nick called for her to come in, and she slipped into the room, shot forward to drop the package on his big desk and started to retreat.

He tipped back his swivel chair, giving her a smile that didn't touch his gentle brown eyes. "Everything going okay, Sophie? I haven't seen you all day."

She didn't remind him that he'd been with her in the kitchen that morning. "Everything's terrific." Her hand closed on the solid edge of the door.

"Don't run off," Nick insisted. He looked at his watch. "Tell me how those children of mine are behaving."

Sophie felt sorry for him. In recent weeks she'd got the impression he was trying to cover up some sort of strain. Now she was sure of it. There had been moments when she'd feared a rift between Nick and Abby, but at least she could now put that idea aside. The tension she'd sensed was a result of business difficulties rather than personal differences, and she could cope with that. She couldn't have borne it if two gentle people, so well suited and obviously in love, were drifting apart.

"Are they behaving?"

She jumped when Nick repeated his question. "They sure are," she assured him. Just outside her line of vision, somewhere behind her left shoulder, she felt Michael. She felt his eyes boring into her and pulled awkwardly at the hem of her T-shirt.

Nick was smiling and rocking, evidently trying to think of something to say. He was such a good-looking man and so thoughtful—the kind of man she'd like to meet. Sophie looked away, vaguely uncomfortable with the thought. She glanced over her shoulder and directly into Michael's deep blue eyes. He smiled and she wished the smile weren't quite so lacking in guile.

"Michael," Nick said, and she jumped again. "We've really found a gem in Sophie. Abby says so every day, and I agree. She makes it possible for us both to do our jobs without worrying about those two rascals of ours."

Overkill, Sophie thought and lowered her eyes quickly. Saint Sophie Peters was on the block before Michael Harris again. Why were Abby and Nick so determined to push them together?

"I know how wonderful she is," Michael said in a soft voice that caused Sophie to glare suspiciously at him. "I certainly wouldn't want my nephew and niece in any other hands."

He was making fun of her, but she inclined her head and smiled what she hoped was a modest smile. "Thank you,

Michael. I'd better get back before my halo grows any mold.''

Before she could make another move, the door was knocked from her hand, and Justin squeezed past her legs, holding Maren firmly by the hand. "We're here, Daddy," he announced stoutly in a voice that said he knew he shouldn't be interrupting but intended to bluster his way through. "I can't find Mommy or Sophie and look what Maren did.''

Nick leaned over his desk to look down at his blond daughter whose diaper rested on top of bare feet. The bottom of her sundress was soaked. "I see," Nick said and coughed into a fist. "That's a bit of a problem, particularly if she wants to walk. But Mommy's working in the kitchen, and Sophie's over there, Son. You just trod on her coming through the door.''

Justin didn't look at her. "What are we gonna do about this kid, Daddy?" he went on as if Nick hadn't spoken. "Is she ever gonna get trained or what?''

Sophie grinned and felt sad simultaneously. The boy would always go directly for what he wanted, and right now he wanted more of his father's attention than he'd been getting recently. Justin was Nick's adopted son, Abby's child by a first, very unsuccessful marriage, but Nick left no doubt as to how much he cared for the youngster.

"It's a worry, this training, Justin," Nick said gravely. "But we'll lick it, the same as your mom and I did with you. I'd help out now, but I really have a lot of work to get through, so how about letting Sophie take over?''

"Yeah, Justin," Michael broke in. "Your dad's busy and so's your mom. I'll give a hand, though." He swept up a shrieking Maren by a hand beneath each of her arms and set off for the stairs.

Justin followed at a trot, yelling instructions, and Sophie turned, too. In the doorway she looked at Nick and frowned. He was part of a conspiracy against her, and it wasn't going to work. Nick lifted his palms and shrugged before turning to the computer. As she entered the hall, Sophie realized he'd been using the machine to play black-jack.

She shut out her concern over the Dorsets' money worries and took the stairs two at a time. Michael Harris was going to bug out and quickly.

In the nursery, Maren sat naked and laughing on the changing table, while Michael did an imitation of a rabbit scratching its nose. The more he sniffled, rubbed imaginary ears on top of his head and preened supposedly two-foot-long whiskers, the more Justin and Maren howled. Maren was hiccupping.

Sophie watched from the doorway for a minute before they noticed her. Michael was great with the children. He really loved them and it showed. But he was getting them too excited.

"I'll take over, thank you," she announced, entering the room. "Calm down, you two, or you'll be sick."

Justin groaned and leaned against his uncle's legs. "She's all right," he said, looking balefully at Sophie. "But she fusses lots. Are we going to the park?" he added without missing a beat.

"I don't know," Sophie said. "We'll have to see how good you are."

"She always says that," Justin remarked conspiratorially to Michael. "It means we're going."

Sophie couldn't help returning Michael's grin. He took a disposable diaper from a box and tipped Maren onto her back. "Okay, young lady. Let's get you comfortable for your outing." He deftly stripped backing from sticky tabs and pressed them in place. "Better wear pants if we're going to the park."

We? Sophie already held cotton pants and a tank top for the toddler. His face blank, Michael took the clothes from her and slipped them on Maren, who promptly drooled on the clean top. She was cutting a molar and had crammed four fingers into her sore mouth.

"I think we should wait for another afternoon when we can leave earlier," Sophie said. She wasn't about to be marooned in the park with Michael and only a couple of tots as chaperons.

"You promised," Justin wailed.

"Promised," Maren echoed around her dripping fingers.

Both children fixed her with doleful gray eyes.

"I did not promise. And Maren's teething. Her mouth hurts."

"We'll find somewhere to buy her a nice cold ice cream," Michael said helpfully. "That'll do the trick."

"Yeah," Justin agreed. "That'll do the trick. Can we go now?"

She was losing ground. "There isn't much time before dinner." She attempted a matter-of-fact tone. "You wouldn't want to get there and have to come right home."

"With two of us to help, we'll make twice as much of the time," Michael interjected. He gave her a cherubic smile. "And after all, Sophie, it's not quantity that counts, it's quality—in all things."

Chapter Two

"There's a name for what you just pulled."

Michael stared innocently ahead at the road, wind whipping his dark hair this way and that. "Do you like convertibles?"

Sophie couldn't help smiling. He was impossible. "Do you always avoid answering questions? This is a nice car. What is it?" She glanced over her shoulder at Justin and Maren who were securely buckled into a minuscule back seat.

"Triumph," Michael said, turning a brilliant grin in her direction. "English car. Glad you like it."

He rotated the wheel sharply, and Sophie automatically leaned into a curve. The little red sports car swept onto the floating bridge over Lake Washington and headed away from Seattle and toward Mercer Island.

"I thought we were going to Seward Park," Sophie shouted.

"Luther Burbank's better," Michael responded, narrowing his eyes against the sun. "And I'll bet you always take the kids to Seward because it's close to Leshi and home. You need to get out of your rut."

Exasperated, Sophie shook her head. Even when he seemed to be trying for peace he managed to be insulting. She quelled an impulse to say that since Luther Burbank

Park was close to his Mercer Island town house, he was probably the one in a rut.

"Ice cream first," Michael announced. He detoured through a shopping district and bought cones for himself and the children. Sophie didn't feel like ice cream. Agitation made even the thought of food revolting. She prayed she would survive the next hour, or however long it took to extricate herself from Michael's company, without incident.

By the time they'd parked and lifted Justin and Maren from the car, both children were covered with winding rivulets of melted ice cream. Sophie mopped at them with a cloth from Maren's diaper bag. "They aren't allowed to eat in cars," she informed Michael tartly. "Particularly messy things. Oh, no, look at that seat." Melted ice cream puddles dotted the supple black leather.

Michael shrugged and waited until she'd finished cleaning Maren's grimy legs. "She is a pretty fussy lady," he said with a wink at Justin and took the cloth. In seconds he'd restored the car to a fair facsimile of its former impeccable condition. He slung the diaper bag over one shoulder, picked up Maren and led the way toward a grassy slope leading down to the lake.

"We can't stay long," Sophie said and immediately realized she was talking to herself. Justin was dashing for the playground, and Maren, released on the grass, toddled happily from daisy to buttercup, squatting to tear at slender stems and laughing as they slithered between her fingers.

Michael had dropped the bag and stood, hands thrust into the pockets of his jeans, face lifted to the breeze. She stopped, too, and stared at the sharp line of his jaw outlined against an azure sky. Michael Harris was too attractive for his own good—for her good. And she didn't understand what he wanted from her.

He looked at her. For once he wasn't smiling. He had a wonderful, sensitive face in repose; or was that part of an act, something that worked on unresponsive subjects?

"Sophie? *Is* this okay?" he asked, and she registered that he was repeating the question.

"Fine." She sat down a few feet from him. "Maren, sweetie, stay close. That's a good girl," she said. Michael was watching her, and she took refuge in monitoring the children's movements.

"What a day," he said, expelling a long breath. "Can you believe it's this hot so late in the afternoon?"

He was offering an olive branch again, but Sophie couldn't unwind. "It's too hot for me."

Without warning, he dragged his shirt over his head and tossed it aside. She swallowed, averting her eyes.

"You can look," he commented lightly. "I'm not shy."

She broke off a blade of grass and chewed it, ignoring him.

"You are shy, aren't you, Sophie?"

"No." She dropped on her back, shading her eyes. "What is it about me that turns you into a tormentor?"

He was silent for so long she wondered if he'd heard her question. Finally he said, very quietly, "I don't want to torment you. I like you."

She didn't know what to say.

A second later he stretched out beside her. Sophie turned her head and looked directly into speculative blue eyes, too close for comfort. She sat up immediately.

"Relax," he said. "You don't have to be frightened of me."

"I'm not frightened," Sophie retorted. She wanted to go home now. "Someone has to watch the children."

"Mmmm." One hand rested on his flat stomach.

Sophie looked rapidly at his body, from broad, heavily muscled shoulders, downward over the dark hair that covered his chest, past his waist to narrow hips and long legs.

Oh, but Michael Harris was a knockout—classic heart-break material—and Sophie had gone that route once. Her heart was beginning to fill in quite nicely, and she intended to keep it that way.

"Will I do?"

Caught! She started and felt heat blast into her face. "You'll do very nicely, Mr. Harris, as I'm sure you know. I always appreciate a good male body." She silently congratulated herself for calling his bluff.

"Thanks." He locked his hands behind his neck and peered at her. "So if I pass inspection, why do you keep me at arm's length?"

She cleared her throat and met his gaze squarely. "I'm employed by your sister and her husband. I like them, and I think they like me. I also think they're so happy together that they think everyone should be involved with someone. They want me to have someone, too, and you're the only available candidate they know, so they've asked you to be nice to me. You're simply following orders. Isn't that the way it goes?"

He frowned. "Go on. Finish your theory."

She felt a little sick. "That's about it. Except you're not giving up on me because you can't take rejection. If I hadn't been shoved under your nose, you'd never have noticed I was alive. I'm not your type."

"Too skinny, huh?" He sat up slowly and leaned closer until she squirmed.

"That and other things."

"I'm a sex fiend and you're frigid?"

"Don't be disgusting."

"Sorry, but you sure as hell drive a man to say all the wrong things. Like I said before, I like you. Simply *like* you. That doesn't mean I spend every second of my life trying to figure a way into your bed. I just want us to be friends."

Her skin burned. He sounded reasonable, and she sounded like a shrew. "We didn't get off to a very good start, Michael,'' she said. Maren scampered up and dumped a handful of sand from the water's edge into Michael's lap. He rolled over and tickled the little girl until she squealed and took off screaming for Justin.

''Are you ever going to forgive me for that movie fiasco?'' Michael asked softly as he scooted even closer. ''I told you the truth. I intended to hold your hand and missed.'' He bowed his face, laughing. ''I thought the roof was falling when you threw that popcorn at me.''

Sophie laughed, too. She drew up her legs and rested her chin on her knees. ''I felt such a fool afterward.''

''So did I.''

''I'm sorry.''

''Truce?''

She breathed deeply. ''Consider the whole thing forgotten.'' Michael was near enough for her to smell the scent of cedar that was always a part of him. Whenever she thought of him she smelled that scent.

''You enjoy working for Abby and Nick, don't you?'' He hunched his shoulders forward, and muscles rippled.

''I've never enjoyed anything more. The children are lovely. A handful, but lovely.''

''Abby told me you came from Iowa.''

''Uh-huh. Just outside Winterset. John Wayne country. He was born in Winterset.''

''Really?'' Michael flicked sand from his jeans. ''Do you still have family there?''

Sophie's jaw tightened a little. She shouldn't mind discussing personal things. She knew how to talk about her past without really saying anything. ''My parents still run a farm. Times are tough for them—at least I suppose they are, they always were. We aren't close.''

''That's too bad.''

She met his eyes sharply. ''You say that because you're close to Abby and your mother. My folks were always too busy making a living to spend a lot of time on...on...

They're good people, they did the best they could with what they had. I love them in my own way.''

"I wish you could have met my dad," Michael said, a faraway expression in his eyes. "He was something. Not brilliant or witty or a great conversationalist—just solid. He was a baker. He used to make special things for Abby and me. My mom always behaved like she was in charge, and he let her. He was quiet—but he was the strength in the family. Something went away when he died. Even after two years my mother isn't over it—none of us is, really, Nick included.''

"You're lucky to have someone like him to remember," Sophie said and immediately regretted sounding wistful. She must try to be more understanding of Wilma Harris. From time to time the woman mentioned "her George", and never without a pause in whatever she was doing and a little twitch at the corners of her mouth.

"You were married." Michael made the statement without inflection, not looking at her.

"Yes. For seven years." The familiar prickling started in her scalp.

"You must have been young."

"Nineteen. Jack and I met in high school."

"Abby said he died. He couldn't have been very old."

Michael looked toward the lake as he spoke. Sophie studied one large hand, resting on his knee. At this moment she wished he would touch her.

"He was twenty-six." She might as well finish her pat little story. "He picked up a virus and something went wrong. The doctors said it got into his brain. He went into a coma and never came out again." She could almost say it as if those two people, Sophie and Jack, were people she'd met in another time and place; they weren't she and her dead husband.

"Rotten luck." Michael had pushed his hands into his hair, and she couldn't see his face. "Did you feel helpless, like you should be able to do something about it?"

The question surprised her. "I'd felt like that for years, I—" She stopped, appalled at what she'd almost said: that she'd blamed herself for Jack's steady self-destruction, for his wild drinking bouts, even for the way his love for her had turned to hate—and what he did to her out of that hate. That was past. She squeezed her eyes shut. Jack had been a special man, a good man with problems like everyone had problems.

"Are you okay?"

She opened her eyes. Michael was staring at her. "Of course I am." She must change the subject. "Michael, can I ask you something personal?"

"Sure."

"Don't answer if you don't want to."

"Ask."

"Earlier, when I came to Nick's study, I . . . heard something."

He straightened his back.

"Um . . . this is none of my business."

"Sophie, will you spit it out. I'm not going to eat you." But his eyes bored into her.

"Abby and Nick have been kind of uptight lately. It's been worrying me. I thought maybe they were having troubles—"

Michael gave a shout of laughter. "Abby and Nick? Forget that. They've got your one hundred percent solid marriage. They could give how-to lessons in that department. One day I'll tell you the whole story of how they came to where they are now, and you'll understand. Nick and I go back a long way. I know him almost as well as I know myself. When he met Abby she was on the bottom and he helped her up. They've been through more together already than most people face in a lifetime. You don't have to worry about Nick and Abby. Those two are a permanent item.''

She let him finish, then touched his hand briefly. "I know that now. But I heard Nick say something about cutting corners. He was talking about Islands Unlimited, wasn't he? You're having some money troubles with the business.'' She shouldn't be prying. This wasn't her affair. Once she'd have taken such a challenge between her teeth and wrestled out a solution. She hadn't developed a successful travel agency because she gave up easily. But all that was behind her now.

He realized one of the things he really admired about this woman: her honesty. She approached a point directly, by the shortest route. He wrinkled his nose and glanced at the children. They were yelling, rolling over and over downhill. "We jumped in too soon," he said. "The idea was Nick's at first—way back when we were getting out of the service. We both started flying for the same commercial airline, and he soon had me hooked on starting a seaplane service of our own. After he and Abby got together, he really wanted it badly. So did I, but we should have looked longer and harder at all the angles. The concept's good, and we're going to make it work, but right now we aren't doing so well.''

"I see. Is cash flow your main problem?''

He stared at her for an instant, mildly taken aback. Her heavy lashes cast shadows into her intensely dark eyes. The lady was bright. "Exactly," he agreed. "On the nose. We need capital, but who's going to rush to lend funds to an operation as shaky as ours still is?''

"Maybe you need a fresh approach.''

"What do you mean?''

She looked away, and he thought he saw an odd sadness cross her face. "Oh, I don't know. I was just thinking out loud. You'll come up with something.''

What *had* drawn him to her at first? As soon as the question formed, he knew the answer. She was like him. Speak first, think later. Carefree and optimistic, convinced she could cope with anything. He gave a short laugh and tried to turn it into a cough when she looked at him. Who was he kidding, certainly not himself? Sophie Peters was like the man Michael Harris used to be, not the man he'd become.

"Did you give up your other flying job to get going with Nick?"

He started. "What? No. What made you think that?"

"Nick said you'd given up a lot to join him. And you said—" she hesitated "—you said you were finished as a flier...." Her voice dwindled away.

She was getting too close to something he didn't want to—couldn't—talk about. "I didn't give up a job the way you mean. I flew in the air force first. That's where I met Nick. Then we both went with a big commercial line. But I got tired of never sleeping in the same bed two nights in a row, so I signed on with a commuter service that operates out of Seatac. That meant I was at my own place every night."

Her pale face was turned up to his, her lips slightly parted as she concentrated on what he said. Damn, she was lovely in a fascinating, delicate way. And he didn't want to go on talking about himself.

"What made you stop wanting to fly the commuter planes?"

He gave a shrug that felt elaborate and phony. "I got shaken up and I lost my nerve. Simple as that." He made himself keep looking at her. Nothing in his life had been less simple than that stinking day. It would color everything he did for as long as he lived.

"You mean you were in a crash?" Her brow puckered, and she unconsciously rested a hand on his knee. "That's awful. What happened?"

Oh, no. He wasn't going into this. Not now, not ever. He got to his feet and pulled her up. "Nothing so awful, really. A bit of a bang up, but it took the wind out of me for a while. A scare always does. But that's in the past now. Within a few months Nick helped me through the jitters, and we got started on the new business." He glanced at his watch and pulled on his shirt. "We'd better get you back to Leshi. I don't want to throw off your dinner schedule."

He scanned the area and started to run. "Look at that little crumb dropper. He's going to get them both soaked." Justin stood in the shallows of the lake kicking sheets of water over Maren, who flapped her hands and shrieked.

Sophie grabbed the bag and ran after Michael. She'd misjudged him. He was just a nice man who liked to be friendly with everyone. In future when they met she'd make sure she was just as nice. Instantly, a shred of caution tempered her forgiving mood. She mustn't be too nice, or he might misunderstand her motives.

"They're going out in a canoe." Justin shouted as she drew near. He pointed at a swaying blue boat. "Uncle Mike, can we go in a canoe?"

Justin loved the water and boats. The Dorsets had a catamaran. Sophie's rooms were over the boat house where the craft was moored. Nick never seemed to have time to take it out, and on several occasions Sophie had heard Justin beg for a ride, then cry when his father refused.

The boy scrambled onto a wooden dock and stared longingly at the bright blue canoe paddled by a man and a teenage boy. "Can we take one out?" Justin repeated.

Michael raised one brow at Sophie. She picked up Maren and climbed on the dock to get Justin. "We have to go home, Justin. Maybe another day we can rent a canoe."

"I want to go now," the boy said crossly. "Daddy always says that. Another day."

"Hey, guy," Michael said, reaching to hold the boy's shoulders. "I know what we'll do. I've got a free afternoon on Wednesday. That's four days from now. How about you and Maren and Sophie and I going over by the University of Washington and renting a canoe? Huh?"

"Yes, please." Justin's frown disappeared.

Sophie caught Michael's eye and shook her head slightly. He didn't seem to notice. "We'll get two boats. Sophie can take one of you and I'll take the other." She untensed slightly. She had to stop second-guessing him. "Is that okay with you, Sophie?" he continued. "Picnic on me? I'm flying in the morning, but I'll come straight over when I'm done."

What could she say? "If Justin and Maren would like that—"

"We would. We would." Justin hopped from foot to foot.

"Would." Maren, pouting in concentration, tried to copy his antics.

"Great." Michael smiled at her. "Wednesday it is, then."

MICHAEL WATCHED NICK'S PLANE touch down on the smooth waters of Lake Union. He jiggled coins and keys in his jeans pockets and took a deep breath through his mouth. This was going to be tough.

The tan De Havilland Beaver sprayed wide blades of sun-dappled water, then it slowed, settled deeper on its floats and cruised toward the dock. Nick wouldn't laugh... but what if he did? No, Michael decided, if there was one man who wouldn't laugh at him for needing help with a woman, it was Nick Dorset. Nick had conquered incredible odds after he met Abby. Michael himself had been one of those odds. Nick might have been his best friend at the time, a friend who had shared a lot of tough times, but seeing that man falling for Abby while she was pregnant and still married to someone else had almost ended the friendship—until the truth came out.

Abby's husband had already left her, and Nick stepped in, buoying her up, proving he had enough love to give her and a baby, even a baby who was not his. Michael still remembered with vague shock that on the morning after Justin was born he'd walked into the hospital and been met by Nick.

Nick had been with Abby throughout labor and delivery. Later Michael had discovered that Nick had attended childbirth education classes with Abby and become the support system her husband should have been. Until that morning, in a hospital corridor, Michael had never really considered how it might feel to love a woman. But at that moment, looking into Nick's haggard but euphoric face, he had known he would want to find out some day. The day seemed to have come, and Michael believed Nick would understand all about wanting to know a special woman better.

Too quickly, the Beaver nudged the dock, and Nick opened his door. He bent his tall body almost double to clamber from the cockpit before he stood by, offering a hand to each of the Beaver's seven disembarking passengers. At least this had been a full load, Michael mused. There were too few of those. He'd just made the return flight from Friday Harbor with only two customers aboard. He and Nick were caught in a vicious cycle. Too little business to provide the capital for more planes, and not enough planes to lay on the frequent service that would attract the repeat payload or give them the reputation they needed. Only last week another small operation had gone under. How long could they hold on? The old, comforting theme played again: Nick Dorset and Michael Harris were a team, always had been, always would be, and as long as they hung together they'd make out okay.

"Hiya, Mike. What's up?" Nick approached with his characteristic long stride, the confident swing of wide shoulders. The heels of his boots scuffed worn boards.

"You lay that baby down like a snowflake, Nick," Mike said when his friend drew close. "Boy, I wish I could reach your pinnacle of perfection."

Nick grinned broadly and punched his arm. "Eat your heart out. Takes a natural talent, boy. Some have it, some don't. But you show promise, Mike. A few more years—"

"Okay, okay. Enough." Michael draped an arm around Nick's shoulders and walked with him toward the office they rented in a warehouse beside the lake. "I've got to talk to you, Nick. I want ... I need ... Hell, I've got to have some help or I'll blow it again."

Nick stood still and stared him directly in the eye. They matched each other almost inch for inch in height, but Nick had a slight weight advantage, and every ounce was solid muscle. A gentle giant, Michael thought abstractedly, a man who always saw the good side—of anyone. That was something else Nick had taught him over the years, that it was worth hoping to find the best in people. Michael looked steadily back at Nick, who raised his straight brows questioningly.

Seconds passed. "You do have a problem," Nick said when the silence had gone on and on. "Let's have it, Mike. What's wrong now? Did they cut off the electricity in the office or what?"

Michael managed a laugh. "This is personal."

"*That* would be pretty personal to me, friend."

"Come on." He urged Nick forward and pushed open the door to the tiny room where they took reservations and sometimes came when they wanted to talk away from Abby's worried ear.

"Mike," Nick said, hoisting himself onto a cluttered table by the window, "we both have flights in the next hour, so this had better not take long."

Michael looked at his palms. Sweat gleamed there, and he rubbed them together. He cleared his throat and went to stare through the window. The parking lot between the warehouse and the docks was crammed with cars belonging to lunchtime diners. The lake was convenient to downtown Seattle workers, and almost every building in the area housed a restaurant or a bar.

"Are you with me, Mike? I thought you wanted to talk."

He closed his eyes. "Are you ready for a good laugh, buddy? This is probably going to give you one."

"Something tells me—"

"Let me get this out," Michael cut in. "You know I'm, uh, I'm kind of interested in Sophie Peters." He swallowed and sniffed. "Don't interrupt me, please."

Nick had folded his arms and was studying his boots, crossed at the ankle. Michael narrowed his eyes, almost certain he saw the hint of a smile on the other man's face.

"Well, I am interested. Don't ask me why. She's too small and too bossy—and she doesn't seem to like me. But I like her and I've managed to get her to agree to come out with me and your kids on Wednesday afternoon. We're going to take a picnic and go canoeing, and she'll be in one canoe with one kid and I'll be in another with the other kid. Nick, I think I've made a little ground with her. I'm sure I have. After what happened when I took her to the movies I thought I was dead in the water. I never told you what went wrong. It was dumb." He paused for breath. "I'm not going to tell you, so don't ask. It just took a while for her to get over it. She's not completely over it. But I think she's ready to be.

"Oh, God, Nick, I think I'm getting a case on this woman. Can you believe that? She's shy with men. I'm sure that's why she doesn't react when I come on to her—I don't come on to her that way, not anymore—I'm damned careful, polite. Mostly polite, when I don't forget. And that's the deal, Nick, I forget, and if I mess up on Wednesday I'm going to kill myself because I don't think she'll ever speak to me again if—"

A choking noise made him close his mouth tightly and stare at Nick. He grabbed his shoulders and shook him. "Are you laughing, you rotten son of a bitch? Are you? Nick, so help me—"

"I'm not laughing. I'm not." Nick held up his hands and shook his head. "Would I laugh at you?"

Michael ran his tongue over dry lips. "You...damn you, Nick Dorset. You *are* laughing at me. I convinced myself you wouldn't, but you are." And he started to laugh himself. He swung to sit beside Nick and covered his face, laughing until he had to rub tears from his eyes.

When they were quiet again, Nick shifted to a chair where he could look up at Michael. "So how am I supposed to be able to help you?"

"You've got to tell me how to handle her, Nick. You've got to."

"Me?" Nick's voice rose to a squeak.

"You. You understand shy women. You managed to get to know my sister and make her fall in love with you. And she was divorced and pregnant and an emotional mess. You must know all the right things to do and say with a woman who isn't ... you know ..."

"Who isn't what?"

Michael gave him a slitted glare. "You aren't going to make this easier on me, are you?"

"I just want to know the facts, that's all. What exactly is Sophie? Sure, Abby was a challenge, but with my charm there was no problem. I could try giving you some lessons, but I don't know ..."

"Nick," Michael warned. "This is serious. I swear, every time I open my mouth around her I insert my big foot, and this matters to me."

"What do you want from her?"

"Want?" Michael frowned.

Nick wasn't smiling anymore. "Want, Mike. Is she a thorn in your side because she isn't falling over herself to jump into bed with you? Do you just want to reassure yourself you can have any woman you want, or are you interested in her for some other reason? Abby and I have both encouraged you to take her out, but I haven't been all that sure it was such a great idea. She isn't your type, is she?"

"I'm so sick of hearing that." He leaned forward and hung his hands between his knees. "Sophie said that. Hell, *I* said it—before I'd been around her as much as I have now. I can't tell you why she turns me on, Nick, but she does. She's different. Maybe I'm ready for a woman who's different. Yeah, that'll do for now. I need a different kind of woman and she's it. So will you help me figure out the right things to say to her on Wednesday or not?"

Nick considered, tracing circles on one thigh. "Okay. I'm no expert, but maybe two heads are better than one."

"No, Nick. Not two heads. Yours. Wait." He pulled a notebook from his back pocket and scrabbled on the table until he found a pencil. "Now I'm ready. Give me some lines. I'll get 'em memorized."

When Nick didn't speak, he glanced up. "Go on. I'm paddling through the lilies over by the university, the sun's shining, it's quiet because it's Wednesday and there aren't many people out. She smiles at me and I say..." He waved the pencil.

Nick shook his head. "This isn't going to work."

"Sure it is. What do I say? Your hair looks great, maybe? That's nonthreatening. Then I could say I'd like to see it spread out...she always wears it tied back. Yeah, spread out." He thought about her hair and whistled. "It would look like something on a pillow."

"Oh, God," Nick said with a sigh. "You do need help. Okay, we'll work it through. But make sure you say the right lines in the right places."

"You think I'm mad?"

Nick didn't answer.

"I shouldn't say anything about the way she looks, is that it?"

"We'll get to that. First we've got to figure out a way to make sure this is a canoe trip for two."

"But the kids are coming."

"No, they're not," Nick said, grinning slightly. "Leave it to me."

Chapter Three

She would keep calm. She would remember her resolve to be kind to this woman, to remember all she had lost. Sophie smiled at Wilma Harris, who stood in the middle of Justin's room, her hands clasped beneath her ample bosom.

"Uncle Mike's taking us in a canoe," Justin said for the third time. "He said Wednesday and this is Wednesday."

"Granny's taking you to the Seattle Center," Wilma said, undeterred. "You can go with Uncle Michael another day. We're going to have a lovely time. Rides and ice cream—"

"Uncle Mike always buys us ice cream," Justin said stubbornly.

"That's enough, Justin," Sophie said. "Please go and play with Maren."

Wilma Harris stood between the boy and the door. Her chest appeared to expand like a nesting hen. "You're too hard on Justin," she said to Sophie, her magenta-coated lips pursing. "Get Maren, Justin. Your daddy called. He wants you children home in time for supper." She flashed a combative stare at Sophie. The rouged spots on her cheeks stood out starkly against a powdered face.

"But, Granny—"

"Do as your grandmother tells you," Sophie ordered and waited while the boy hesitated a few more seconds before slamming from the room. "Nick asked you to take the children today, Mrs. Harris?"

Wilma patted at upswept puffs of gray hair on each side of her face. "He knows I'd like to spend more time with them. He's been so thoughtful since..." She lifted her chin. "Some people who should be thinking about others are too busy with their own wants," she said significantly. "But Nick always remembers. *He'd* be glad if the children were with someone of their own, instead of a stranger who'll go away one day."

Sophie hardly heard the last comment. Wilma was only repeating what she'd found a dozen other opportunities to suggest, that Maren and Justin should be with her instead of Sophie. She never missed an opportunity to remind Sophie that her position in this household could only be temporary, or to imply that Abby was an insensitive daughter.

"Nick knows you're taking Maren and Justin," Sophie repeated slowly. "When did you talk to him?"

"Are you saying you think I'm lying?" Wilma's voice rose several pitches. "You can call him if you think that."

"No, no, of course not." Sophie made herself smile again. "I guess we all got our signals crossed, that's all. I thought I'd mentioned to Nick and Abby that Michael promised the children a canoe ride and a picnic. I'm sure they'll have a wonderful time with you at the Center. Thank you for taking them." But she would call Nick as soon as she could.

"I don't have to be thanked for taking my own grandchildren anywhere," Wilma said, but she blinked too rapidly. The woman was insecure and trying to cover her vulnerability with bravado.

Half an hour later Wilma hurried the children to her car. Maren left the house happily, but Justin cast a reproachful look at Sophie before she closed the door.

Immediately she ran to the closest phone in the small library off the hall. The phone at the Islands Unlimited office rang twelve times before Nick answered and put her on hold. Sophie sat on the edge of a tiny tapestry chair and drummed her fingers on the receiver. She waited for several infuriating minutes before Nick came back on the line with a cheerful, "Hi, Islands Unlimited."

"This is Sophie."

He took a second to answer. "Is anything wrong? The children—"

"The children are fine, Nick. They just left with Abby's mother."

Again he was silent.

"Is Michael there?"

"Ah no. He left."

Oh, no. "I did tell you Michael was taking the children canoeing this afternoon, didn't I?"

"Ah . . . oh, yes, I guess you did."

"But you told Mrs. Harris she should take them out instead? I guess I don't understand."

The silences were making her uncomfortable. Nick coughed and said, "I messed you up, huh? Sorry, Sophie. I'll try to keep things straight next time. I'm sure there will be other chances to take the kids on the lake."

Now he sounded as if he thought she was overreacting. She sat straighter. "Did Michael say if he was going to his apartment before coming here?" There had to be some way to head him off.

"No," Nick said. "He'd gone by the time I got in from my last flight."

She wasn't going to get any help from Nick Dorset. The man was so straightforward he would never understand her apprehension at the thought of facing Michael alone. "Okay then, Nick. Don't give it another thought. See you this evening. Goodbye."

A key turning in the front door lock paralyzed Sophie. Michael came in, whistling, his key ring dangling from a forefinger. He wore shorts and a tank top, and she was struck again by the man's height and breadth, his vitality. A second later he must have sensed he was watched and turned those deep blue eyes in her direction. He smiled broadly, his teeth very white against tanned skin.

Sophie slid back in the chair.

"What are you doing in there? Hiding from the minor monsters? Don't tell me they've finally broken your spirit."

"They...they aren't here."

He clamped his hands on his hips, a frown replacing his smile, and came into the room. "Where are they? We said two and it's two now." He checked his watch. "On the nose."

His nose was spectacular, straight, narrow at the bridge. And his cheekbones were well-defined. And his mouth was one of those beautiful mouths men shouldn't have, wide, tilted up at the corners, the kind that made dimples in lean cheeks when he smiled. Sophie touched her own bottom lip.

"The picnic's in the car," Michael said. He stared at her, his eyes narrowed. "What's the matter with you?"

"Hmm? Nothing." She stood up and immediately wished she hadn't. Michael was a parquet tile width from her, and she had to crane her neck to look at his face. "Mrs. Harris has taken Justin and Maren to the Seattle Center for the afternoon. I'm very sorry, Michael. I tried to reach you, but you'd already left Lake Union." No point in mentioning that Nick had ruined the afternoon; he certainly hadn't done so intentionally.

"You mean it's all off?" His eyes clouded. "I looked forward to this since Saturday. Oh, hell, Mother chooses the darnedest times to butt in."

"She didn't mean to upset you," Sophie said quickly. "I think she's a bit lonely, Michael. It's hard getting over losing someone you've known for so long." She plucked at the belt of the cover-up she wore over shorts and a halter top and felt she'd said too much.

"You're kind, Sophie Peters," Michael said thoughtfully. "And I'm glad you're kind to my mother. Right now I wish someone would be kind to me." He waved his hand. "Forget I said that. Things have been a bit hairy, that's all. I guess I'd better get out of your way."

She took in the dejected slope of his shoulders as he turned away. He was having a hard time with the business, and his usual I've-got-the-world-by-the-tail act had slipped for once. He'd actually been looking forward to an afternoon with the children and forgetting his worries for a while.

"Michael." She caught up with him in the hall and grasped his elbow. "I'm really sorry."

His lips turned up in a smile, but a sad shadow remained in his eyes. "Thanks."

"You can still go on the lake. Then find a quiet place to picnic and get some sun—and don't think about a thing that bothers you for a while."

"Sounds great," he said wryly. "Or it would if I had someone to go with."

Sophie took a deep breath. She couldn't let him leave like this. "Look, say no if you want to—really, just say no. But, if it would help, I'll come with you. At least we could be quiet together if that'll help."

An expression she couldn't define crossed his features. He looked...guilty? Guilty because he'd made her feel bad? She wouldn't let that happen.

"I'd really like to come with you, Michael," she insisted. "I was looking forward to it as much as you were." She made a fist at her side. What she said was true.

"HAVE YOU EVER PADDLED a canoe before?" Michael shouted.

They wobbled wildly, and she took her paddle completely out of the water. "No, I've never paddled a canoe before."

"How did you think you were going to manage alone with one of the children?"

Sophie grimaced and bowed her face. "This is going to sound really stupid, but I thought it would be a cinch. I thought I'd just know how."

"Okay," Michael said, "take it slowly. Stroke the water, don't dig."

She tried to do as he asked and missed the surface completely. Michael laughed behind her, and she leaned forward and drove the paddle firmly down and back. She'd got the hang of it now.

"Stop!" Michael yelled.

"Why?" She looked over her shoulder and almost dropped the paddle overboard. "Oh, no, Michael. Did I do that? Oh, no."

He blinked at her. Water from his hair streamed over his face. His blue tank top clung, sodden and dark, to his chest.

Sophie pushed the paddle beneath her feet and unbelted her cover-up. "Hold on, Michael—" she pulled it off "—use this to dry off. Jeez, I'm sorry. What an idiot I am."

A strong hand on each bare shoulder, squeezing, pushing her back into her seat, stopped her from turning around.

"Sit still," Michael ordered. "Please, Sophie. Sit very, very still. Don't paddle. Don't turn around. Don't do anything. Enjoy the sunshine and let me do the work. You're tired, I know you are, so I'm going to give you a ride." They were already moving smoothly ahead. "I know the area and I've got just the spot in mind for a perfect picnic."

"But, Michael," she said, distressed, "I want to help. I want to learn." She started to turn again but changed her mind.

"Of course you do, and I'll teach you—later. While we eat."

"I thought we were going ashore somewhere to eat."

"We are."

Sophie looked straight ahead and smiled ruefully. She'd almost dumped them both in the lake. The least she could do now was cooperate.

The University of Washington's soaring football stadium loomed on their right, its banks of sand defined against the dazzling sky. Michael propelled them beneath the Evergreen Point Bridge. On each side of the channel tall rushes swayed, a whispering forest of sticks.

"You've never done this before, then," Michael said and added quickly, "Don't turn around. I can hear you."

"I haven't done this before," Sophie said and heard the asperity in her own voice. "But I've watched from shore and it seems to me I always see people talking to each other. And they turn around, too."

"Carefully, Sophie. They do it carefully. Aren't the lilies, er, aren't these the most beautiful water lilies you've ever seen?"

"Very beautiful," Sophie agreed. The canoe nosed a path through floating bowls of dark polished leaves. In direct sunlight, they opened wide to show the lilies, yellow, lavender, some almost purple. Along the shady banks, close to the rushes, only slits of color peered from their green armor.

Michael paddled on in silence.

"It's so quiet," Sophie said. "Feels like we're the only people on the lake today." They'd left the open expanses of water, and Michael steered the craft farther along a channel that narrowed until one side of the canoe's hull brushed rushes.

"This is it." Michael worked the stern around and drove the bow through a narrow cut and onto a grassy bank. He leaped into the water, waded ashore and hauled in the canoe. "How's this? Perfect for that quiet picnic and some sun, huh?"

Sophie took his hand and climbed cautiously onto the soggy turf. Willows, their branches overhanging the water, created a gently swaying curtain around a grotto where the sun was no more than a shifting chiaroscuro on lush grass.

"Are you sure the water won't rise much?" Sophie asked dubiously. "There doesn't seem to be any higher ground around here."

"No problem," Michael assured her. He pulled a picnic basket from the canoe and set it well back from the lake edge. "Good thing I put the blanket in a waterproof bag." He grinned and spread a plaid throw.

"Boy, I really did a number with the paddle, didn't I?" Sophie said, laughing. "The mad splasher."

Michael wrinkled his nose and raked back still damp hair that was drying into unruly curls. He grinned at her, and his eyes crinkled in a way that did interesting things to her insides.

She sat down and watched him unpack sandwiches and fruit—and a bottle of wine and paper cups. He emptied the entire contents of the basket, finishing with a wedge of Brie. Sophie sat on her heels and examined the feast. "Michael—" she chuckled, then sobered "—what were the children going to eat? Or drink? Pâté sandwiches and Brie and wine?"

He looked from the food to the wine to Sophie, a stricken expression crossing his face. "I, uh... Oh, well..." While he stumbled over his words he fished a notebook from a pocket in his shorts and glanced at it.

"What's that?"

He shoved the book away. "Um, notes. Just notes. I was sure I wrote down what I intended to bring. I must have forgotten the children's juice. That's it." He sank down, cross-legged, smiling apologetically. "I must have left it in the refrigerator."

"Never mind. Next time I'll help." Immediately she blushed and bowed her head. *Next time?* "I mean...Justin won't be happy till he gets his canoe trip with you. When you go, I'll make the picnic." She took the sandwich he proffered without meeting his eyes.

Michael didn't answer. She glanced at him, but he was engrossed in opening the bottle of wine. A scent she didn't recognize hung in the air—sun-dried clover, perhaps. There hadn't been time for smelling flowers recently—not for years. She accepted a paper cup of white wine from Michael. They were very alone here. It felt right. He needed space and peace, but he also needed someone to share that peace—he'd said so, and she was glad she was the one who was here for him.

They ate in silence and drank wine, and Michael refilled his cup. Sophie studied his capable hands, the play of muscle and tendon beneath tanned skin on his forearms, the way fine dark hair covered those arms and his long, well-muscled legs. She looked at her own pale skin and fidgeted, pulling her ankles beneath her.

Still Michael said nothing.

Sophie coughed and tucked an escaped wisp of hair behind her ear. What did she really know about Michael Harris?

"It's a wonderful day, isn't it?" he said loudly.

She stopped plucking blades of grass. "Yes, yes, it is."

He smiled at her and poured himself more wine. Sophie had barely touched her first cup. Her back ached, and she changed positions. She wished he hadn't brought the wine.

"The kind of day you want to hold on to."

"What?" She stared at him. He was removed, different.

"Oh, yes. Special days make you want to stop the world."

He returned her gaze intently, his lips slightly parted. She hadn't thought of him as the deeply reflective man he obviously was. Still looking at her, he took out the notebook once more but returned it to his pocket without looking at its pages.

Could there be something he should be doing—paperwork perhaps that he'd expected to tackle while the children were playing? "Michael, if you've got something to do, don't worry about me. I'm happy just sitting here."

"Do?"

She nodded to his pocket. "Notes to look over for business or something. Go ahead. I may take a nap."

He was staring again.

Sophie put down her cup, bunched a corner of the blanket for her head and lay down. She'd be here for him, but she mustn't intrude on his need for quiet.

Michael leaned forward and rested his elbows on his knees. This was hopeless. He couldn't remember the things Nick had suggested as conversation starters. Damn. She'd closed her eyes now. If he didn't think of something to say she'd be asleep. He couldn't believe this was happening to him.

She clasped her hands behind her head. Her skin was pale, the pulse in her arched throat beating visibly. Good Lord, she was a small woman. Her delicate body was lovely, perfectly formed. He wanted to touch her, to hold her.

"Are you all right, Michael?"

He started violently. "Fine, fine," he said, and his voice broke. Even as a teenager he'd been more collected with women than this. "I was just thinking you're pale. We'd better be careful you don't burn."

She peered at him. "There's almost no sun here."

They were in total shade. "Right. Of course, you're right. I wasn't thinking." He seemed to have lost whatever he had to think with. "Um...what do you think about the way Seattle's growing?"

She sat up. "I'm sorry, Michael. What did you say?"

He was damned if he knew what he'd said. Something inane. "How old are you, Sophie?" *Hell.*

"Thirty-one. How about you?"

"Thirty-four. Sorry. Gentlemen don't ask ladies' ages, I guess." Fate was on his side. Even with the blunders, he didn't appear to have turned her off.

"I don't mind." Sophie smiled at him. She had a lovely mouth.

"Do you suppose I could kiss you?" His skin turned cold. She hugged her knees, and her eyes were huge. He couldn't have asked to kiss her. He'd never asked a woman that in his life.

"Sophie—" she wasn't moving, only keeping her eyes on his "—Sophie, I don't know where I am with you. I'm...attracted to you. Is that okay? Do you mind?" Any minute she would slap him or throw something—he knew it.

She rested her forehead on crossed arms. "It's okay." He hardly heard her.

"You don't mind?"

"No."

Tentatively, he reached out a hand until it hovered inches above her hair. "You said I didn't frighten you." He stroked the back of her head and rested his fingers lightly on her neck.

She didn't look up. "I'm not frightened."

"But you don't want me." He swallowed. His stomach contracted sharply.

Sophie raised her face. "What do you mean?" She was even paler.

Michael rubbed the soft skin behind her ear and brought his face carefully, slowly, closer. "I'm not sure what I mean at the moment. But I do know I've wanted to kiss you for a very long time. A very long time, Sophie." And when he touched his lips to hers, she held quite still. His own eyes closed, and when he opened them again he saw her lids, lowered, but not quite closed. Had he done this right? Nick had said to wait for her to be calm and until he felt she was softening toward him. She seemed softer, somehow, and withdrawn.

"You are so special, Sophie." He knelt beside her and tipped up her chin. "I've never met a woman like you." She kept her arms around her knees, but he kissed her again, slowly moving his mouth over hers.

When he put his arms around her and pulled her near, she clutched his shirt where it stretched across his sides. Her fingers dug into his skin, but her lips parted, slightly at first, then wider as he pressed his tongue into her mouth.

Slowly, gently, he eased her down and rested an elbow at each side of her shoulders. She gazed up at him, unblinking, unsmiling. Her eyes glistened, and he thought the corners of her mouth quivered downward. He rubbed his cheek against hers, blew softly at her ear and lay on his side, drawing her into his arms.

"You are one tiny female," he said. "Is everyone in your family so small?" Maybe if he lightened the atmosphere she'd loosen up.

"No."

So much for that approach. He kept smiling. Her skin was smooth. She was soft, supple. He stroked her back. "Just you, huh? I like the way you are."

His next kiss found the corner of her mouth, and she immediately buried her face beneath his chin. His legs turned to water. Whatever was so different about her aroused him almost unbearably. Her ribs, bare beneath the halter, were raised as if she held her breath. He ran his hand downward to the dip at her waist, downward over firm hips, and back to the side of her breast. And he nipped the skin at her throat, her collarbone.

She'd made a noise. An odd, tight little noise. He held still, waiting. Oh, God, she was shaking. He lay motionless, his hand spread over her shoulder. Every few seconds a fresh tremor passed through her inert body.

Michael closed his eyes tightly. She was frightened of him. Not repulsed, he was sure she didn't find him unattractive, but she didn't want this. She'd tried to go through the motions with him and failed. Why had she tried? Because she felt sorry for him? He sat up, bringing Sophie with him. He'd been so damn clever engineering this jaunt, making her feel she should keep him company, and he'd ended up scaring her to death.

"I'm sorry, Sophie," he managed. "I guess I blew it with you again."

Her hand on his jaw surprised him. She turned his face toward her. "*I'm* sorry," she said almost inaudibly. "I just ... I guess I'm not ready for this yet."

"Particularly with me." He couldn't bring off a smile.

"Not with anyone."

The tears that sprang to her eyes tore at him. The lady had something on her mind he knew nothing about. Thirty-one-year-olds who'd been married seven years didn't go to pieces over a kiss or being held—or a man putting his hand on their leg. He pressed her face to his chest. They didn't go to pieces unless they were still hung up over a husband. But she'd been widowed five years. The problem had to be with him.

Sophie flattened her palms on Michael's chest. He was a tender man, she was sure of it—wasn't she? Couldn't a man be tender? Jack had been, once. But he'd changed. Michael's kiss had been what she'd dreamed of, firm, erotic. She'd wanted him to kiss her, so why couldn't she respond?

He thought he'd done something wrong. She couldn't allow him to think that. "Thank you, Michael," she said.

"For what?" A bitter edge entered his voice.

"For not pushing too soon."

He breathed against her forehead for several seconds. "You mean there's a chance that another time could be the right time?"

She couldn't believe he cared enough to want to be with her again. "You're a nice man, Michael."

He laughed, and the sound made her wince. "Nice? Just what I always wanted to be."

"I mean that I appreciate your understanding."

He pulled away, tilted his head and looked at her. "Who says I understand? But if you appreciate whatever I am, will you have dinner with me tomorrow night? I promise I won't try to put the make on you again—not until you let me know it's what you want.''

His smile was there again, slight at first, gradually widening, and she smiled back. "I don't know why you want to, Michael, but yes, I'll have dinner with you tomorrow.''

SOPHIE DRAGGED ON JEANS AND A SHIRT and ran downstairs to the kitchen. Nick stood at a counter island chopping red onions while Abby poked more holes in the steak she was marinating.

Abby saw her first. "Aha, the wanderer returns. Nick, here's Sophie.''

She raised her brows, puzzled.

"So I see,'' Nick commented, his eyes tearing from the onions. "How was your canoe trip?''

Blood pumped into her cheeks. How did they know? An instant later she frowned at Justin who sat at the kitchen table coloring an empty egg carton. "The trip was fine,'' she said.

Wilma had been returning the children just as Michael dropped Sophie at the door. Michael had told Justin they'd been on the lake and promised to take the boy soon. Justin must have mentioned it to his parents.

"Where did Michael take you?'' Abby asked.

Sophie saw Nick frown quickly at his wife. Abby might be intrigued by the role of matchmaker, but Sophie had a hunch Nick was becoming less enamored of the idea of his partner being involved with his children's nanny.

"Sophie?'' Abby prompted.

"Over by the arboretum at the university,'' she said noncommittally. "Justin, this isn't the time to start a project. Wash your hands and get Maren. She went around to the sandbox. And, by the way, I just looked in your room. If you want to play with Markus tomorrow, you'd better work on that toy box after dinner.''

"Ooh, Sophie, no," Justin moaned.

"You'll do as you're told, young man," Nick said, winking at Sophie over the boy's head.

The front door, slamming into its jamb, brought them all to attention. Before anyone could react, Wilma Harris stormed into the kitchen, Maren clutched to her chest.

"Hello, Mom—" Abby began.

Wilma scowled at her daughter and turned her attention to Sophie. "How dare you! How *dare* you, you—you—"

Sophie swallowed. "Mrs. Harris," she said faintly. "What is it?"

"What...of course you ask what's the matter. You don't know, do you? You're too busy gallivanting around with hardly any clothes on, flaunting yourself in front of my son to know what's going on."

"I—"

"No, Sophie," Nick broke in. His mouth came together in a grim line before he spoke to his mother-in-law. "That's about enough, Mom. If you've got something to say, say it. And don't make insulting comments to Sophie."

Wilma's face turned a deep, ugly red. "You won't defend her when you find out what she's done. You'll get her out of this house as soon as you can—only it won't be soon enough. She's irresponsible, completely unsuitable to care for your children, my grandchildren."

"Mother!" Abby slammed the flat of one hand on the counter.

"This child," Wilma said, holding Maren closer. "I brought this child back a few minutes ago and left her in Sophie's care." She quivered, narrowed her eyes on Sophie. "I left both my grandchildren in her care and went home—or started to go home."

Sophie's legs trembled. She crossed her arms tightly.

"Thank God I realized the diaper bag was still in the trunk of my car. I came back and do you know what I found?" She aimed an accusing stare at Sophie. "I found this child wandering in the street. I left Maren in your care, and you were too busy to look after her. She was in the middle of the road when I saw her." She was almost screaming now. "She could have been killed! Killed!"

Chapter Four

Sophie saw a spear of light dart across the blade of the knife Nick was using, heard the thunk of its handle as he set it down. Then the only sounds in the room were Wilma's breathing and her own. Sand drizzled slowly from Maren's sandals and settled in two small heaps on the floor.

"Well?" Wilma said and shifted Maren to her other hip.

Nick cleared his throat. "Thanks for bringing Maren in." He took the child into his arms. "Did you want to stay for dinner, Mom?"

Wilma's jaw slackened, but not for long. "Dinner? I just found your child running around in the street, and you ask me to stay for dinner? Cool as you please?" She leveled a finger at Sophie and looked at Abby. "Are you going to let her get away with this? Nick may not understand how mothers feel about their children's safety, but you do, Abby. You remember how careful I always was with you and Michael when you were children, and I know you're the same way."

Maren began to whimper softly, and Nick hoisted her higher, rubbed his cheek against her hair. His mouth was tight, and he stared hard at Abby.

Sophie felt shaky and cold. "I'm so sorry...." She faltered, unsure whether she should speak or stay silent. "I— I sent the children in when Michael dropped me off. Mrs.

Harris—"she spread her hands "—you saw me send them in here. I told Justin to let Maren go out to the sandbox while I changed. The gate to the backyard is always closed, and she can't get near the lake."

"Sophie," Abby interposed, "you don't have to defend yourself. Maren did come through the kitchen with Justin, and he told me you'd said she could play in the sandbox for a while. Whatever happened isn't your fault, and everything's all right now, thank God."

"All right?" Wilma sputtered. "Everything's all right and she doesn't have to defend herself? What's the matter with you, and you, Nick? This woman should be out of this house immediately. She isn't fit to take charge of my grandchildren. Do you hear me? If I hadn't had to come back, Maren might be dead! And you say everything's all right!" Her cheeks had turned a dull puce.

Maren had progressed quickly through sniffling sobs to loud wails. Nick jiggled her more rapidly, apparently unaware that he was increasing her agitation.

"Don't do that, Nick," Abby said suddenly. "Can't you see you're upsetting her, throwing her around like that?"

Sophie took an involuntary step backward. She didn't want to be here.

A muscle knotted in Nick's jaw. She wondered what control was costing him. "This isn't getting anyone anywhere," he said. "If we want to get technical, Sophie's off duty. As you know, Mom, if we're here in the evening, Sophie doesn't have to be. We're here, so I guess we're to blame if Maren got out of the yard."

Wilma opened and closed her mouth several times like a beached fish. She seemed to swell as Sophie watched, horribly fascinated.

"Mom," Abby said gently, "let it go, please. Thank you for bringing Maren in. Really, this isn't Sophie's fault, if it's anyone's fault at all."

"If? *If* Maren got out? For me to find her wandering among cars she must have gotten out. And for her to get out, someone has to be to blame. She—" her finger, once more jabbing air in Sophie's direction, wobbled "—she took the children from me, so it was her job to make sure they were safe."

"Mommy, what's the matter?"

Sophie had forgotten Justin. He still stood by the sliding door where he'd been the instant Wilma came in.

"Nothing's wrong, Son. Come here," Nick said. Justin immediately hurried to hold his father's hand.

"Mrs. Harris's right," Sophie said. She locked her trembling knees. "I should have come into the kitchen with them. I wanted to get my things from upstairs to take them back to my apartment, but that could have waited."

"You see." Wilma gave a triumphant smile. "She knows she was wrong. If I hadn't come back we all know what might have happened."

Abby slowly tore off sheets of paper towel and wiped her hands. Absently, she pushed the pan of meat to the back of the counter. "You've made your point, Mother," she said, not looking up. "And we've made ours. Nick and I were in charge around here when Maren went outside, not Sophie. We are, and always have been, extremely satisfied with the work she does for us. Justin and Maren are happy and well adjusted. I know what you want us to say, and it's not going to happen. I have to work and I need Sophie. I want Sophie. We're all grateful you saved us from a tragedy. Thank you. End of discussion."

Sophie held her breath, expecting a fresh outburst from Wilma. None came. Casting a last, sweeping glare around the room, she turned on her heel and left without another word.

Nick sank onto a ladder-back chair. He smiled weakly as he hiked Justin onto his lap. "That's been coming for a long time,'' he said, hugging the children, rocking. Maren was quiet except for loud sucking on her fingers.

"I feel dreadful,'' Sophie said, and her voice sounded scratchy. "This is my fault, all this trouble. No wonder Mrs. Harris is upset. How could Maren have got to the street? I'll have to rig up some sort of safety catch on the gate.'' She was grateful, deeply grateful for Nick and Abby's quick defense of her.

"Nick,'' Abby interjected, "what do you mean: this has been coming for a long time?''

"Just—''

"Can I color again now, Daddy?'' Justin interrupted.

"Sh.'' Nick frowned at the boy. "We're talking.''

Justin slid to the floor. "I want to color now. Can Markus come over, too?''

Sophie itched to take the child out of the room and tell him to behave, but she never interfered when his parents were present.

"Be quiet, Justin,'' Abby snapped. "Nick, what did you mean?'' The towels in her hands were a tight sodden ball.

"Exactly what I said. I've been expecting your mother to bring her campaign into the open for a long time.''

"Campaign?''

"Can Markus come?'' Justin tugged on his mother's sleeve. "Can he?''

"That's enough, Justin,'' Nick said, clearly exasperated. "Be quiet or go to your room. In fact, that's a good idea. Go and clean up your room the way Sophie asked you to. Dinner's going to be late anyway.''

The boy didn't budge.

"Nick, I asked you a question.'' A trace of color stained Abby's cheeks. "What were you trying to say about what just happened?''

He let out a long sigh. Maren wriggled, and he set her down. "You know what I meant, Abby. Your mother never approved of your going back to work in the first place. She used to say you shouldn't waste your talents, and as soon as you decided to use them again, she jumped all over us about how you should be at home 'where you belong.'"

Abby opened the refrigerator and stared inside, shut it again and stood, hands on hips, with her back to Nick. Sophie could see the side of her face, and her eyes were closed. Damn, why hadn't she headed this situation off?

"I know what you're saying," Abby said finally. "Mother does interfere. But she's had a rough time, Nick, you know that. She and Dad were together a long time. They married at eighteen and they'd known each other since they were kids. She's got a big hole in her life."

"And she fills it by trying to make a mess out of ours."

Sophie's heart thumped uncomfortably. There was no graceful escape route, yet she didn't belong where she was.

"That's not fair," Abby muttered. "She doesn't want to upset things between us. She loves you, Nick. And she loves me. But she doesn't have enough to do with her time, and she thinks she should spend more of it with the children. In her mind, if I were here all day, she'd be able to come most of the time, too. But—"

"Oh, terrific," Nick interrupted. "Exactly what I need at the moment. I don't have enough to worry about, so I should welcome my mother-in-law underfoot every waking hour. Over my dead body."

Abby turned. "You don't have to be so nasty. And it's not going to happen."

What Abby hadn't said was that the second-best solution in Wilma's mind would be for her to take Sophie's place. Sophie realized she was winding her fingers together and deliberately clasped a wrist behind her back.

Nick and Abby looked unwaveringly at each other. Sophie cleared her throat, but they didn't notice.

"Mine!" Maren screamed suddenly. "Mine! Mine!"

Justin held the half-colored egg carton firmly in the middle while the toddler scrabbled for possession of one end.

"Mom," Justin moaned. "Stop her, will ya? S'my thing. She's always taking my things."

"Be quiet." Abby didn't look away from Nick.

Justin promptly gave Maren a shove, sending her backward into a wailing heap.

A steady thudding started in Sophie's temples. She broke her rule and set Maren back on her feet. "Hush," she whispered. "And you quiet down, too, Justin. Let's take you two upstairs and get you ready for bed. You can eat dinner in your pajamas. That'll be okay, won't it, Abby?"

Abby wasn't listening. "Ill take care of my mother," she said, a suspicion of a sheen in her eyes. "She won't bother you, so don't worry. I'll make sure she keeps out of your way."

"Damn it all, Abby. You're missing the point and you know it. Look at the way these kids behave after an afternoon with her. She spoils them rotten, and they come back impossible."

"Didn't I hear it was your idea for them to go with my mother today?"

The hand Nick rammed into his hair told more about his frame of mind than any words. Sophie had seen the mannerism before. He was running out of patience.

"Okay, okay," he said carefully. "Yes, I suggested the children spend the afternoon with their grandmother. Why couldn't that be enough for her? Why did she have to pull the stunt she just pulled?"

Abby's color darkened. "What are you accusing her of?"

"Wait here. Just wait. Nobody move a muscle." Nick opened the sliding door to the patio with enough force to rattle the tracks and strode outside. Within seconds, he returned, not bothering to close the door again.

"Well?" Abby asked. "What did that prove?"

"That your mother didn't find Maren in the street. The gate is closed. Did Maren close it behind her as she left, d'you suppose?"

"Are you saying . . ."

"That your mother got Maren from the sandbox and took her around to the front door? I sure am. Then she stormed in here with her little bombshell and expected us to fire Sophie."

"Oh, Nick, she wouldn't do that. She interferes too much, but she isn't mean." Abby's voice broke.

"This little number was more than mean, it was vicious."

She had to say something, she had to. "Mrs. Harris wouldn't deliberately make something up. She wouldn't—"

"You're too generous, Sophie," Nick interrupted.

Abby pursed her mouth and passed him to open the door to the hall. She leaned on the jamb, looking outside for a moment, then left to return with the brightly colored diaper bag dangling from one outstretched hand. "By the front door, Nick. Like Mom said, she came back because she'd forgotten to leave this."

He let out a long, tuneless whistle before he dropped to his knees on the stone-tiled floor. "What do you suppose this is?" Sophie couldn't see what he was showing Abby.

"Sand," Abby commented. "From Maren's feet. So what?"

"If Maren had been tripping the light fantastic in traffic, if she'd even run through the backyard and across the grass in front, she'd have shaken most of this loose. She didn't. Why, do you suppose?"

"Why don't you tell me, Nick? You seem to have all the answers." Abby put down the bag and crossed her arms.

"Because she didn't leave the sandbox until your mother picked her up and carried her in here."

"Are you . . . no, Nick, no." Abby shook her head emphatically. "Mom isn't some kind of a criminal mastermind who's saved her talents all these years. And neither are you some sort of detective. I want to drop this. Now."

"I know you do. And we will, but not before you open your eyes to what Wilma Harris is trying to do."

"Don't talk about her that way."

"Calm down, please Abby. I'm not saying this was a premeditated act. I believe she came back with the diaper bag just the way she said she did. But that's where I stop believing her. She probably heard Maren. You know how she talks to herself when she's playing. Well, your mother heard and did what she did on the spur of the moment. By now she probably wishes she hadn't, but she doesn't know how to get out of it without feeling a fool, so she'll bluff it through."

There was no mistaking the tears that stood in Abby's eyes now. "I can't believe she would... Oh, Nick, what are we going to do? She needs us. I can't hurt her."

Sophie's insides tightened. She wanted to cry herself. Her presence was causing problems these people didn't need. Yet they needed someone. Why not her? And she needed to be here.

Nick stood and gathered Abby into his arms. He smoothed the puckered place between her brows and kissed her there. "It's okay, sweetheart. We'll cope. But we're both going to have to be firmer with her."

"But, Nick—"

He kissed her mouth, cutting off whatever she'd intended to say. Sophie felt close to hysterical laughter. Pressure in the room had evaporated, leaving her relieved but weak. She smiled and studied her shoes. For Nick and Abby Dorset, she no longer existed. Her purse and the clothes she'd worn today were on a chair by the table. On tiptoe, she moved to retrieve them and headed back to the door. Justin, who had evidently decided he'd be safer playing quietly with his sister, glanced up from the defaced egg carton and opened his mouth. Sophie silenced him with a finger on her lips and slipped outside, carefully pulling the door shut behind her.

The backyard sloped down from a trellis-enclosed patio and play area to the lake. The lawn, emerald green and finely manicured, was divided by flights of white stone steps that zigzagged between beds of marigolds and startlingly blue lobelia. At the top of each flight stood twin tubs of riotous impatiens. Sophie trotted, as quickly as her wobbly legs would allow, toward the water and her own precious haven in an apartment above the brick boat house.

She found her key in her purse and mounted the wooden staircase at one side of the building. Designed for two large pleasure vessels, it housed only the catamaran so far, but Sophie knew Nick hoped to have a second boat one day, something he and his family could take on long trips.

Inside her apartment, she went quickly into the bedroom. She kicked off her sandals, tossed her purse and the bundle of clothes on the bed and went to run a bath. She felt grimy, and anyway, she needed the relaxation the warm water always brought. She'd soak and think only pleasant thoughts. Today's events with Wilma weren't likely to be quickly forgotten, but worrying would solve nothing. Careful plans for dealing with any future episodes might help, but for the moment, Sophie's brain felt like mush.

In less than five minutes she stepped into the tub. The steady beat of Billy Joel singing words she couldn't quite hear reached her from the living room stereo, distracting if not soothing her jumpy nerves. She had pulled the laundry hamper near the bath and set one of Nick's old copies of *GQ* magazine and a glass of Coke where she could reach them. She slid down until her chin touched the water, waiting for her muscles to relax. But even the warmth didn't penetrate her tense body.

She picked up the magazine and leafed through pages of sulking male models until she found an article on famous men and their cars. Concentration was impossible. Her eyes refused to focus, and her mind slid away from the words' meaning. The vision of Wilma, mouth open, finger pointing imperiously, formed, garish and vivid. The woman might back off for a while, but not forever.

Sophie stared again at the pictures but saw Michael Harris's face instead. His image came so clearly, too clearly, and the sensation of his mouth on hers, his hands on her skin. The feelings weren't new. Jack had made the same sort of magic for her when they'd first met. She closed her eyes, conscious of her own tremulous smile and a nostalgic warmth in her belly.

Jack, laughing, young, invincible, had been the high school prize, and she'd won him. They'd faced the world fearlessly, convinced they'd have it all, whatever they wanted. He'd had a wonderful sense of humor, and his appetite for fun had swept her along, swept her free of a naturally reserved nature and made her part of everything he cared about. Michael reminded her of Jack. The warmth inside cooled slightly, her muscles tensed even tighter. Michael was...no, he wasn't the way Jack had been in the early years; he was a reflection of what she'd expected Jack to become. Only it hadn't happened. Sophie closed the magazine. Their dreams, hers and Jack's, had been so big and beautiful, and they'd all died, died with Jack. Some would say she should be glad of her freedom and usually she was, but she still grieved for the loss of Jack's promise and sometimes even for the man.

A hollow sensation, a falling away, started in her stomach, and she opened her eyes, but the image that had started to form didn't fade: Jack as he'd been in the weeks before he died. Still handsome, the dark hair still thick and tousled, his blue eyes arresting, even though they'd become distant in an increasingly gaunt face. Jack had been disintegrating while she watched, and she couldn't help him. He no longer wanted her help. The bottle at his elbow was all he relied on then. And his wild rages were his only communication with her. She felt suddenly sick. The end wasn't what counted...she wouldn't think about any of that.

Something rested on her ribs. She glanced down and sat up with a jolt, shaking the sodden edges of the magazine she'd forgotten.

There was a similarity between Jack and Michael Harris. Sophie got out of the bath and set the magazine on a towel to dry before rubbing herself vigorously. She wouldn't go out with Michael tomorrow after all. She didn't need another disaster in her life. Being here, with the Dorsets and Justin and Maren, made her happy. Times weren't too smooth at the moment, but they would be, and this was where she wanted to stay. Even if Michael were perfect, Mr. Solid Citizen—which he might be—she didn't want to run the risk of finding out he wasn't, she didn't need to. Having another man in her life wasn't important. Not now anyway. And getting involved with Michael could definitely be dangerous to her job if they got in too deeply and then things didn't work out. She wouldn't be able to face him day in and day out after that. No, she'd call him and cancel the date. Even as she lectured herself, formed logical arguments for what she intended to do, the doubts didn't fade, nor the apprehension. She was far from settling her differences with Wilma Harris and maybe even further from reconciling her true feelings for Michael.

Wrapped in a short terry cloth robe, she walked barefoot over the deep-piled teal-blue carpet, through the living room to the kitchen. She'd better make something to eat for dinner and take it to the bedroom. She'd sit in her favorite spot on her king-size bed recessed cozily into a dormer window, and when she'd eaten she'd call Michael. The conversation would be pleasant. He was a reasonable man. She paused with a bunch of grapes in one hand, a colander in the other. Michael Harris *was* reasonable, wasn't he? She shook her head and began washing the fruit.

Her apartment had been designed by the previous owner of Abby and Nick's house to serve as his studio and getaway. Sophie had never heard what he was getting away from, but the man had been an artist who had painted in what was now her dining area, and she loved what he'd done with a fairly small space. A huge Palladian window dominated the wall overlooking the lake. Its vertical support beams fell between living room and kitchen, kitchen and bedroom. No dividing walls reached the sharply sloped walnut ceiling, and the etched glass of the window could be seen in a great dome from any point in the apartment except the bathroom. In the bathroom a bubble skylight was splattered by rain or sun-washed by day and became a window on the dark skies Sophie loved by night.

Half an hour later, she sat cross-legged on her bed, a plate of fruit and cheese untouched on a bedside table... beside the phone.

Michael might not even be at home. She hauled the open phone book onto the bed. A circle around his name and number stood out clearly from the rest of the listings.

What was really eating her? She leaned forward, rested her elbows on her knees and supported her chin. If she were honest, she'd admit that she was afraid, afraid she could just come to care for Michael.

The phone rang at the same moment she turned her head to look at it. She jumped violently, clenched and unclenched her hand and listened to another shrill ring before snatching up the receiver.

"Sophie?" *Michael.*

"Yes."

"Sophie, it's Michael. Look, I called Nick about something, and he gave me the rundown on... on what happened earlier with my mother. I'm sorry, Sophie."

For a moment she couldn't reply. He was a kind man, truly kind. "Thanks, Michael. You're... thanks for bothering to call, but like I said before, Wilma's lonely. Things will work out, I'm sure." A lump formed in her throat.

"Nick said he thought you were pretty upset, and I don't blame you. Abby and I are going to have to spend a bit more time with Mom. And I think we need to figure out something to keep her busy. The main thing is, you mustn't let this get to you. Nick and Abby think you're wonderful...and so do I...."

Sophie was silent. Her skin turned hot and cold by turns. He sounded so sincere. She *wanted* him to be sincere.

"Are you still with me?" His voice was soft.

"I'm with you, Michael. It's hard to say what I feel, that's all. I needed a few kind words, and you came up with them."

"My pleasure. Well, I didn't call to bend your ear, just to let you know I feel partly responsible for this and I'll do my part to make sure it doesn't happen again. All right?"

"All right. Thanks." She should tell him she couldn't make it tomorrow.

"Great. That's my girl. Listen, we didn't set a time for dinner tomorrow. I checked with Nick, and he said they'll be home early and don't intend to go out, so there's no need to find a baby-sitter. How about me picking you up at six, if that's not too early? I thought we could drive somewhere and go for a walk. Then dinner. Have you been to Ray's Downtown?"

She could visualize his mouth and the way he lowered his eyelids a fraction when he looked at her. "No," she said, "I haven't been there."

"Good. We'll go to Ray's. You'll love it. Then, if we're not too beat, we'll find somewhere with music, any kind of music you like. How does that sound?"

The telephone receiver was slippery. She gripped it in both hands.

"Hey there, Sophie. Give me a sign. Does that sound good, or would you rather do something else? A movie? A play?"

"No, no," she said hastily. "That sounds wonderful."

"Terrific. I'll make our reservations. See you at six. Bye."

"Yes...well...." But he'd hung up.

Spineless. That had been one of the things Jack had called her when he was angry and she wouldn't fight back. Was she too spineless to make up her own mind and act upon her decisions?

She flopped on her back and stared at the rich wood overhead. Not turning Michael down hadn't been an act of indecision. Sophie wanted to be with him...more than she'd ever wanted anything.

Chapter Five

He'd never seen her hair down before. Even first thing in the morning when she was giving the children their breakfast she either tied it back loosely or made a single braid that swung across her back as she walked. Now it slithered softly about her shoulders in the breeze, and a lowering sun caught pale highlights in its smooth, gently wavy length.

"I like it here." Sophie strolled beside him along the waterfront, her face turned toward Elliott Bay where sightseeing boats threaded between ferries and container ships and a dozen other types of craft. "There's no smell like the water to me. Tar, or creosote, or whatever that is, and fish cooking. When I was a kid I always wanted to see the sea." She laughed. "See the sea. Computer headache, huh? No spell checker's going to sort that one out."

The comment surprised Michael. "Have you worked with computers?"

She glanced up at him. Those velvet-brown eyes did something to him, and he liked it. He could see them in his sleep. But she looked hesitant.

"I...I played around with them years ago," she remarked and faced the water again.

Michael frowned. The strangest questions seemed to bother her. "How old were you when you first saw the sea?"

"Nineteen. My husband and I went to Mexico for our honeymoon—Puerto Vallarta." Her voice was expressionless. "I expect it seems funny to you not to have seen a wave until you were nineteen."

"In a way. We take some things for granted." Michael considered taking her hand and changed his mind instantly. Possibly he'd made a little ground with the lady. A very little ground. One wrong step and he'd be back in the blocks. "We could go out to the end of one of the piers if you like," he said. "Then there's the market. If we're feeling energetic we can take the Pike Place Hill Climb." He nodded across Alaskan Way to a steep flight of steps switchbacking upward to a row of rickety buildings clinging to the side and top of a hill. The buildings were part of Pike Place Market.

"The piers. That's what I'd like. Let's go down this one," Sophie said and surprised him by slipping her hand into his and pulling him along frayed wooden planking beside a row of dilapidated warehouses jutting into the bay. "Come on." She looked up at him over her shoulder and laughed. "You aren't too old to run, are you?"

He grinned broadly and broke into a jog. Soon she was at a full run to keep up with him, but he didn't stop. He felt good, young and incredibly happy.

"S-stop," she sputtered when they were almost at the end of the pier. "I think I'm dying."

He slowed, turned and kept trotting backward, smiling into her flushed face. "Come on, come on, Sophie. I thought I was the one who was too old to run."

She planted her feet, pulling him to a halt. "Okay, macho friend," she managed around gasps, "you're king of the condition race—for now. We'll have a rematch when I've worked on my muscles and lungs a bit." As soon as she spoke, her pink cheeks darkened. Why couldn't she let her guard down with him for more than two minutes without being embarrassed?

"It's a deal," he said quickly. "Want to sit on one of those benches for a while? Fresh air should be part of your fitness program." He didn't say what he wanted to say, that she seemed in great shape to him, perfect in every way.

Silently she passed him and made for one of the benches he'd indicated. She wore a light rose-colored cotton dress, the bodice tight and held at the shoulders by narrow straps tied in bows. Beneath a tiny waist, the soft skirt alternately billowed and then flattened to her small hips. Her bare legs were well shaped. She didn't have to do a thing about her shape for him. True, she was small, in every way. She'd sat, and he stood beside her a moment, looking down, smiling involuntarily. "Quality not quantity," she'd said to her reflection in the refrigerator. Her breasts might be small, but they matched the rest of her, and the whole package was sexy enough to take up far more of his mental energy than was good, either for him or Islands Unlimited.

Sophie looked at him, and it was his turn to blush—an unfamiliar and uncomfortable sensation. He sat beside her. Time to make some more progress with this woman, no matter how little or how slow.

"What do you like to do, Sophie?"

Her shoulders, glimpsed between the shifting blond hair, were pale and smooth.

She stared at the sky. "I like to read and listen to music. I used to like to dance and play tennis and swim—in a lake or a pool, of course. And horses, I like riding horses. But I guess what I enjoy most of all now is being with the children."

Well, Michael thought, what had he expected? It hardly made sense to be disappointed that she hadn't included him in her list. He pressed on. "We've got a lot in common." That much was true. "I like all those things, too. Tonight we'll try the dancing. Will you play tennis with me soon?"

"I don't have a racket anymore."

"We'll find you one."

She didn't answer.

"Have you ever swum off a boat?"

"No."

"I'll take you out on Lake Sammamish, and we'll swim. It's great. So clear you can see the bottom in places." He got a quick image of Sophie in a bathing suit, or better yet, skinny-dipping at night, the moon in her eyes and glistening on her wet hair and naked skin. He puffed out his cheeks. Imagination could be a dangerous thing.

She stood and walked to lean on a railing. Michael joined her. "Would you like to go swimming, maybe next weekend?"

An arrogant sea gull swooped to perch a few feet from Sophie. "This guy isn't afraid of a thing," she said. "Look him in the eye, and he looks right back."

He'd try one more time. "Swimming, Sophie? Are you still on my wavelength? Will you come with me?"

"Maybe," she said, turning her head away. "I'll have to see what Nick and Abby have on, and I expect you'll need to check your schedule. What other things do you like to do?"

She was adept at avoidance tactics, but he'd go along. He planted his chin on a fist and considered. "You won't laugh?"

Sophie faced him, her arms crossed. He had her interest. "Of course I won't laugh. Tell me what you like to do. No, no, let me guess." She frowned, pressing her lips tightly together. "Needlepoint?" No trace of a smile showed. Her eyes were wide and innocent. "Ballet. That's it, you're a closet ballet dancer."

He gave a hoot of laughter. "Wrong on both counts. But you are going to laugh, I know you are. So I'm not going to tell you."

"Oh, Michael. I'm sorry, honestly I am. Couldn't resist. Tell me, please." She pulled his fist from beneath his chin. "Come on, don't tease."

"Well, it's no big deal, and I'm terrible at it, but I like to paint. Abby's the real family artist, but I like to mess around with oils from time to time.

Her lips parted slightly before she smiled, and delight shone in her eyes. "You paint? How lovely. What do you like to paint best?"

He'd never told another woman about his hobby. The fear that they'd think it didn't fit his image had always made him self-conscious about the subject—not that it had tended to come up.

"Don't clam up on me now, Michael. Seascapes, still life, what's your favorite?"

"I'm very bad at it. I chose oils because they're forgiving. You can always change your mind when you mess up."

"Michael," she let out a gusty sigh, "stop hedging. What do you paint?"

"Everyday scenes," he said, watching her carefully. She looked interested. "Things like people doing what they do for a living. Fishing, repairing cars, cooking. People's faces are great when they aren't thinking about themselves."

He hadn't meant to put it that way. But it was true, ordinary man doing his thing fascinated him.

"I'd like to see some of your paintings."

"Oh, no. I never show them to anyone. They're awful."

"I bet they're not. But be secretive if you like." She touched his arm, smiling that wonderful unaffected smile of hers. "I'll probably ask again, though, so be warned."

He flipped some errant strands of hair back from her shoulder, and his fingers brushed the smooth skin at the side of her neck. "Fair enough. You warned me." He glanced at her eyes, her mouth and turned to lean his elbows on the railing. Below, an oily film, glossy mauve, pink and silver, slithered over the surface of the opaque green waters that swirled around the blackened pilings. She'd virtually asked to see his etchings and he'd refused! Fortunately, he was past the point where he fostered myths about his sex life. He shook his head faintly. Michael Harris was either slipping, or... He'd grown up, that was all. Time had finally taught him to recognize specialness in a woman. Sophie was special, and he was learning that the old rules for the male-female dance, the ones he'd known for so long, didn't apply with her.

The sea gull, content to perch and stare for just so long, abruptly flapped its wings, let out a screech and soared away with enough force to make Michael flinch.

Sophie was laughing, her face tipped up to watch the bird. She had beautiful teeth and the kind of skin that looked as if some magic brush had tinted it in all the right spots with exactly the right shades. He checked his watch. More time had passed than he'd realized.

"We'd better start back," he said. "I'd like to move the car closer to the restaurant, and parking could be a problem." Staying here, intensely aware of her yet unable to touch her or say an intimate word, was definitely becoming a problem.

Ray's Downtown was on Second Avenue. At this time of year stone planter boxes filled with brilliant blossoms dotted the forecourt and deciduous trees lining the sidewalk rustled, their leaves soft and still tender.

Sophie slipped her hand through the elbow Michael offered and walked side by side with him into the restaurant, taking pleasure in the glances women gave him.

Seated at a table by windows overlooking the street, she settled the folds of her skirt around her, suddenly certain she should have dressed more formally.

"What is it, Sophie? You look edgy."

"This dress is all wrong," she blurted and immediately wished she hadn't. He seemed to have that effect on her—the ability to make her say the first thing that came into her head. "I mean that everyone is a lot more dressed up than I am."

He regarded her solemnly until she had to look away. "Mmmm," he said at last. "The truth is, my dear, that everyone else is overdressed beside you. Some people need a lot of—whatever you call all that stuff. You don't. In fact, I'd say the less you wear the better. I mean..."

She narrowed her eyes at him, laughing. "You blew it, Michael. The true you sneaked out when you didn't expect it to."

"No, no," he insisted seriously. "That wasn't what I meant. I meant you look lovely in very little—"

"Michael!" She winced and met the curious stare of a man at a nearby table. "Michael," she said more softly. "Quit while you're—while you might be ahead. And thanks for the vote of confidence I think you just gave me. You look pretty terrific yourself, by the way." Pleased with her aplomb, she studied the menu.

She declined a cocktail, but Michael ordered himself a martini.

"Memorized that yet?"

Over the menu, she returned his smiling gaze. Evening sun sent its gold glow along the window. His face was half in shade, and light from a candle on the table reflected in his dark, almost navy-blue, eyes. "I'm trying to choose between salmon and swordfish," she said and looked down again. The twisting ache came in her belly, not for the first time since she'd known this man.

"Why don't you have one and I'll have the other and we can trade halfway through?"

Relaxing with him would be so easy. "Maybe you don't want fish at all. Aren't you a steak man?" Anything too easy was dangerous, experience had let her know that.

"I prefer fish."

She knew he was looking at her. "You're not just trying to be nice?"

"No. But I don't have to try to be nice with you, Sophie."

No brilliant response came to mind. She was warmer—too warm.

"Are you nervous?"

"Why should I be nervous?" She swallowed the last word but met his eyes squarely. Oh, but he was right. She *was* nervous.

"I'm not sure. Maybe I just thought you might be, too."

"*Too*, Michael?"

He appeared uncomfortable. The martini had been served, and he drank it like water. Watching him, Sophie felt her own throat tighten. Michael showed no reaction to the drink except to hail the waiter and order another.

She opened her mouth to comment and took in a deep breath instead. One day she'd stop panicking every time she was around alcohol. Michael was having a few social drinks, nothing more.

"Do you mean you're nervous?" she persisted when he faced her again.

"I guess so." He moved his knife back and forth on the table. "Funny, huh? I guess you think I'm always in control? Always on top of the situation? Isn't that what you think?"

Impulsively, she reached across the table and covered his hand. "I'm nervous, too, Michael. I guess I don't know what to expect when I'm with you. I don't know what you're thinking. I don't even have an idea of why you'd want to be with me."

"Do you want to be with me?" He turned his hand and twined his fingers in hers.

Before she could reply, the waiter came with the second martini and took their dinner order.

When the man left, Michael increased his pressure on her hand and repeated his question, "Sophie, are you glad to be here with me?"

"Yes," she said simply.

"Good. That's what I wanted to hear. I can't tell you exactly what I'm thinking, but a lot of what I think these days seems to have to do with you. I can't tell you exactly what I want from you either, except I like being together like this. And that's what makes me nervous, I guess. You're—you're kind of new territory for me."

Sophie digested the idea of being territory of any kind. "You mean I'm not what you're comfortable with in a woman. I'm not much of a conversationalist or..." She let the rest of the thought trail away. Most of the women he'd known were undoubtedly a lot more physically responsive than she knew how to be. No, she'd known how to be demonstrative once, before her marriage turned sour.

Michael had said something. "I'm sorry?" she said.

"You were miles away there." He grinned. "That's some of what interests me about you, Sophie: you're a mystery. I wonder what goes on inside your head, too. So I guess we're even."

A mystery, Sophie thought, and moved her shoulder aside as her salad was served. She was no mystery.

Dinner was excellent. As Michael had suggested, they sampled each other's fish and made round eyes of appreciation until they laughed aloud. From other tables came the subdued hum of conversation, the clink of crystal and the sound of silver on fine china. Sophie absorbed the ambiance and felt herself surrounded by it while she and Michael were drawn closer and closer.

Their plates were taken away, and Michael ordered coffee for them both and Pernod for himself. Sophie continued to sip the glass of wine he'd insisted on pouring for her.

He took a long, thoughtful swallow from his own wineglass. "You really are happy at Abby and Nick's, aren't you? Being with the children makes you feel secure."

She looked at him sharply, hit with the unnerving sensation that he'd been looking into her head. "I enjoy my job. It's what I want to do."

"For now, you mean?"

She hesitated before she said, "For as long as I'm thinking about. I make it a rule not to look too far into the future. Planning ahead sets you up for disappointment." Again she'd said more than she'd intended.

Michael was silent, and when she looked at him he was studying the wine he was swirling in his glass. He seemed . . . sad? She was imagining things.

She was glad when the waiter brought coffee and Michael's after-dinner drink. He offered her the small glass of licorice-scented liqueur. "Taste this. It's so good it's addictive."

"No, thanks." She began to feel uneasy again.

"I promised you dancing after dinner. Four Seasons okay?"

Dancing. How many years had it been since she danced? "Sounds wonderful," she agreed while she wondered if she'd even remember how or if she'd step all over his feet. Her next thought was that being held by him again would feel so good.

"We can walk from here," he said. "It'll help with that conditioning program we're going to get into."

Sophie returned his grin before she glanced at a woman who had been about to leave the restaurant. Slightly plump but pretty, with stylishly cut honey-blond hair, she stopped a few feet from Michael and stared at him, frowning. Her uncertain expression cleared, and she said a few words to the man with her before hurrying to their table. She rested a hand familiarly on Michael's back, and he looked up.

"Michael Harris," the woman said. "I wasn't sure it was you for a minute. You old fraud. You promised to keep in touch, and I haven't heard from you in months. How are you?"

Sophie put her hands in her lap and watched Michael's reaction. Within seconds she was winding her fingers together until they hurt. Michael had turned waxen beneath his tan, and Sophie was almost certain she saw beads of sweat pop out at his temples. He didn't answer the woman.

"Michael? Earth calling Michael?" she bowed over him, jutting her chin slightly. "It's me, Maxine. A little heavier than you remember, perhaps, but not a stranger...or a ghost, old friend."

He cleared his throat, laughed and leaped to his feet. "Maxine, I'm sorry." He embraced her, held her close, and Sophie saw his eyes close. Something...something like misery washed over his rigid face. He opened his eyes, settled a forced smile on his lips and held her away. "You surprised me, that's all. How are you? You look great." He pretended to survey her carefully. "You used to be too thin, now you're just right."

"Oh, Michael. You always were a silver-tongued devil. Still giving the women a run for their money?" She immediately gave Sophie a wry grin. "Forgive me. Habit makes me talk to Michael this way. Introduce your friend, Michael."

"Yes, yes, of course." The hand he waved toward Sophie jerked. "Sophie Peters, this is Maxine Jones, an old friend, the wife of...Maxine was married to my friend Dallas Jones."

The squeeze Maxine gave Michael's arm was accompanied by a gentle smile. "Maxine Bell now, Michael. I'm remarried."

He bowed his head.

"We all need someone," Maxine went on quietly. "I'm a lucky woman to have found two wonderful men in one lifetime." She glanced back at the man she'd been with. He smiled and gestured toward the reception area. When she nodded he made his way out. "I intended to let you know about John, Michael. I guess I wasn't sure how you'd react. Do you understand?" An anxious light entered her brown eyes.

"Sure," Michael said, but muscles in his jaw stood out. "I'm glad you're happy."

"Thanks. We'd like to have you over if you'll come. Will you Michael?"

"Yeah, yeah, of course I will. I'll call you though, okay? This is the busy time of year for me."

Sophie rubbed her upper arms, embarrassed at the perfunctory way Michael had reacted to Maxine's invitation.

The woman watched him for a few seconds, then took a pen and pad of paper from her purse. She scribbled briefly and tore off a sheet. "Here's the new number. I hope you will call. Be happy, Michael." She smiled at him, briefly, tightly, nodded at Sophie and hurried from the restaurant.

For several minutes Michael remained standing, evidently oblivious of stares from other diners. Slowly he folded the paper Maxine had given him and slid it into the breast pocket of his white shirt.

When he sat, his movements seemed slow and heavy. He raised his hand to summon the waiter without ever looking at Sophie. Instead of asking for the bill, he ordered another martini, a double. Sophie's stomach felt sucked up beneath her ribs. She could hardly breathe.

He'd drunk half the fresh drink before Sophie found the courage to break the silence. "Is something wrong?" she asked uncertainly.

When he looked at her it was with glazed eyes. He tossed back the rest of the martini and signaled the waiter yet again.

Sophie's heart pounded. This was the kind of thing she'd been afraid of in getting involved with this man. With any other she could walk out, but not with her boss's brother. She ran her fingers into the hair at her temples and propped her elbows on the table. Even if he weren't Abby's brother, she couldn't have left him like this.

"You're quiet," he said suddenly.

"You're the quiet one, Michael," she commented in a low voice. "What happened just now—with Maxine Bell? She upset you, didn't she?"

"No!"

His raised voice attracted attention once more, and Sophie pressed a palm to her fiery cheek. "Don't shout, Michael. I'm sorry if I butted in where I don't belong. Look, maybe we should call it a night."

"Maxine didn't upset me." This time he spoke almost inaudibly.

He drank some more, his mobile mouth unfamiliarly drawn down. His gaze, when it connected with hers, seemed pleading. "Sophie, I don't think I'm ready to call it a night. This is one night I may never be ready to call."

Now she felt sick—and trapped. The sensation was familiar. "Okay," she said in a voice she'd heard herself use so many times before. "We'll do whatever you feel like doing, Michael. Just let me know when you're ready to make a move." She even used the same phrases in the same placating, parent-to-child voice that had usually managed only to make Jack more difficult to handle.

"I'd like to leave now. Is that okay?" He looked not at Sophie, but at the window, a black mirror reflecting shapes and colors inside the restaurant.

Sophie managed a smile. "Of course. Let's go."

Michael got to his feet, jarring the table, rattling glasses. His napkin fell to the floor as he pushed back his chair and waited for her to stand. Sophie walked past him, eyes down, wedging her small purse beneath her arm. In the foyer, he dropped a credit card on the desk and signed the receipt in silence, then held her elbow as they went out to the sidewalk.

Sophie felt too emotionally insubstantial to deal with whatever troubled him. The desire for flight hit her again, harder this time, but he put his arm around her shoulders, holding her tightly against his side. He was a big man, strong....

"I don't feel like the Four Seasons anymore," he announced without preamble. "If it's all right with you, we'll go to my place and dance. Music's better anyway—and we'll be alone. I don't feel like being with a lot of people."

They reached the Triumph. Sophie's skin turned icy. She watched him open the door and motion her absently inside, but she stood her ground.

"Get in." He motioned again.

"I don't think so, Michael," she said distinctly. "You need to be completely alone. That includes not with me. And I don't want to be with you while you're like this. I also don't want to go to your place to dance. Dinner was lovely, and the walk. Thank you."

He let the door open fully and shoved his hands in his pockets. "Are all women the same?" he asked indistinctly on an expelled breath. "Do they all suck everything out of a man for as long as it pleases them, then move on without looking back?" Sophie thought he swayed slightly. He was definitely deeply upset.

"I wish I could help you, Michael, but I don't know how. Look, I'm going to catch a cab. Thanks again for everything."

His hand on her shoulder stopped her from turning away. "I brought you and I've got to take you home. Please, get in." He urged her into the car and slammed the door.

Sophie sat very still, every nerve and muscle in her body jumping. She didn't want him to drive. But how could she stop him? He did seem steady enough. Michael walked around the car, sorting through the bundle of keys in his hand as he went, and climbed in beside her. He didn't speak all the way back to Leshi, and Sophie was glad. By the time he pulled into the driveway at the Dorsets her neck and shoulders ached with tension.

"Right." He switched off the ignition and climbed out of the car. She was already standing on the grass when he came around to her side. "I'll see you to your place," he said.

"That's not necessary. You're tired. Go on home and get some rest."

He ignored her and put a hand on her shoulder once more. The sky was a great soft bowl of silver and indigo speckled with stars. A shimmering glow surrounded the moon. Sophie took a deep breath, looking up, trying to calm down. She gained some comfort from lights at the windows of Nick and Abby's house, a renewed connection with safety. Michael unlatched the gate to the backyard, and she walked through with him.

"Look at the sky," she said, trying to lighten the mood for him. "I don't even paint, but it appeals to the artist in me."

"It's beautiful," he said, and she relaxed slightly. He sounded more normal again. The fresh air must be doing its work.

At the bottom of the stairs to her apartment, she turned to him and smiled up in the twilight. "I'm fine from here. Thanks again, Michael."

He didn't move or speak.

"Good night." Surely he didn't expect her to kiss him after the tension they'd just gone through.

"Can I come in for a while?"

Her blood seemed to drain to her feet. "Ah...I really do think you should get home, don't you, Michael? You're obviously uptight."

"Can I come in Sophie?" he repeated. "I can't take being alone right now."

She wished she knew what was going on in his head, that she could give in to the empathy she wanted to feel and let go of the anxiety. "Well..."

"Please, Sophie. I won't stay long."

Several seconds passed before, resigned, she led the way to the front door and into her apartment. She walked around the living room, busily snapping on lights, sweeping up the pile of newspapers on the coffee table and putting them in the kitchen garbage. When she finally stood still she found Michael had taken off his jacket and gone to stare through the window at wavering reflections across the lake.

The one thing she mustn't do was show insecurity. She knew what that could produce in certain men, particularly when they'd been drinking.

"Would you like some coffee?" she asked tentatively.

"Coffee?" Michael didn't turn around. "I don't suppose you've got any gin?"

"No." Swallowing was hard.

"Scotch?"

"No. I don't have any reason to keep any of those things around."

He looked at her over his shoulder. The melancholy, almost lost expression in his eyes turned her awkwardness to desperation. "You only have coffee?" he asked.

Sophie rubbed her palms together. "Coffee or tea."

"I need something alcoholic." He bowed his head. "I need something."

The base of her neck knotted painfully. "I don't usually drink. I . . . I don't."

"Maybe you've got some wine you forgot." Michael turned, hitting the corner of the dining table as he headed for the kitchen. His low curse made Sophie step backward. She shouldn't have let him come in.

Bottles and jars rattled as he opened the refrigerator. "Hah!" he called. "Thought as much. What have we here? Champagne? Just the ticket, Sophie, my love. We'll celebrate. Put on some dancing music." Now he sounded wild. Mood swings. Sophie remembered those too well.

The next noise she heard was the popping of the champagne cork, followed by the sound of Michael rummaging for glasses. He muttered something she couldn't make out and emerged with two water glasses filled to the brim.

"Thought you didn't keep anything like this." He smiled engagingly, and Sophie's heart twisted a little.

She took the glass he held out to her and let him clink his own against it. She made no attempt to drink. "I'd forgotten I was given the champagne when I moved in."

"Who gave it to you?" He looked into the pale bubbles as he drank.

"A friend. Someone I know back home. He was passing through Seattle and he knew from my folks I was here."

Michael's eyes cleared, and he stared at her intently. "A guy? I've never seen you with a man, but I guess I don't see everyone who comes and goes here."

Irritation flattened her anxiety. "No, you don't see everyone who comes and goes here. Not that anyone does except the children and me."

He went to the stereo, checked the cassette still in the machine and turned it on. Billy Joel; the tape she hadn't changed from the day before.

"At least this one guy has come and gone, though. Who is he?"

She set her glass carefully on the counter between the dining room and kitchen. "Luke Shumsky is a very nice man who grew up on the spread next to my folks. I've known him all my life."

"Cozy. Is there something between you?"

"Oh, Michael," Sophie exploded, "are you ever going to hate yourself in the morning. What are you talking about? If there *was* someone in my life it wouldn't be your business. As a matter of fact, Luke is twenty years older than I am and married with four kids. He came by more to be able to tell my folks I was okay than anything else. And you're drunk."

She was shaking and the palms of her hands were damp when she rubbed them together.

Michael lifted his glass to the light and gave an uncomfortable little laugh. "I'm sorry. Guess I did overstep the mark there." He walked slowly across the soft rug and put his glass beside Sophie's. "And I won't drink any more, okay? Can I be forgiven if I'm good?"

More familiar words. "How about that cup of coffee, Michael? I think you should have one before you go home."

"Yup. Coffee. I'll have some coffee...if you'll dance with me."

She stared at him in disbelief. Shaking her head, she went to put on the kettle. "It'll be instant, I'm afraid."

He was behind her when she turned away from the stove. "Sometimes I speak first and think later," he murmured. "Do you ever do that?"

"I guess so," she said. He was trying, clumsily, to apologize, but she was still uneasy.

"You are beautiful, Sophie. Elusive and beautiful." With a finger and thumb he gently tilted up her chin.

"Michael—"

His lips cut off the rest of what she might have said. His mouth met hers softly while he spread trembling fingers over her back. Sophie closed her eyes. For seconds she kept her hands at her sides, then, hesitantly, she touched his sides. She couldn't help responding to him. He was suffering and in need. The warning came then, distant first, then loud and insistent. The world was made up of givers and takers. Sophie didn't want to take, but neither did she want to give, then be left alone to bleed again.

"Stop it, Michael." She struggled to put distance between them, but he kissed her again, more insistently this time, and his grip tightened. Another place and time, another man, entered her mind as vividly as if she were there with him now. Sweat broke out all over her body. "Let me go," she begged. And she pushed hard against his chest until he released her.

"What? You...what is it?" He reached for her again, confusion dulling his eyes.

Sophie turned her back on him. "Leave. Go away, Michael."

"Don't make me go tonight, Sophie," he said, his breath coming in short gasps. "Let me stay with you."

This was a nightmare she'd never expected with him. "You know I can't do that."

"I need you." His voice broke. "A man's only got so long. He doesn't know when the day he's in is his last day. Then he's gone and forgotten."

"You...you aren't sick, are you?" A cold wad formed in her throat, and she swung around to face him.

He rolled his head from side to side. "I just need to feel I'm alive now. Don't you understand? Being with a woman lets a man know he's still alive and kicking, and I have to have that tonight."

Tonight. Over and over again he talked about tonight. "You mean like a man who just came through a battle and has to have sex with the first female in sight to celebrate his survival? What battle did you just survive? Sorry, Michael, you're out of luck." Sophie walked past him, holding her breath, expecting him to shoot out a hand and stop her.

She reached the front door and swept it wide, moved outside on the small deck and waited. The time that passed before he joined her seemed endless. His jacket trailed from one hand.

"I didn't mean what you just said," he murmured very softly. "All I really wanted was to be with you. Just feeling you near would have been enough."

"Yes, sure. Good night."

As soon as he started down the steps Sophie went inside and shut the door, shot home the dead bolt and leaned against the frame.

He'd never know what he'd made her pay this evening, how she'd relived a thousand little cameos from her life with Jack, cameos she'd thought buried.

On rubbery legs she made it to the couch and sat down. She ought to cry. Normal people cried when they'd just been through a crisis. But she wasn't normal anymore, Jack had seen to that. What was it about her that attracted men who wanted to dominate women?

Her breathing slowly calmed. Was that what Michael was, another Jack, another potentially violent drunk? As soon as she had asked herself the question she knew the answer. Michael wasn't like Jack. Something in that restaurant, something about Maxine Bell had upset him, otherwise he would never have behaved as he had. The man who had treated her with such gentleness when they'd picnicked was the real Michael Harris. She sensed it instinctively. But old fears and patterns had stopped her from offering him even a little of the comfort he had needed. With patience and trust she might have drawn out of him whatever was wrong and been able to help. Now it was too late. She'd sent him away.

Too tired to get up and go to the bedroom, she stretched out where she was.

"Just feeling you near would have been enough." A tear did slip free then, coursed across her temple to her hair. Just feeling Michael near would have been enough for her too. More than enough.

Chapter Six

"We're going down! Mike, for God's sake, we're going down!"

"Not now. Don't do this now." Michael covered his ears and stumbled from the bottom of the boat house steps toward the edge of the lake. Water, scalloping in over shiny pebbles, hissed, then sucked as it went out again. The water was another of those things that pulled, a relentless pulling, like gravity, the gravity that could pull down great heavy metal machines full of people. Safer to fly than drive, everyone said, trying to convince themselves as much as their listeners. And they were right if odds were all you counted. But if you got on the wrong side of their wonderful statistics, became part of the minority chalked off in history as rare disasters, flying wasn't safe. Thanks to Michael, Dallas Jones became one of those statistics.

"Damn!" His shoe caught the edge of a rock, and he fell, slamming his hands into sand loaded with ragged shell fragments.

"Pull her back!"

His head swelled inside with the power of that remembered voice. He was going to burst wide open.

"Get the nose up! We're going in! Can't see the bloody runway!"

"Stop it. For God's sake, Dallas, stop it." His hands hurt like hell, and his wrists, but the sand was cool. He scrunched it between his fingers, knelt and let coarse grains pour from his palms.

"Mike..."

"No, no!" He pressed the heels of his hands to his temples, but the pumping only got stronger. He felt the blood in his veins; behind closed eyelids he felt as if he could see the blood pumping through the veins in his head. "Please stop." His own voice sounded far away. It had to be loud enough to shut out that other voice. "I'm sorry." He'd shouted, hadn't he? "I'm sorry!"

"Mike. Help me... help... Mike!"

Glass buckling, bulging into a milky bubble, then fracturing in a flying cloud of glittering fragments. He saw it all again in slow motion. "Oh, God." The breath in his lungs had pushed to the top, crammed into his throat. He was going to die, too. *Too.*

Hot tears, like singed grit, welled up. Dallas had begged for help, and he hadn't given it. He'd decided he was some sort of god himself, decided there was time to get the others out of the plane and come back for a man who was a better man than Michael ever hoped to be. Because of him, Dallas Jones had died and everyone had forgotten him, everyone but Michael, and he'd never forget, had no right to expect to forget.

The noise, the tearing, screaming sound of bursting rubber when the tires went and the fuselage ripped wide open...and then the fire. He curled into a ball on the damp sand. He'd felt the fire, the pain, but Dallas... No, he couldn't go through that again. His fault. His lousy judgment. Why had he decided that Dallas would be any less jammed under the control panel after the passengers were out than he was before? The passengers had been okay, hardly a scratch on most of them, and the attendant had been doing fine, but Michael had made his judgment, made sure he was the hero who saved the helpless. And his judgment had killed Dallas.

"I am so sorry." He heard his own moaning whisper. But Dallas didn't hear it. Thanks to him, Dallas would never hear anything again.

Dallas was gone. Michael pushed himself up until he knelt once more. In front of him, the water was a black flickering mass shot with laser chips. Slowly he shifted to sit, elbows on knees, and cradled his aching head. The rushing noise in his skull receded, and he could smell the pungent air again.

What had he done tonight to Sophie? Tears pricked at his eyes again. Big, invincible Michael was turning into a blubbering heap, and he deserved it. He'd frightened a sweet, gentle woman. But maybe that's the way it was intended to be, that from here on he'd never be allowed to get close to anything decent. He was a destroyer, and anyone vulnerable should be protected from him.

Sophie had looked at the sky, and he looked at it now. It was beautiful. Up there, looking down, flying, free, he'd always felt in control, until one bum engine had taken it all away. Oh, he flew now, and most of the time it was okay. But it wasn't the same, would never be the same.

An arc of light from the Palladian window in Sophie's apartment shimmered on the lake's ripples. The scene he'd just put her through played before him like a high-grade video, and he wanted to vomit at its cold reality. He'd opened his old box of personal trash that was supposed to stay hidden and dumped the contents on what might have turned out to be the best thing that had happened to him in years—Sophie Peters. She'd never agree to be alone with him again, and he didn't blame her. Why should she put up with a crazy man who came on like Jekyll and Hyde?

He pushed to his feet. Slowly, on legs that felt like lead, he started back up the flight of steps toward Abby and Nick's house. Halfway up he stopped and glanced over his shoulder at Sophie's place. He hadn't been lying when he'd told her he just wanted to be with her. Not that what he'd meant mattered anymore. And stopping whatever had started between them was just as well for Sophie.

Skirting the house, he arrived on the small terrace outside Nick's study. The sliding door was open a crack, and a fold of thin drape, stolen by the breeze, snapped to and fro.

Michael hesitated and heard the soft click of computer keys. Nick was in there trying to come up with the solution they had to have within a few weeks if their operation was going to stay alive.

It wasn't worry about the business that drew Michael close to the window. Nick understood what he'd been through two years ago as only another flier could possibly understand. Abby had been great, gentle the way she always was, but she didn't really comprehend what had gone on in his head. He had to talk to someone who understood.

Through the sheer drapes, he saw Nick bent over the keyboard. His head was down, his hands in his lap. They hadn't thought far enough ahead, either of them. Administrators they weren't. Financial wizards were made of different stuff than Nick Dorset and Michael Harris. He straightened his shoulders and tapped the glass. Unless he could get his act together he was no use to anyone.

Nick's chair, slamming against the credenza, startled Michael. Nick leaped at the window and wrenched open the door, his face hostile. When he saw Michael he looked first surprised, then angry. "Damn it, Mike. You about gave me cardiac arrest. What the hell are you doing skulking around my yard in the middle of the night?"

Michael gave him a sheepish grin. "It's only ten or so." His tongue felt thick, and the words were muffled. Like Sophie had said, he was drunk.

"Get in here." Nick stood back and peered closely at him as he entered the room, almost tripping over the metal door track. Once inside he stood still while he heard Nick close the door again.

"I thought you and Sophie went out for the evening."

"We did."

"And?"

His palms stung. He turned them over and picked a piece of shell from the base of his thumb.

"Sit down." Nick walked around him and pulled out a chair. "Here, old buddy. You look like hell."

Michael followed directions, slumping onto the wooden seat of the chair.

Nick returned to his own chair, rolled it from its spot between the computer table and his desk until he sat a few feet from Michael.

"I need a drink, Nick." He started to get up but Nick rose enough to shove him back down.

"From the looks of you, you've had enough, my friend."

When he looked at Nick's face he had to turn his head sideways to focus. "You aren't my keeper. Anymore'n she is." He nodded in the direction of the lake. "And how do you know when I've had enough to drink? The whole damn world wants to tell me how to live. Then they won't let me live. They won't let me feel like I'm alive. I tell you there isn't enough time. You think you got forever, buddy, but you don't have any more time than...than... You don't know how long it's gonna be before you're gone and they forget you. They go on when you're gone and they forget you." He wiped the back of his hand across his mouth. His nose was running. Damn it all, he was going to blubber like a kid again.

His eyes were closed when he felt Nick's arms go around him. He rested his face on his friend's shoulder. Nick thumped his back and Michael first gripped his shirt, then returned the hug. He let the tears come, silent tears mounting to choking sobs, and he felt no shame. He'd been an only son, but through Abby he'd gained the best brother a man could have.

"I'm sorry," he mumbled and sniffled again. Nick released him, and he lifted his head. "You sure I can't have that drink?" He found a handkerchief in his pocket and held it over his nose and mouth.

"It isn't my choice, Mike. I wish you wouldn't, though. You've never been a drinker and you don't hold the stuff well."

"Yeah." Nausea rose and washed over him. Even his skin turned clammy. "It all fell apart for me again tonight, Nick. He...it all came back. Ah, hell, Dallas, Dallas." He covered his face with both hands.

"Hey, Mike." Nick's arms went around him again. He held the hair at Michael's nape and pulled his head onto his shoulder. "I thought you'd put all that behind you. It's been two years, and it wasn't your fault."

"Says who?" The words came, fuzzy, against Nick's chest.

"Said the guys who ought to know, the investigators. And they were right. When are you going to let go and get on with the rest of your life?"

"Dallas doesn't get a chance to get on with his life. I made sure of that."

Nick made an incoherent noise and gripped his arms, pushing him back until he could look into his face. "You sound like you want to suffer. Is that it, you enjoy wallowing in a tragedy that wasn't your fault no matter what you say?"

"Damn you, Nick." He raised a hand to shove Nick away but let it drop into his lap. "I thought you understood."

"I do, but I also understand that if you can't cope with this thing and heal yourself you'd better get some professional help."

"I don't need professional help. And I don't need you, or anyone. I don't need Sophie." But as he said it his mind pounded back that he did need her, more and more he needed her.

Nick held his bottom lip in his teeth, apparently waiting for Michael to continue.

He scrubbed at his face, working for control. "I took Sophie to Ray's Downtown for dinner."

"Nice place. How was the food?"

He wadded the handkerchief between his palms. Holding on was everything. If he didn't hold on he'd go to pieces again. "The food was great. Sophie and I have a lot in common. We both like fish, and music and...dancing." His mouth tingled when he tried to smile. "We went for a walk on the waterfront first. She's something, Nick, really something." Each breath hurt his throat. "And she's never going to speak to me again."

"What the hell did you do this time?" Nick leaned forward. "I thought you two were starting to work things out."

"We were." He stood, went to the credenza near the door and poured scotch into a tumbler. Nick called his name but he ignored him. "Maxine Jones was at the restaurant, Nick."

"Maxine Jones?"

Michael swung around, tipping the glass up to his lips. The liquor burned all the way down. "Maxine Jones. Dallas's wife—widow. Maxine Bell now. She married again, Nick. Dallas has been dead two years, two years next month, and his wife is already remarried."

He didn't want the drink after all. When he set it down, the glass almost slipped from his fingers. "That guy was the best. He was my friend and he relied on me. I let him down. I should have been able to—"

"Knock it off." Nick crossed the room in a couple of long strides and grasped his wrists. "Oh, Mike, I thought you'd finally let it go. Think, man. Think hard and straight, if you can with all the crap you've obviously poured into you. Dead on impact, the coroner said, remember?"

"No. Don't." He wouldn't listen.

"Yes, Mike, yes. Dallas was a great guy and if he was here now he'd tell you to stop making a melodrama out of something that's over. You had a crash. Equipment failure was the verdict. And Captain Harris was cited for bravery. Remember that, Michael?"

"Oh, yeah, I remember. Michael Harris the hero. I should have gotten my friend out."

"He was already dead," Nick said deliberately. "You made the choice between getting a dead man out and helping save a bunch of live passengers. You chose the living, and the choice was right, Mike."

"He'd yelled for help. I wasn't sure he was dead."

"Weren't you? He didn't say anything when you went to him, did he?"

"I left him there."

"Because you knew you couldn't do anything for him."

"I'll never be sure of that."

"For some sick reason you're hanging on to this. You're using it like a stick to beat yourself with, like you get some sort of charge out of being maudlin."

"Maudlin? Thanks." He shook free. "I'm enjoying myself, right? What I heard out there—out there when Sophie kicked me out—was what I wanted to hear because I enjoy remembering the good times, huh?"

Nick leaned against the wall and bowed his chin to his chest. "I'm sorry. You heard Dallas again, I guess. I didn't think that was still happening."

"It wasn't until I saw Maxine and realized how fast the earth really covers us up. How could she marry someone else after what she had with Dallas?"

Nick let out a low whistle and moved away from the wall. "Listen to yourself, will you? What do you want the woman to do, sleep on his grave? She loved him, you know that. She mourned him. You know that, too. But she's gone through the process and she's ready to live again. That's healthy, Michael. Take a lesson from her and give Dallas up.''

"I'll never forget him, never.''

"I didn't ask you to forget him, just to admit his death wasn't your fault and get on with your own life.''

"I heard him call my name. The last thing he said was my name.''

"Yeah. It's got to be rough. What happened with Sophie?''

The pounding started in his head again. "I botched it, Nick. Ruined everything. I...oh, God, I think I scared her. Like you said, I'm drunk. She said I was drunk. I came on to her, and she threw me out.''

"Is she all right?'' Nick came very close, and Michael flinched. "Did you...touch her?''

He couldn't look away. "She's okay, except she probably won't ever want to be alone with me again. She's tougher than you think. She let me know what she thought of me. I should get the hell out of the area for a while. All I do is mess up everything I touch.''

"You stupid son of a bitch.'' Nick's voice came low and menacing. "You aren't going anywhere. Right now you'll get yourself up to the spare bedroom and sleep off that fat head you've made for yourself. In the morning you get on with the business in hand—our business. How you mend your fences with Sophie is up to you, *if* you can manage to mend your fences. But so help me you'd better not hurt her. Abby and I feel responsible for Sophie, and we won't stand by while you make the woman's life a misery.''

Michael stared at Nick. Space and silence seemed to open up between them. He squared his shoulders. "Don't worry about that. I won't go near her, not that she'd let me anyway.'' A disconnected calm drifted over him. "And don't lose any sleep over me. I don't need anyone. From here on nobody's going to have to worry about what goes on in my head. It'll be all business.''

He considered leaving, driving home. Instead, he opened
the door to the hall and headed for the stairs. Nick had
sounded so logical. And the arguments made sense, only
they didn't seem to work for Michael. Sure, the past had had
its day. But forgetting would be tough, he'd already found
that out. All he could shoot for was trying to live each day
as it came. Excess baggage had weighed him down for too
long. It wouldn't be easy, but maybe he could do something about letting it go. Maybe.

On the way to the guest room he passed the little suite he
knew was Sophie's when she stayed overnight with the children. He pushed open the door. The drapes were drawn
back, and moonlight washed over a pale bedspread. Was it
his imagination, still too much in gear, or could he smell her
perfume?

He backed away. Getting her to even speak to him again
might take a miracle, but having to let her go completely was
an idea he wasn't ready to accept.

Chapter Seven

Sophie pulled the floppy brim of her straw hat lower over her eyes and paused, peering at the screw in her hand. She needed to make a hole in the gatepost to insert the metal eye she'd found in the toolshed, but she couldn't make much more than a dent with the screw she'd chosen for the job.

"Sophie! She's at it again!"

She grinned and looked over her shoulder in the direction of Justin's yell. "Get along, you two, or—" She closed her mouth, exasperated, and dropped the screw. "Maren!"

The little girl sat on the dirt in the middle of the vegetable patch. Her back was to Sophie, but her elbows, waggling fiercely, were a familiar sight. She was systematically stripping the fruit from a cherry tomato plant.

"Stop that, Maren!" Sophie shouted, leaping over an edge board and dodging plants to reach her charge. "Oh, Maren. You *did* do it again." She sank to her knees and pulled two small clenched fists toward her.

"Mine," Maren said, her gray eyes baleful. Her mouth started to tremble.

Sophie gave a long sigh and ruffled the girl's hair. "Okay, sweetie pie, let's go through this again." She sat on the soil and pulled Maren onto her lap. "Don't cry. It's okay. Open your hands and show me what you've got."

Pudgy palms slowly unfurled to reveal two small green tomatoes. Sophie took them and settled Maren against her chest.

"You gonna tell her off, Sophie?" Justin came to squat beside them. "She doesn't know *anything*. Maybe I should get Granny. Granny'll give the kid something to eat. That keeps her busy for a while. Then maybe she'll forget 'bout what she was doing before."

Wilma Harris had arrived earlier in the morning, insisting she would help Abby out by doing her laundry while she and Nick were spending a couple of days in the San Juan Islands. The woman had turned pure charm on Sophie, who was beginning to feel she'd been too hard on Wilma. The incident over the accusation that Sophie was careless with the children seemed to have been forgotten, and Sophie was glad.

"Hush, Justin," Sophie admonished. "Granny's busy with the laundry. Anyway, Maren has to learn just like you did." And, she thought, giving a treat to take a child's mind off mischief wasn't in her own unwritten book of child-rearing rules.

He snorted. "I never did the dumb things she does."

Sophie kept her face straight. "You've always been very grown-up. Your mom and dad have told me that. But you don't remember everything you did when you were little, Justin. You're four and a half now. That's pretty old. But don't you think you could have done a few dumb things? A long time ago, of course."

He pursed his lips and played with the fallen tomatoes, rolling them like marbles. "Maybe," he said at last, "but not like *she* does."

"Okay. But let's you and me teach Maren about how things grow so we can use them."

"I guess so," Justin said doubtfully.

Maren's left thumb was firmly in her mouth, her cheek warm and damp against Sophie's arm. She held her tighter and rocked. These children were becoming more and more a part of her life.

"First, Maren, these are Mommy's tomatoes, not yours. Right?"

She felt the child nod.

"Your mommy spends a lot of her spare time planting vegetables so you can have fresh things to eat. You have to plant things when they're little, then look after them while they grow—just the way your mom and dad are looking after you while you grow."

"And you, Sophie," Justin put in. "You look after us, too."

Her throat tightened a little. "And me. We all make sure nothing happens to hurt you while you're growing, don't we?"

A small hand found a wisp of Sophie's hair and wound it through the fingers. "Mmmm," Maren mumbled around her thumb.

"Anyway, if you pick off the tomatoes before they're ripe, they won't grow up and be good for us. Do you understand, honey? And the little lettuces and cucumbers, and the flowers Mommy starts along the edges of the beds. We have to be careful of them. You can smell the flowers and look at them. They're pretty. And you can check the vegetables every day if you like. You'll see how these tomatoes change color if you let them. These—" she picked up several of the rocklike green fruits "—will never ripen now so they're wasted. But never mind. You'll know next time, won't you?"

A cough startled her from the comfortable place that had formed about her and the children. She looked up, knowing who she'd see. Her stomach seemed to scrunch into a knot.

"You're wonderful with the children," Michael said quietly. "No wonder they love you. And Nick and Abby. It doesn't take much to figure out why they're so pleased with having you around.''

Sophie stayed on the ground looking up. A week had passed since her disturbing evening with him. Since she hadn't seen him at all in that time, even coming or going from Nick's office, she'd assumed he was avoiding her. The conflicting feelings he caused her, simply by his presence now, sharpened her conviction that they should stay away from each other.

"If you're looking for your mother, Michael, she's probably in the laundry room."

He was paler, thinner even. "I'm not looking for my mother."

Sophie rubbed Maren's back and bent over her. It was important for her to deal effectively with Michael, to make sure no shred of the personal encounters that had passed between them became a problem.

"Hi, Uncle Mike. You didn't take me canoeing yet." Justin was evidently tired of the adult conversation circling him and had decided to exert his presence.

"No, Justin, I haven't. I've been busy."

"I heard my dad tell my mom you haven't been working much. He said you were feeling sorry for yourself."

Sophie's cheeks flamed. She was embarrassed, for Nick and Abby, but most of all for Michael, who had turned his face away.

"That's enough, Justin—" she began.

"Michael! I didn't know you were here. Why didn't you tell me you were coming over?" Wilma bustled from the house, her pleasure obvious at the sight of her son. "I'd have had lunch ready for you."

"That's not necessary, Mom. Thanks anyway. I need to do some work on the computer."

Wilma, Sophie noted, wore a flour-dusted apron. No doubt there would be fresh-baked cookies and a pie or two waiting in the kitchen. This must be Wilma's new approach to her takeover goal: good works to help the family out, little homey touches neither Abby nor Sophie always had time for. No sooner had the idea come than Sophie felt mean.

"You're as bad as Sophie. Too tied up with work." Wilma folded her hands fatuously. "I was telling her this morning that it's about time a young woman like her took more time doing the things young people do." She turned bright eyes on Sophie. "Wasn't I telling you that?"

"Yes," Sophie agreed. "Michael, you're lucky to have a mother who thinks so much about your welfare. If she had her way, I'd be laying out in a chaise drinking iced tea while she worked." She caught Wilma's pleased look and gave her a broad smile.

"Maybe you should take Mom's advice," Michael commented. "You never know, you might even get a tan."

The lightness of his remarks didn't fool Sophie. He was acutely uncomfortable with her, and the feeling was mutual. She carried Maren from the vegetable garden and set her down on the lawn. "I don't tan," she said matter-of-factly. "A red nose and a rash are my usual reward for coveting a golden glow. Anyway, I've got work to do."

"Well," Wilma announced, as if she hadn't heard a word Sophie said. "I'll leave you two to sit in the sun. Give me a few minutes and I'll bring you something nice and cold to drink."

Sophie didn't wait for Wilma to leave before she told the children to stay on the lawn and returned to her carpentry efforts. Once more she took up screw and screwdriver and worked at starting a hole.

She felt Michael behind her but gave him no sign.

"What are you trying to do, Sophie?"

"I'm putting a second latch on the gate," she responded shortly. "Fail-safe precaution. I worry about one of the children getting out of the backyard." She made no reference to the incident with Wilma.

"You going to use a hook and eye?"

"Yes," she said through gritted teeth. She wasn't making any progress.

"Hold on," Michael said and made for the shed. He returned in minutes with an electric drill and an extension cord, which he plugged into an exterior electrical outlet.

Seconds later he'd drilled holes in both post and gate. "See if that works," he said, and she glanced up at him. Many men would have finished the job in their own way. He was simply trying to help, and she liked him for it.

"Thanks. I wasn't getting very far on my own." Quickly, she rigged a solid catch above the existing bolt. "There we go." She stood back. "Try it. No one's going to knock that loose accidentally."

Michael did as she asked and grinned. "Terrific, ma'am. We should go into business. We make a great team...." His cheerful smile dissolved into a frown, and he bent to gather the tools. "I'll put these back if you like."

Sophie avoided looking at him. "Please. Justin's been waiting for me to play ball."

Hopping from one foot to the other to roll up her cotton pants, she ran toward Justin. Basics of soccer were her current project. Justin was good with the ball, and she could already imagine him on a team in a year or so.

"Ready, Justin?" With one toe, she stopped the ball he tossed, then dribbled it around Maren. "Remember, Justin, no hands. Feet only. Come and get it from me."

Justin, fearless in all things, waded in, feet pumping like small steam engine pistons. His hands were used to keep a firm purchase on Sophie while he walloped the ball downhill and set off after it, whooping in triumph.

She laughed and watched, hands on hips. Maren came and wrapped her arms around one of her legs. "Get the ball?" She smiled up at Sophie. "Maren get the ball?"

"Go for it," Sophie encouraged and laughed again as the little girl ran after her brother, plopping down for a second whenever her balance failed, only to bob up again and toddle on rapidly.

"That's the way, Maren. Way to go, you two. Next stop Olympics." Life didn't get any better than this, Sophie thought.

"Iced tea!" Wilma's voice trilled from the terrace, and Sophie turned, shading her eyes against the sun. "Come on, Sophie. You too, Michael." She must have sensed Sophie's hesitation because she added, "I'll keep the children busy for half an hour. They can help me in the kitchen."

Before Sophie could protest, Wilma had set a tray on a low wrought iron table and pulled two chairs beside it. She passed Sophie, smiling cheerily and collected Justin and Maren from the lower reaches of the yard.

From the corner of her eye, Sophie saw Michael hovering near the shed where he must have stood, watching while she played with the children. She waved at him, wishing fervently she didn't give a damn about Michael Harris.

"We're going to make jam roly-polies," Justin announced, galloping by.

Sophie patted the boy's head and smiled at Wilma who carried Maren. The trio went into the house, and Sophie took a deep breath. If she didn't know better she'd think Wilma was deliberately encouraging her to be alone with Michael.

He walked slowly to the terrace, rubbing his hands on his jeans. His blue polo shirt, as dark as his eyes, made the most of a body that didn't need any help.

"May I pour some for you, Sophie?"

On your best behavior, Michael? "Yes, please." He'd already filled one glass with iced tea and followed with the second.

Sophie flopped in a chair, took off her hat and fanned her face. Absently, she ran a hand over sticky skin beneath the V-neck of her bleached cotton shirt and longed for a breeze, but the day was still. A dull band of gunmetal gray underscored the innocent blue of the higher sky. There could be thunder lying in wait.

"Too warm for you?"

She looked up directly into Michael's eyes. His lashes did that thing she'd noticed before, brushed a shadow over his eyes and made him look pensive. She accepted the glass he offered. "I don't do so well when it gets hot. That's one of the things I like so much about living here. There aren't too many really boiling days."

He sat on the other chair and stretched out his legs. He crossed his ankles, bare in boat shoes. A sprinkling of fine dark hair covered his ankles, as it did the backs of his tanned hands and muscular forearms. Sophie had replaced her hat, and she studied him covertly from beneath its brim.

"How did you manage in Iowa?" he asked, his head bowed.

"What do you mean?"

"With the heat. I imagine midwestern summers can be pretty deadly if you're a cold weather animal."

She closed her eyes and shook her head. "Boy, you're right. How they ever came up with a name like Winterset for my hometown, I'll never figure out. I remember the summer nights when I was a kid. I could never sleep. I used to move my head to a cool spot on the pillow, and in seconds that was hot, so I moved again."

"Miserable," he said sympathetically.

"Mmmm."

"Mom's iced tea is good," he said. "She says it's the mint leaves that make the difference."

Sophie started to sip and realized how thirsty she was. She downed half the glass and sighed. "It's very good. I'll tell her so."

"Sophie..."

She looked at him. "Yes."

"I do have work to do here, but more than that I wanted to say... Oh, hell, I'm not good at this."

He was going to say something about the other night. Sophie finished her drink quickly and made leave-taking motions.

"Don't go," he said with something like desperation in his voice. "Look, sorry isn't enough, but I *am* sorry. I was disgusting. I hate myself for the way I behaved. You won't understand this, and I don't expect you to, but I had a bit of a shock that night, and then some...some things I've been trying to forget kind of piled up on me. I—"

"It's okay," she broke in hastily, shifting to the edge of the chair. "I realized later that you must have been upset."

His laugh was bitter. "That wasn't a good enough excuse for the way I treated you. I scared you, didn't I?"

She fiddled with a loose thread on her shirt.

"You don't have to say so," he said ruefully. "I know I did, and I don't know what else to say except, yet again, I'm sorry, Sophie. Can we at least be friends?"

If she looked at him now she'd be lost. "Forget it," she said. "We all have bad times." She ought to know about hard times, ought to be able to help him with his, only she wasn't sure she was ready to be someone else's prop.

"I guess that means I'm kind of forgiven?"

She did look at him now, at the little-boy-hopeful expression in his eyes. Resisting was impossible. "Forgiven," she agreed and smiled. "Okay? Let's shake on it."

He hesitated an instant before taking the hand she extended. "You're a surprise a minute, Sophie Peters," he said and gripped her fingers a little too tightly. "I really like you. A man is lucky if he can have a friend like you. I won't overstep the bounds again, I promise."

Promise, Sophie thought fleetingly, one of her least favorite words, the English language's least-likely-to-succeed word.

Michael released her and jumped up from his chair. He jogged toward the house and pulled a flat package from behind a juniper bush.

As he returned, Sophie noticed that a flush had risen over his cheeks. In front of her, he stopped, turning the brown paper wrapped parcel over and over before thrusting it into her hands. "I thought you might like this. It's a peace offering."

"You don't have to give me anything," she said awkwardly, holding his gift out like a tray. He must have decided to stash it out of sight until he'd felt out the climate with her.

"If you hate the thing, say so. You'll probably hate it...you won't like it." He stuffed his hands into his pockets.

She glanced at his serious face and couldn't contain her smile. "You really don't expect me to like whatever this is, do you?"

He caught her eye and laughed self-consciously.

She set the package on her lap and tore away the paper. "Michael!" she said, delighted with what she saw. "Justin and Maren. I thought you said you were a hopeless painter. This is wonderful. I love it." The unframed canvas showed the children in the bath, splashing, arms outstretched to fend off flying water. There was a photographic quality about the work. M. Harris was inscribed, very small, in one corner. "You are really talented," she said, first holding the painting away, then looking closely at the brushwork.

"You aren't just saying that?"

"No!"

He let out a noisy breath. "I never gave anything I've painted away before—except to Mom. She thinks anything her children do is wonderful, so I felt pretty safe." He laughed nervously.

"I'm going to get this framed and put it in my apartment." She bent over the painting. He mustn't see how affected she was. His diffidence over his art wasn't an act. Deciding to bring this particular gift must have taken courage.

"I'll have it framed for you. I wanted to be sure you'd like it first and find out what sort of frame you'd prefer." He sounded relieved, grateful for her acceptance.

She considered refusing his offer. Instead she said, "Thanks. But there's no hurry."

He cleared his throat. "I really owe you a consolation dinner," he said.

Sophie wrapped the picture and tucked it under her arm. "Nonsense," she said, getting up. "Forget it." She didn't meet his eyes. To pass him, she had to step sideways.

"I'm not ever going to forget it, Sophie," he said very low. "Is it too soon to ask you to take another chance on spending an evening with me?"

Her heart took an uncomfortable leap. What she'd like to say would be wrong, for both of them. "Yes, Michael, it's too soon." She touched his cheek lightly, tried to smile but failed. "I think we should be the kind of friends who don't do couple things, at least for a while, don't you?"

"But—"

"If you think about it, you'll agree. I'd better get in and take over from Wilma before those two little ragamuffins wear her out." She saluted him with the painting. "A million thanks for this. It means so much to me." And she meant it more than she could ever risk telling him.

Michael watched her walk into the house, then turned to look toward the lake. She wasn't as convinced as she'd intended to sound about not wanting to see him again soon. Not that the thought gave him enough satisfaction to make up for the disappointment of her refusal.

She liked the painting, that had been obvious. He bit the inside of his cheek and winced. What *did* he want from Sophie? This last week had been a misery, and only partly because of the freshened memories of Dallas. Between the old nightmares, and his self-recriminations, and his repeated resolutions not to pursue her anymore, had come the persistent longing to be with Sophie.

The first breeze he'd felt all day gusted, unexpectedly cold, and was gone. He lifted his face, automatically sniffing the air. There could be a storm before the day was out, one of those marvelous summer storms he'd always loved.

There was work waiting. Reluctantly he made his way into the house. Sophie and the children were at the front door saying goodbye to his mother. Things seemed to be smoothing out there, thank God. He moved silently on and closed himself into the study.

In the middle of the room he stopped. The stirring in his body was familiar and confusing at the same time. Of course he knew what he wanted from Sophie. He wanted her in his bed. Why not? She was a healthy, attractive woman, an available woman. But was she so available to him? And even if she was, why did she appeal to him with such force? She was almost opposite to any other woman who had ever played an intimate part in his life.

He sat in front of the computer, switched it on and slipped in a disk. Available? Since when had he chosen women on the basis of their availability? And if he had, would a Sophie have been one of them?

Not my type.

"You're losing it, Harris." Maybe there was some expert somewhere who could sort out his interest in this pint-size female; he sure couldn't.

SOPHIE CHECKED HER WATCH. Ten-thirty. She'd just tucked Justin back into bed for the third time and given him yet another glass of water. Finally he seemed tired enough to fall asleep.

She went down to the kitchen and made a cup of hot chocolate. Distant thunder rumbled through the night, and despite the humidity, she craved the childhood comfort the chocolate represented.

Going through the hall on her way to the stairs, she paused, listening. Michael hadn't appeared again all afternoon or evening, although she had heard him cross the corridor to the bathroom earlier. Should she offer him something, at least to drink? He hadn't even had dinner. She knew the answer. No. The less contact the better.

Upstairs in the room she used when she spent the night in the main house, she set down the cup and took out the nightgown and robe she kept in the closet.

Abby had made this room a wonderfully comfortable home away from home for Sophie. Stereo, a television, even a small refrigerator had been installed. She switched on the television, picked up her cup again and went into the bathroom to shower. She sipped her chocolate while she undressed and adjusted the shower water to her satisfaction.

The stinging spray invigorated her. Pine-scented shampoo tingled on her scalp and left her hair squeaky, the way she liked it.

This had been a good day, a good evening. The thought caused Sophie a twinge of guilt. The reason was too easily identified. Michael. She'd been aware of his presence in the house and drawn comfort from it. Without seeing him, she'd felt him close by doing his thing while she did hers. The most simple, natural setup in the world. Like . . . like a couple.

Sophie turned off the water. After their talk in the garden, his sweet apology, when every word he spoke suggested he expected rejection, she had felt drawn closer to him. She wouldn't push, but in time he might decide to share those things he'd said he was trying to forget. Then their picture together could change. Relationships must be founded on honesty.

Honesty. Sophie stepped from the shower and picked up her towel. If they did ever try to get together on other than a friend-to-friend basis, the openness would have to go both ways.

As quickly as she acknowledged the thought she discarded it and finished drying her hair and body. For now there was no reason to reach beyond the moment and the pleasure Michael gave her simply by being near. She pulled her simple cotton nightshirt over her head and winked in the mirror at the stenciled image draped across her chest. Garfield looking smug. "They don't call this woman Sexy Sophie for nothing," she said, wrapping a towel around her head.

She lifted her chin, tossed her robe over her shoulder, and strutted into the bedroom.

Michael stood in the open doorway to the corridor.

Chapter Eight

"Hi."

All the blood in her body had plummeted to her feet. He'd taken ten years off her life. And all he could say was "hi"?

As rapidly as the blood had rushed down, it now returned to pulse in every part of her.

"Hi," she managed. She should ask him what he was doing in her room, then tell him to get out. "Finished working?" *Oh, feet of clay. Oh, weak one.*

"Uh-huh. Thought I'd just come and see if you were okay." He shuffled from one foot to the other. "If there was anything you needed before I go."

Sophie regained some composure. "Good thing I didn't decide to come out of the bathroom in the buff, Michael. We'd both have had a shock." She shut her mouth firmly. The downward flicker of his eyes suggested he might not have minded the shock.

"I did shout."

"I didn't hear you."

"The water was running."

Aha, Michael, she thought triumphantly, *you opened your mouth and inserted your foot.* He'd known she was showering and deliberately stood there waiting for her. Her next thought was anything but triumphant. Please, in the name of fairness, he hadn't heard her stupid comment to herself, had he? Not again?

With what she hoped was nonchalance, she put on her robe. "Everything's fine with me, Michael," she said. "The children are asleep at last, and I'm going to curl up with my hot chocolate—or what's left of it—and watch a movie."

A brief swell of brilliance paled the drapes, and within seconds of the lightning, thunder boomed, long and rolling. Summer storms unnerved Sophie.

"You don't mind being alone here at night?" Michael asked. He looked very tired.

Usually she quite enjoyed having the big house to herself. The thunder spoiled the pleasure a little, but she wouldn't let him know that. "I'm used to it. And I'm glad Nick took Abby away for a couple of days. They need more time together...I mean, it's good for any marriage when..." She must curb her loose tongue.

"I know what you mean." He leaned against the door frame, arms crossed, apparently deeply interested in his feet. "Things have been pretty tough on all of us, businesswise. But I expect you can tell nothing's better there. That kind of tension wears on any relationship. Just getting away helps. It's easy for Nick to fly in and out of Friday Harbor for a day or so. And that way he and Abby can be alone when he's not working. I thought that was a great idea. They couldn't do it if they didn't have someone like you to rely on, though."

"No, I guess they couldn't," she agreed slowly. Her attention moved away. She heard his voice, the words, but her mind stayed removed. *A great idea.* Somewhere there was a great idea waiting to be pulled out for Islands Unlimited. It could be a versatile operation. Nick and Michael didn't have to be stuck on the concept of simple transportation between two main points. *Unlimited.* They called themselves unlimited while they continued to squirrel around in the same small circles, never attempting to experiment.

Michael watched her face. "What's the movie?" he asked. He appeared to have lost her, he thought. She was gazing past his shoulder. He coughed and repeated, "Sophie, what's the movie you're going to watch?"

He saw her eyes come into focus, and she smiled at him, then looked at the screen. The picture was on without sound. "A Western, I think."

She never ceased to catch him off balance. "You like Westerns?"

"Of course. Don't you? The right guy always wins."

"The right guy, huh? Even if he shoots a few dozen black hats on the way and treats his women mean?" He raised his brows. "Don't tell me you're one of those women who likes her men tough and rough?"

"No!" She turned away so abruptly that the towel slipped, and her hair fell in wet tangles about her shoulders.

Now what had he said? "Hey, hey, Sophie, that was meant to be a joke, okay?"

She lifted the hair from her back where it was wetting her cotton robe. For a moment she stayed like that, her hand beneath her hair before she said, "Of course you were joking. I know that."

He shrugged and swept up the towel, took a hesitant step toward her, put a hand on her shoulder. The immediate jolt he felt in her muscles startled him, but he didn't move away.

"Your hair's making your robe wet," he said and hoped she didn't hear him swallow. "I'm an expert hair dryer. I used to do it for Abby."

"Did you?"

Carefully he wound the towel around the wet mass and rubbed the ends between his palms. She was going into her motionless act again. He couldn't get her measure. Vaguely he recalled that she'd begun to respond when he'd kissed her at her place. The desire to kiss her now was so strong his gut pulled in hard.

"I usually let it dry on its own," Sophie said in a small voice. She turned toward him and took the towel. Her face was pale, her eyes downcast. "Thanks."

His hands felt useless. He tapped his fingertips together. The top of her head reached somewhere below his shoulders. The thin cotton robe and nightshirt clung to her slender shoulders, her breasts and hips. A battle was in progress between his inhaling and exhaling. Must be the humidity. "Don't you brush it?" Humidity had nothing to do with what he felt.

"What?" She looked directly up at him, and he knew he should leave now.

"Your hair. Shouldn't you brush it before it dries?"

Her laugh surprised him. "You have been around women, haven't you? Yes, I need to brush my hair." She tilted her head to one side and began rubbing it with the towel again while she walked away from him.

He didn't know if he was relieved. "I'd better be getting home."

"Listen." Sophie silenced him with a hand. "Listen to that rain, will you? Boy, what a relief. I always feel I'm suffocating when it thunders and the rain never comes. We used to get a lot of that back home."

When he didn't immediately answer, she looked at him. That shadow was in his eyes again, that ... sadness. She didn't know what was troubling him, but after their earlier talk she was even more convinced that he had some old and powerful demon on his mind. And intuition told her he hadn't been lying the other night when he'd said he didn't want to be alone. He didn't want to be alone now, she was sure.

She took a deep breath. For once she could let down her defenses and allow the old impetuousness out. "Michael, you'll get soaked just getting to your car. The rain probably won't last long. You should wait a while. I want some more hot chocolate. Can I make you some?"

He still said nothing, and she started to feel warm. "Of course, you probably have something else to do."

"No. I'd love a hot drink. Thank you."

Did he sound as pathetically grateful as she thought he did? "We can have it in the kitchen if you like." She paused. His weariness was almost palpable. "Or you could sit over in that chair." She nodded to the white corduroy armchair and ottoman on the far side of her bed. "It's so soft I'm afraid to sit in it if I want to stay awake."

"I'd like that," he said simply. "Thanks."

She wished he'd stop thanking her every few minutes. "The movie's starting. Shall I turn up the sound for you?"

"I'll do it, thanks, Sophie."

"You don't—" No, she wouldn't tell him what he should or shouldn't say. And she'd stop reacting to innocent comments, the way she had to his remark about liking rough men, as if he meant anything significant. How could he? He didn't know about her life with Jack. "Make yourself comfortable. I'll be right back."

Halfway down the stairs she stopped and retraced her steps, running this time. "Michael! Is the top down on your car? You'll have to bail the thing out if it is."

He stood where she'd left him. "I put it up already," he said, his voice a little gravelly. He grinned suddenly, the old mischief back in his eyes. "Although I almost wish I hadn't. I'd make you come and help me, and that outfit should be quite something in the rain, Sexy Sophie."

Her instant grimace was followed by a wave of clammy goose bumps before she joined his laughter. "I suppose you think I go around saying those things all the time."

"Yup."

"Well, Michael Harris, I certainly don't."

"You expect me to believe that?"

She shook her head. "You're impossible. It just so happens that I'm a very serious woman. And I'm going to get more serious because every time I break out a bit I get caught."

"Please, don't."

Sophie raised a questioning brow. "Don't what?"

"Don't get more serious," Michael said. "I like you just the way you are, although I'm not always sure what that is."

For what seemed a long time, they stared at each other. She must be careful around him. Very, very careful. His feelings at this moment were naked in his eyes. Michael's mind was on sex. Her thoughts skittered around the images that followed, the two of them together in bed, naked. How would it feel to make love to a man after so long? How would Michael be?

He let out a sigh. "Sophie..."

"I'll get the hot chocolate," she muttered and left him quickly, rushing downstairs, arriving breathless in the kitchen.

When she started back up with two cups and a massive tuna fish sandwich and potato chips balanced on a tray, every half-forgotten insecurity crowded in. She'd made a mistake in asking him to stay. He was bound to think the suggestion had a deeper meaning. Nick and Abby were away, the children were asleep. She was a fool if she expected a man like Michael not to think she had something other than hot chocolate in mind.

She peeked in on Justin and Maren in their separate rooms. Each slept soundly.

With one bare foot, she nudged her bedroom door open wider. Michael had turned up the sound on the television and settled himself in the chair. The room was soft, subtle, all white and mauve and pale blue gray. Michael seemed almost out of place, powerful, cardinal against the gentle backdrop.

"Here we are," Sophie said brightly, pushing the door to slightly. "Sustenance. You didn't have dinner, Michael. I realized that when I was in the kitchen. I hope you don't hate tuna fish.'' A little glass table flanked the chair, and she set down the tray.

"My favorite food," he assured her, immediately lifting the plate and taking a giant bite from one half of the sandwich. "S'wonderful," he managed with his mouth full.

"Good." With her own cup, she retreated to the bed and plumped up her pillows. Careful not to spill, she maneuvered herself into her favorite television-watching spot.

On the screen, a lone man, his sweat-stained black hat tilted over pale blue eyes, galloped astride a gleaming palomino. Sophie sighed contentedly. Her cozy nest, the children asleep, Clint Eastwood...and Michael to keep her company. Immediately, she shifted and glanced at him. He was finishing the sandwich, his attention on the film.

Eastwood crested the rise of a barren hill. Pink mesa stood against a blindingly blue sky, and the man squinted, surveying the horizon. "Couldn't you just look at him, exactly like that, forever?" Sophie said dreamily.

She felt Michael looking at her and glanced in his direction. He was grinning. "What's so funny?" she said.

"You. 'Couldn't you just look at him like that forever?'" he said in a falsetto voice. "Frankly, my dear, I don't give a damn about Clint Eastwood. Can't understand why any woman would prefer all that lean, sinewy, and I presume sexy, masculinity. Too obvious, Sophie. Now take a man like me. I'm subtle. I understand all the little nuances of attracting a woman that only a true master of the art knows." He sniffed and popped a potato chip into his mouth.

Sophie's mouth was full of hot chocolate, and she almost choked. "Arrogant," she sputtered. "And you say I'm the one with the off-the-wall comments. Look at him." Her forefinger jabbed imperiously in the direction of the close-up of Eastwood. He held a toothpick between miraculously white teeth and still studied the horizon. "Don't tell me you can't see why he turns women on by the million."

Michael made a bored face and wiped his mouth and hands on his napkin. "Not truly discerning women, my dear. What's he got that's so great, anyway?"

"Those eyes for one thing." She pulled up her feet and sat cross-legged, leaning forward. "They look right through you."

"What about my eyes? Have you taken a good look at them?"

She had, too often, but she did so again and immediately fell back on the pillows, giggling. Michael had squinched up his face, flared his nostrils and raised one eyebrow in a supercilious arch.

"Oh, thanks. You know how to stroke a man's ego."

When her laughter subsided, Sophie struggled to sit again. "Watch the movie," she commanded. "This is one of my favorites."

"Yes, ma'am," he said and put his feet on the ottoman.

They fell into a companionable silence. Even during the commercials Michael said nothing. Perfect, Sophie decided, quelling a shred of apprehension. This was the most peaceful, special evening she'd spent for a long time. Was it possible for a man and a woman to be simply the best of friends?

When the credits started to roll up the screen, Sophie set down the cold cup she'd unconsciously held throughout the film and remembered in the same moment that she'd never brushed her hair. Damn. It would take ages now.

She swung her feet from the bed and stopped. Michael's head leaned at an awkward angle. His elbow, propped on the arm of the chair and supporting his chin, was gradually slipping sideways. He was asleep.

Careful to make no sound, Sophie took one of her own pillows and went to his side. Standing over him she saw the flicker of his eyes beneath the lids, the fanning shadows of his lashes on his cheekbones. In repose, his mouth was incredibly vulnerable.

She dropped to her knees and braced his elbow the second it was about to drop. It took all the strength she had to hold him. He didn't stir. With a hand behind his neck, she pulled his face gently against her shoulder and settled the pillow behind him. Something had to break for Michael and Nick soon, for their sakes and for Abby's. They were all far too strung out.

He was heavy. Trying to push him back smoothly made her legs and arms shake. She made it to her feet and gradually leaned over the chair.

When her feet left the ground she was too startled to react—until she'd been twisted and plunked in his lap with one of his arms looped around her. "Michael!"

His eyes were still closed, but a smile turned his mouth up at the corners. He spread a hand over the side of her head and guided her face into the hollow of his shoulder.

"Michael..." She wasn't sure what else she wanted to say. The spot where her head rested was warm and firm and smelled clean. His hand stroked gently over her hair.

Snuggling closer was so natural, so good, and he adjusted his body to hers until she felt she'd sat with him like this enough times to count it a habit. Uncertainly, she brushed the tips of her fingers over his chest until they rested at the open neck of his shirt.

Sophie looked up. Those blue eyes were open now. They were amused, definitely slightly sleepy, and so very appealing.

"This isn't fair, you know." But as she said it, she made no attempt to stop him from running his thumb along her bottom lip. He bent forward, kissed her quickly and rested his head back, closing his eyes once more, settling her even more comfortably against him.

He was again the man she'd thought him to be, gentle, nonthreatening, in tune with her need for them to go slowly.

Another program came on the television. Sophie heard music and voices but had no idea what the voices said.

"Michael," she whispered. His steady breathing answered her. She couldn't stay here. What if one of the children decided to come looking for her? She wiggled and his grip tightened.

The remote control for the television was on the table beside the chair. Sophie managed to reach it and flip off the set. She lay still, expecting the silence to elicit some response from him. Only his breath against her hair, the splatter of light rain on the window, responded to her waiting senses.

Half an hour passed. Her neck began to ache unbearably, but she liked being where she was. Cautiously she flexed her spine and peered up... into Michael's wide open eyes. He wasn't smiling anymore.

When she slipped from his lap he made no attempt to restrain her. "You're exhausted, aren't you, Michael?"

"'Fraid so. Exhausted and frustrated. But I don't want to dump on you."

"Dump. I'm a good listener." She sat on the edge of the bed. Longing still darkened his eyes, but clearly Michael was a man who knew when to back off.

He got up and went to the window. He lifted the drapes, and Sophie saw the rain, glittering droplets hanging on the glass, constantly assaulted by fresh squalls.

"This is our best time of year," Michael said absently. "And we're barely keeping our heads above water. We don't have any cushion, and within a few weeks we'll be slacking off and facing bare bones traffic." He let the drape drop and hooked his thumbs into his jeans' pockets. "I guess it's time to admit we could fail."

"Garbage!" Sophie thumped the bed with both fists. "Absolute garbage, Michael. You're too narrow, that's the trouble. Think big. Think bigger and bigger." She scooted back to sit cross-legged once more. "Why do you and Nick think of yourselves as simply carriers, passenger carriers?"

She passed a hand over her tangled hair, aware Michael stood by the bed now. She waved him down beside her. "Sit. I can't think with you hovering like that."

He lowered his big body close to her thigh. "What are you talking about, Sophie? We *are* carriers. Carriers carry, period."

"Why period?" She stared at him. "That isn't all you could do with what you've got to work with. If I—" She stopped abruptly, felt her cheeks color. The old enthusiasm was running off again. Retreat time had arrived.

"Go on, Sophie," Michael said. He regarded her intently. "If you what?"

"Nothing. Nothing at all. I'm sure if there's some brilliant solution you'll come up with it." She prayed he would, and that she wouldn't feel compelled to let down and prompt him if he and Nick took too long about it.

Michael's gaze didn't waver. "You had an idea, didn't you? Tell me."

A few careless words and she was up to her knees in something she didn't want to touch. She'd sworn off anything to do with the travel business. "I don't know what I was thinking for sure, Michael. I guess I'm too simplistic. It always seems to me that there's an easy way out staring us in the face while we make frown lines looking for something more complex." She prayed he wouldn't question her anymore.

He rubbed his jaw with an open palm. "You're probably right. I must be a mass of wrinkles about now."

Unthinking, Sophie massaged between his shoulder blades and kneaded the base of his neck. "Let it go for a while, Michael. Relax. Trying too hard usually backfires." Beneath her fingers she felt the muscles untense. His hair, a little long and very dark even against the blue shirt, passed softly through her massaging fingers.

He tipped his head back and closed his eyes. She paused, but only for a second, before pressing harder into the long tendons over his shoulders, then easing upward to make soft circles below his ears. A long sigh shuddered through him and he half turned his face toward her. If she kissed him, the simplest kiss on his temple, his jaw, the corner of his mouth—if she touched him as her body urged her to touch him, gave one little sign—they would make love.

His neck was strong. She kissed him there, fleetingly, a kiss that signaled this was as far as this encounter could go here tonight. Then she patted his arm lightly and moved beside him. "Feel better, Michael?"

His eyes met hers. "Mmmm." And what he didn't say she read in his face. He didn't want to let the tension between them ease. Briefly, Michael rested a forefinger on her mouth, made a line across her cheek and placed a whisper of a kiss beneath her eye.

Then he shifted, quickly, silently, and before she could protest, he was behind her, pulling her between his outstretched legs. His strong hands went to work on her shoulders and neck, sweeping her hair aside, stroking, pressing, until her head bowed forward. A lambent warmth stole into her. Even while common sense told her she was playing with fire, the long-denied need for physical contact wouldn't let her draw away.

"Where's your brush?"

"In the bathroom," she told him, not quite believing she was doing this.

"Don't move from there."

He left the bed and came back with brush in hand. He turned on the stereo, tuning in light classical music, and returned to his spot behind her. "This is probably going to hurt. Are you a screamer?" Laughter ran through his voice. "Tell me now if you are so I'll be ready."

"I'm not a screamer...usually. And I believe you like to torture people. I can hear it in your voice."

The quick kiss he dropped on her neck silenced her. Patiently he worked knots and snarls from her hair, brushing, parting, brushing with infinite care until he could sweep the brush smoothly downward.

"There," he said very softly, "done, ma'am. You have beautiful hair." His broad hand, passing from crown to shoulder, sent a shivery ache through her. "We feel something special for each other, don't we, Sophie?" His arms, wrapped around her shoulders, pulling her against him, were a tender trap she wanted to stay inside of. Taking her with him, he leaned against her pillow.

The music drifted about them. Sophie smelled Michael's warm cedar scent and rested her head back. His jaw was rough against her temple.

"Don't you feel what I'm talking about?"

She felt it. "There are...I do, Michael, yes, but there are things against us."

"Things?"

He didn't let her answer. Instead he twisted her around until he could kiss her fully on the mouth. The back and forth brushing of his lips, the reaching of his tongue, went on and on until she was breathless. When he lifted his head she pushed her hair back with a shaking hand.

"There aren't any things we can't deal with, are there, Sophie?"

She watched him mutely, wanting to take his face in her hands, to kiss him with all the passion she'd held back, not knowing how, not able to risk trying.

His mouth found hers again, touched the corners, then pressed rapidly, fleetingly, to a dozen spots across her cheek to her ear, along her chin, in the hollow of her neck and when he returned to her mouth she kissed him back without reserve.

"Ah, Sophie," he whispered against her lips. "Don't go away from me again. We've got lots of time. All the time you need."

But she felt his arousal, and at the same moment his hand passed from her shoulder to her breast, searing her flesh through the thin cotton. She couldn't move, couldn't speak. His thumb moved rhythmically over her nipple. Her belly ached and her thighs, and the heat spread throughout her body.

Michael was breathing harder, kissing her harder.

The little cold, distant place came in the center of her mind. "Please," she said and heard the hoarse quality of her own voice. With a struggle she forced her hands between them and pushed him away. He looked into her face, his eyes first puzzled, then wounded. "Please," she repeated. "I can't. Not here."

He trembled, held her arms, and she saw him draw in deep breaths. "When, Sophie—and where? Tell me what I have to do to be with you."

"I don't know. Can't you see I don't know?"

She scrambled to the floor and sat in the chair. The moment was broken. The lovely, close time had been shattered, by her. Was *she* broken? Had the damage gone so deep all those years ago that she was useless to any man now?

Michael lay flat, spread his arms and legs wide and stared at the ceiling. "Is there something wrong with me, Sophie?" he said unevenly. "I mean, do I turn you off? If that's what's wrong, I can take it. I think." He turned his face toward her.

"There's nothing wrong with you, Michael. You're a wonderful man." Her arms, tightly crossed around her ribs, failed to bring her any comfort.

"Is there someone else, then? Am I treading on another man's turf?"

The hollow quality of her laugh sickened her. "There's nobody else. And there's nothing wrong with you. Can we leave it at that? You must have women lined up around the block to be with you, why waste time with a cold fish like me?"

"You aren't a cold fish."

"Oh?" She rubbed a thumb knuckle against her chin, trying to form the right words to say next. "If I'm not a cold fish, Michael, what do you think I am?" How she wished someone could tell her the answer to that question.

He sighed and sat up, holding his hands toward her across the small space that separated them. "Hold on to me, kid. I need the support if you don't." When she slipped her fingers into his he lifted them to his lips and kissed the backs of her hands, grimacing wryly. "I think you are a lovely, warm woman who, and I can't tell you why, but who's afraid to let herself go. And I take comfort in choosing to believe you would let yourself go with me rather than any other man at that moment if you could. Does that sound close?"

"Very close."

"But you can't give me any more clues?"

"No."

"Did I ruin everything again? By pushing things, I mean?"

She smiled. "We said we'd be friends. We are. The best of friends, I hope. Be patient with me, Michael. I'll try to loosen up, I promise." He really did like her. If she could straighten out what was going on in her head, the things she still didn't want to face, maybe she could be what he wanted, if he hadn't lost interest by then.

"Look, Sophie." He dropped her hands and stood. "I think you'd feel a whole lot different if we weren't here, where the children are—in Nick and Abby's house."

Evidently he didn't think her reaction tonight had been the same as it had been after he took her to dinner or when they'd picnicked. She got up, too. "I think you're right," she agreed and prayed fervently they were both right.

"We'll go out again, okay?"

She nodded.

"I'd better go, but I'll see you in the morning. I've still got stuff to do on the computer."

"See you in the morning, then." Walking past him unsettled her. Her spine tingled. The phone, its ring unnaturally loud in the night, brought her spinning around. "Who on earth can that be this late?"

Michael shrugged. "You'd better answer it."

She checked the bedside clock and said, "Good Lord, it's two in the morning." She picked up the receiver. "Hello?"

"Oh, Sophie, I'm so glad I got you." Wilma's high voice grated. "This is awful, disturbing you so late. Did I wake you up?"

"No," she said, frightened. "I'm ready for bed but I can get dressed in a jiffy if something's wrong."

Several seconds ticked by before Wilma said, "There's nothing wrong, dear. At least I don't think so. I only wondered if you knew what time Michael left."

Muscles in Sophie's jaw contracted, and she sucked in her bottom lip. What should she say?

"He was still with you when I left," Wilma went on. "I've been trying to call him all evening, and he's not home. He didn't say where he was going, did he?"

Michael came closer and mouthed, "What's wrong?"

"Wilma, Michael's still here." What else could she say? "He worked very late. Would you like to talk to him?"

There was a short silence. "No, no, dear. As long as he's all right, I'll call him tomorrow. By the way, did you get in touch with Abby?"

Sophie's brain blanked. "Abby?"

"She telephoned from Friday Harbor while you and Michael were outside. I didn't want to interrupt you so I put a note on the side of the refrigerator with a magnet in case I forgot later." She laughed comfortably. "Silly me, I did forget. Didn't you find the note?"

"No, Wilma, I didn't find the note."

"Oh, dear. Abby wanted you to call her this evening and tell her how the children are, but I guess it's too late now. I hope she won't worry."

"She will worry. I do wish you'd told me when she was on the phone."

"Now, don't you worry," Wilma said, sounding more cheerful than Sophie thought she should. "I told her you and Michael were busy and that he was going to work at the house."

She and Michael were busy. Michael reached for the phone, but she shook her head. "I'll contact Abby and Nick first thing in the morning," she said firmly.

"I wouldn't bother, dear. Abby said she was going to go along with Nick on an early flight. They'll be home by afternoon. Anyway, Abby promised she'd stop and see me as soon as she gets in, so I'll explain what happened. You and Michael being so busy and all." She paused an instant. "Don't you worry. Good night."

"Good night," Sophie echoed faintly. She replaced the receiver. "Your mother will call you in the morning, Michael. She likes to know you're okay. That's nice," she said woodenly and walked back to open the door wide. "Do you mind if I don't see you out?"

She hardly heard his parting remarks. He kissed her cheek lightly, and she remembered afterward that he'd been frowning as he left.

Sleep was elusive. Over and over she heard Wilma's voice: *"You and Michael being so busy and all. Don't you worry."* Wilma would explain everything to Nick and Abby. Damn it all. Sophie sat up in bed. There was nothing to explain, but Wilma would explain it anyhow.

Chapter Nine

"Are you gonna listen, Maren? If you want me to read this story to you, you gotta listen."

Sophie, stretched out on the window seat in Justin's room, smiled and lowered her own book. Justin sat in his small fruitwood rocker with Maren at his feet. Every few minutes she lost interest in his storytelling efforts and tried to leave, only to be grabbed and pushed back onto her bottom.

"Justin," Sophie said gently, "maybe Maren isn't old enough for that story yet. Why don't you read it to me?" For Justin "reading" meant turning the pages and repeating the words beneath the pictures from memory, since Sophie had read the story to him dozens of times.

Justin gave Maren an exasperated glare as she made for her battered Cabbage Patch doll and stuffed it unceremoniously beneath the quilt on Justin's bed. "Night-night," she crooned and picked up another book. She turned pages, leaning over the doll, talking earnestly.

"Dumb kid," Justin said. "She's reading to a doll."

Sophie looked at him thoughtfully. He was too much alone or with Maren and herself, or his grandmother. In the fall he should go to a preschool where he could be with other little boys for at least a part of every day.

He pulled his rocker close to Sophie and started reciting the story again. She only half listened. Her thoughts were preoccupied by Wilma's telephone call last night. How would she report the time Sophie had spent with Michael to Abby and Nick? Would she emphasize that Michael had still been there at two in the morning, mention that Sophie had admitted being dressed for bed? She sighed and gazed through diamond-shaped panes in the bay window. The sun was bright again today, and the storm had brushed away the stillness, leaving a clean, airy brilliance in its wake.

At the sound of muffled thuds on the stairs, she stirred and closed her own book. She knew instinctively that the footsteps, wide spaced because their owner was striding up two, three stairs at a time, were Michael's. She swung her feet to the floor as he arrived in the doorway, a wide smile on his lips.

"Morning, all," he said and swept Maren into his arms. He held her above his head, rolling her from side to side between sound kisses while she squealed. "Isn't this one fantastic day? This is a day for all kinds of good things." With Maren slung over his shoulder like a wiggling sack, he knelt on the floor between Sophie and Justin.

"You look wide-awake, Michael," Sophie commented, not without envy. "But I guess you didn't have to be up at six like some of us."

He looked at his watch. "It's only eight, now, my friend. I was up at seven and I feel fantastic."

"Good for you." And he obviously had none of her concerns about his mother's call. Why should he, when he didn't know the details? "Do you know exactly what time Nick and Abby are due in?" For hours she'd toyed with the vain hope of seeing them before Wilma.

"Early afternoon," he said vaguely. "Did my mother say something to upset you when she called?"

She gripped the book tightly. "No. Why do you ask?" Undermining relationships was an activity she would always avoid.

Michael dumped Maren in his lap. Justin leaned on his uncle's back, his arms tightly clasped around his neck. "You seemed a bit far away after you hung up, that's all. And I could tell there was some mention of missing a call from Abby and that it concerned you."

Her laugh couldn't sound as false to him as it did in her own ears. "I was annoyed at myself, that's all. Wilma left me a note, and I missed it. I hate being careless." If the note hadn't been half-hidden by a recipe and pushed almost against the wall on the least visible side of the refrigerator Sophie would have seen it. But she wasn't going to tell Michael that.

"No big thing," he said easily. "They'll be back today, and there's no harm done. You look tired, Sophie."

"I am a bit." Four hours lying more awake than asleep had only made her wish she'd never gone to bed.

"Why don't you go back to bed for an hour? I can give these urchins something to make mischief with in the study while I work."

Unexpectedly, her eyes stung and she blinked. "You're sweet. But no. I know how it is to try working out snags with chaos all around."

"You weren't always a nanny, were you, Sophie?" Curiosity showed in his eyes. "What else did you do?"

The little slips were the ones that could trap her. "I was married. You already know that." Maybe one day she'd feel like talking about everything, but not now.

He took an uncomfortably long time to answer. "Okay, have it your way. But I think you know a lot about things you don't want to discuss. You're a mystery lady."

"Mmmm." She lifted her chin slightly. "A little mystery's a good thing in a woman, isn't it? Keeps a man guessing."

"How true. You sure you won't take me up on my offer of some peace? All I'm doing is hashing and rehashing, looking for nonexistent places to save money. I sure don't want to lower fares again. The bigger outfits can stay in a rate war longer than we can. There's got to be another answer."

"There is—I'm sure there is," she corrected herself quickly. In the next few days she would do a little research of her own, and if she was certain there was no other way, she'd take the plunge and give Nick and Michael an idea or two she'd come up with. They might simply laugh at her, but at least her conscience would be clear.

"I wish I could greet Nick and Abby with some brilliant solution," Michael said wistfully. He disengaged Justin's hands, put Maren down and got to his feet. "I'm probably making too much of the whole thing. Takes time to get a new business off the ground, right?" Before she could respond he grinned and said, "That saying must have been tailor-made for us. I'll see you later, folks."

"Michael," Sophie said before he reached the door, "did you have breakfast?" He didn't seem to spend much time worrying about his diet.

He considered briefly, then smiled as if remembering. "Sure I had breakfast. Leftovers, my favorite morning food."

"Leftovers?" She eyed him suspiciously.

"Yeah. Leftover spaghetti. Nothing like cold spaghetti to fill a hole."

Sophie winced, her own stomach recoiling. "Come on down to the kitchen before you go to work. I didn't feel like breakfast earlier. You can share something that'll do really good things for your body."

"Really?" He smiled innocently. "What will it do? Put hair on our chests?"

"That's what Mommy always says carrots do," Justin cut in brightly. "She says that's why I've gotta eat 'em."

Sophie didn't trust herself to say anything. She managed not to laugh as she led the way downstairs with Michael whistling behind her and the children at the end of the procession.

When she'd sent Justin and Maren outside to play, Sophie plugged in the blender and started gathering ingredients.

Michael hiked himself onto the counter by the sink and sat on his hands, legs swinging. "You do seem a bit gloomy today, my girl."

"I'm fine." She dropped cut bananas into the blender.

"So you say, but I don't think so." He leaned toward her. "Come on. Tell Uncle Michael what's up."

He would keep pushing until she found a way to satisfy him. "Okay, if you must know, I am a bit concerned about not returning Abby's call yesterday."

"I thought as much," he said nodding. "You don't have to be worried. You know Abby. She's hardly the type to get upset about a thing like that. You were busy. If she'd had any misgivings she'd have called back herself."

What he said made sense, but she was still doubtful. "You're probably right, only... Michael, there is something else on my mind about last night."

His expression, when she glanced at him, had become guarded. "I thought we'd decided to start over and—"

"Not that." She touched his forearms lightly and made no attempt to resist when he pulled her loosely toward him. "I'm worried Nick and Abby may think... I don't know how to say this... They might think I was too busy with you to pay attention to looking after the children and the house," she finished in a rush.

He became still. "Why would they think that?"

"Because you were here so late last night."

"So what?" He held her away to see her face. "Nick and Abby wouldn't think anything of my being here. I often am.

Anyway, it doesn't have to bother you, because they don't know."

Sophie opened her mouth to explain about Wilma but changed her mind. "You're right, of course," she said instead. "Now get out of my way so I can finish this."

Michael only scooted over a bit on the counter where he could still watch.

"Eggs," Sophie said to herself, breaking two into the concoction she was preparing, "milk." She got a carton from the refrigerator. The recipe she used in her health shakes was her own creation.

"What's that stuff?"

When she turned to Michael he wrinkled his nose, nodding at the granules she was spooning out. "Lecithin," she said. "Good for thinning the blood. Look after your cardiovascular system now and avoid trouble later."

"If it tastes the way it looks, I probably won't have to worry about my body anymore. It looks poisonous."

Her response was to turn the blender on high. When the mixture was exactly as she liked it, she filled two tall glasses and handed one to Michael with a flourish. "That," she announced, "will set you up for the day. No fitness program works without good nutrition."

He peered into the glass and sniffed the contents doubtfully.

"Drink, Michael. All of it."

His face remained expressionless while he did as she ordered, tipping the glass up to drain every drop. He set it down, shuddered violently and fell from the counter into a motionless heap on the floor.

Sophie covered her mouth with both hands and began to laugh. She poked him, not very gently, with one toe. He didn't move.

Tears prickled in her eyes. "You horror. You wretch. Get up before the kids come in. You'll frighten them."

He didn't budge or make a sound.

She coughed and controlled her laughter. "I'm about to drink my own shake," she announced and took several swallows. "Now I'm going to stand here and see how long it takes for me to drop dead."

When he still said nothing, Sophie knelt by his side and tapped the back of his head. "I'm going to count to ten, and if you aren't on your feet you get the cold water treatment. One, two, three—"

Four never made it past her lips. Michael sprang at her, swept her up in a bear hug and stood, holding her inches off the floor. "See what you've done?" he said gleefully. "You've given me superhuman strength. And my appetite, oh, you have no idea what you've done for my appetite." And he kissed her again and again until she fought to catch her breath.

"Michael Harris, put me down," she managed when he buried his face in her neck.

"Your fault, Sexy Sophie. You did it to me."

She struggled until her feet met solid ground. "You won't let me forget that, will you?"

"Mmmm. Absolutely not. And I want to get deeper into this fitness program of yours. How about that swim we talked about the other night?"

"*You* talked about." The heat and weakness was in her body again.

"Okay, the swim *I* talked about then. I asked you to come swimming with me, and you didn't give me an answer. You said you'd check Nick and Abby's schedule—"

"What do you need to know about our schedule, Sophie?"

Nick's voice, from behind Michael, made her heart thud. Michael turned around, one arm still draped over her shoulders. "Hi, Nick," he said with no trace of the discomfort that threatened to choke Sophie. "I thought you weren't coming in till this afternoon."

"Evidently. Who's watching the shop, Mike?"

Sophie felt Michael inhale deeply. "How was your break, Nick?" he asked, but a coolness had entered his voice.

"The break was good."

"Where's Abby?"

"She'll be right in. She went back to the car for the things she bought the kids." He turned his attention to Sophie. "Where are Justin and Maren?"

She swallowed, moving away from Michael's arm. "In the yard. I'll get them."

"No," he said sharply. "No, thank you, Sophie. We'll call them in a minute. I want a few minutes with Michael . . . before he has to leave for Lake Union."

"Just a minute, Nick. I'll go where I want, when I want." Michael pulled out a chair and sat down. "What's eating you anyway? I've been working my tail off at that damn computer since yesterday morning—"

"Yeah," Nick interrupted. "Your mother told me how you've been overdoing it. She's worried about you—you and Sophie. Wilma told Abby and me the hours you kept yesterday."

The two men stared at each other for a long time. Michael was getting up slowly when Abby came through the door. "Hello, everyone." Her smile was broad. Evidence of time in the sun glowed on her fair skin. "Where are my kids? Outside? I want to see them." She passed through the kitchen carrying a bulging plastic sack. "I've really missed them." She went outside apparently without noticing the frosty atmosphere in the room.

A revelation came slowly to Sophie. Nick didn't like her association with Michael. Nick was the one adding up the evidence, weighing it, as he was weighing the checks and balances for his business. A liaison between his partner, regardless of who he was outside the office, and his children's nanny was another potential stress, and he was already on emotional overload.

"I think we should talk in the study," Michael said evenly. He bowed slightly and motioned toward the hall. "After you, Nick?"

Nick slowly unzipped his windbreaker, took it off and slung it over his shoulder. "Let's do it." He left the room without another word, and Michael followed making a comical face at Sophie as he went.

Uncertain what to do next, Sophie waited several minutes before running upstairs to collect the things she wanted to take back to the boat house. She was going to make sure there was no repeat of the scene that had just taken place. Michael had said she was uncomfortable being with him here, and he was right. She paused with her small overnight bag held in front of her. She did want to be with him somewhere, sometime. The admission confused her and gave her hope at the same time. Now she must start mending fences, particularly with Nick.

She found Abby sitting on the grass showing Justin how to put together a Lego kit. Maren, ever the miniature mother, clutched a soft baby doll in frilly cotton rompers.

Sophie approached quietly, enjoying the sight of them together.

"It's going to be a plane," Abby was saying.

"A seaplane, like Daddy's?" Justin asked.

"If you like."

"We got to make cookies yesterday," Justin said, bending over his task. "Granny let us put in the flour and butter and everything. Even Maren. Granny said it doesn't matter if little kids make a mess. You and Sophie don't like us to make a mess, though, do you, Mommy?"

"Well—"

"Granny said it can always be cleaned up. And she doesn't mind cleaning up. Did you have one of our cookies yet? They're chocolate chip."

Sophie wished she could retreat, but she'd probably be seen. Yet again Wilma was coming off as a saint while she,

Sophie, must be raising a lot of doubts in her employers' minds.

"Sophie!" Maren shouted suddenly. "Look. New dolly."

Abby twisted to look over her shoulder, and her smile reassured Sophie a little.

"It's a lovely dolly, Maren," she said and plopped down beside the little girl. "They've been so good while you've been away, Abby."

"Mmmm. I think you'd say that anyway."

Sophie frowned. What did Abby mean? That Sophie didn't pay enough attention to the children to know how they behaved?

"They are good."

"Oh, I know. It's funny. Sometimes children seem more responsibility than you want to handle when there's...when you have a lot of things to worry about." She flushed a little. "But when you're away from them for a while you can hardly wait to get back. I can't imagine life without these two."

She was talking about money worries, Sophie was certain. She bowed her head, and in that instant she knew what she would do. "Abby, could we walk down by the lake for a while? Justin and Maren will be busy for at least a few minutes. I'd like to talk to you before I drop off my things at the boat house."

Abby looked puzzled but got up immediately and went ahead to open the gate in the trellis fence. She closed it again as soon as Sophie went through and fell into step beside her.

"Is something wrong?" she asked when they neared the water.

"I hope not," Sophie said. She sat on a piece of driftwood, and Abby joined her. "There's nothing wrong with the children or with me. But I know what you mean when you talk about the things you have to worry about. Please don't be offended if I say this, but it's money that's the trouble, isn't it?"

Two ducks waddled close, stretching their long necks, their bright eyes on the lookout for scraps of food. Sophie shooed them off, but they promptly pressed in again. Abby gathered a handful of tiny pebbles and began tossing them, one by one, toward the water. None of them reached, but she didn't appear to notice.

Sophie fiddled with the handle of her bag. "I've annoyed you. I shouldn't have asked a personal question like that."

Abby dropped the rest of the stones. "You haven't annoyed me, and I don't want you to give it another thought. We're doing just fine. A new business always takes a while to get going."

Containing the urge to say that they were all handing out the same platitudes took restraint. This, Sophie told herself, was what they wanted to believe.

"Good," she said. "That makes me feel much better. There is one other thing I'd like to discuss—my salary." She hadn't timed this properly. "You pay me too much—"

"Oh, Sophie," Abby broke in, placing a hand on Sophie's wrist. "You don't believe we're doing all right, do you? But you must. Please. We wouldn't hear of paying you less. One day I want it to be more, much more."

The sincerity of the reassurance warmed Sophie. "Thank you. But I mean what I say. I do have money of my own. Just being here with you and the children is payment enough. I don't need a salary."

"Nonsense." Abby jumped to her feet. "The arrangement we have is absolutely perfect." She paused. "At least, it's perfect for us. Aren't you happy, Sophie? Do you feel too restricted?"

"Oh, no," Sophie protested. "That wasn't what I wanted you to think. I only meant that with the apartment and everything, I don't think I have to be paid as well."

A stubborn line formed around Abby's mouth. "Nick and I think the world of you. We want you, need you here and so do the children. We wouldn't hear of changing a thing, unless it's to give you more for what you do for us. Is that clear?''

"It's...it's clear.''

"You aren't looking for an easy excuse to leave us?'' Abby's gray eyes became anxious.

"No. I love it here.''

"Then there's no more to be said. My nightmare is that you'll decide you have to go away. We'd miss you so much.''

Sophie smiled and felt tears well in her eyes. Abby was very sincere. The only thing that might spoil what she had here would be too many wrong moves that Wilma could use against her. Evidently Abby had no inkling that her mother's desire to take Sophie's place hadn't dwindled. Abby hadn't read the subtle messages in Wilma's comments about last night, but Nick had.

A wail from the trellised play area let them know Justin and Maren were no longer engrossed in their new toys. "You take your things up to the apartment,'' Abby said. "I'll go play referee until lunchtime.''

The sharp butt of a duck's bill against her knee made Sophie jump. She brushed the bird away absently, her attention on Abby's retreating form. Just what did Nick have against the idea of her becoming involved with Michael?

"LET'S MAKE THIS SHORT.''

A surge of anger hit Michael. "Make it as short as you like, Nick. Whatever *this* is. Why the hell did you come into that kitchen like an outraged father? What's changed with you? You know I've seen Sophie a few times, you also know we aren't kids. But you walked in on me holding her, and you didn't like it. I don't know why.''

Nick balled up his jacket and threw it hard into the chair behind his desk. "A lot of things are bothering me. Whether or not you're going to mess up Sophie's life is something I don't want added to the list.''

Michael knew he had to hold his temper. "Have you stopped to consider that this isn't any of your damn business?"

"What you do right here is my business," Nick shouted, then continued more quietly, "I know your reputation with women and sure, that *is* your business, unless you decide to start something with a woman who's important to Abby and me. What the hell do we do when you get bored with whatever game you're playing and drop her? That'll be a real easy situation to deal with, won't it?"

"You talk as if I've made a career of hurting women."

"There've been a few, Mike. We both know that."

"Hold on, buddy. You *don't* know that. Just because I've never been serious over anyone doesn't mean I've used people."

"Haven't you?"

He slumped into a chair and propped his feet on the desk.

"Avoiding the issue won't shut me up, Mike. What is it you want with Sophie? Are you trying to make me think you're in love with her?"

Michael felt as if he'd been kicked. His nerves skittered. "I don't have to answer to you."

"You mean you won't answer because it would embarrass you, don't you?"

The question hung between them. In the distance Michael heard the rumble of jet engines firing at Boeing Airfield. He got up. "I can't answer because I don't have an answer yet. And when I do, *you* won't be the first to know. Now let's attend to business."

He didn't wait for a reply before he strode from the house and vaulted into the driver's seat of the Triumph. He didn't know exactly what his feelings for Sophie were, but he'd find out—in his own good time.

Chapter Ten

Sophie pressed the button for the automatic door opener, waited, and drove the station wagon into the garage. Abby's blue Fiat was already in its spot.

"Come on, pumpkin." Sophie unstrapped Maren from her car seat and lifted the sleeping child into her arms. An afternoon at the pediatrician's office for a routine checkup had tired her out. It had tired Sophie out, too, particularly when Maren had struggled and screamed during her booster shots.

Tonight Sophie would offer to stay at the main house so that Abby and Nick needn't worry about getting up if Maren ran a fever. The little girl whimpered. Her face was already flushed. Sophie smoothed back damp curls and reached behind the seat for the package of brochures she'd picked up from a travel agent. Later she'd find time to go through them, and she hoped fervently she would find what she was looking for, or perhaps *not* find what she was looking for would be more accurate.

Balancing the child, the diaper bag and her precious package, she struggled into the house. "You're home early," she said when she saw Abby standing beside the little black lacquered table in the hall. When she realized the other woman was talking on the phone she murmured, "Sorry," and started upstairs.

"Wait, Sophie," Abby called. "This is for you. I'll take Maren up." She set the receiver on the table.

Sophie retraced her steps and gave up Maren and the bag. "She's worn out, Abby. I hate putting her through all that even though it does have to be done."

"I know." Abby nuzzled Maren's head into her neck. "I'll get her settled. Justin's next door playing. Michael's on the phone. Talk to him."

Before Sophie could respond, Abby had walked away.

Sophie braced her weight on the table with outstretched fingers and looked down at the phone. Almost a week had gone by without a personal word from Michael. He'd been smiling and cheerful each time she'd seen him, but had made no attempt at making anything but superficial conversation. And Sophie had been glad and disappointed by turns. Now she could feel her pulse drumming. He wouldn't call her to discuss the weather.

She picked up the phone and looked straight ahead at elegant sapphire silk wallpaper reflected in a series of oblong mirrors. "Hello, Michael. This is Sophie."

"I know."

Voices were more interesting on the phone. With no face or body language to interfere, tone and quality became intriguing, especially the tone and quality of this voice. She waited, felt them listening to each other.

"How have you been?" Michael asked. Deep but not too deep.

Sophie stirred, concentrating. "I saw you this morning, Michael. And yesterday. And the day before. I've been just wonderful. You sound as if we'd been parted for a year."

"I like the way you say that—parted. Sounds intimate. And I do feel like we've been parted a year."

The air about her became very still. "I know what you mean." She could not, would not play games, would not pretend.

"Good. I wanted you to say that." His sigh came to her clearly. "Sophie, would you come up to the San Juans with me on Sunday morning?"

An almost childish excitement made her shiver. "You mean come on a flight with you? I've never been in a sea-plane."

"You'll enjoy the ride. It'll be a cargo run—some marine parts for a wooden boat builder up there—so we won't have passengers to worry about."

Just the two of them. "I'm not sure I can."

"Why? Abby said there was no reason you couldn't be away for a couple of days."

He wasn't just asking her to go for a little flight to the San Juan Islands. He wanted her to go away with him. She turned and leaned against the table, winding the telephone cord through her fingers. *Go away with him.* The phrase had its own meaning.

"Sophie? Are you still there?"

"I'm here."

"I said, Abby told me there was no problem with you going."

"I heard what you said."

"So you'll come?"

"Do you think that's such a good idea?"

He was silent.

"Michael, I can tell Nick doesn't approve of us seeing each other and—"

"The hell with—"

"No, Michael," she interrupted, "let me finish, please. I don't want to be the cause of any trouble between you and Nick or in this household at all."

"Are you sure it's not just that you don't want to go any-where with me?"

"No!" And she really meant it, body and soul; she wanted to be with Michael.

He clicked his tongue as if calculating. "Okay, I believe you, so it's my turn to talk and your turn to listen. We talked—correction—*I* talked about going swimming. How would you like swimming off a boat in a cove that looks like something from a Hawaiian travel film?"

Sophie gnawed her lip. He'd obviously seen this magical cove before. With whom? she wondered.

"Taken your breath away, huh? You're so impressed you're speechless. All right. There are two cabins, the main one and a second one the guy who owns it uses for guests. This guy is a friend of mine, and he said we could use the cabins and the boat on Sunday. *Cabins*, Sophie, plural. One for you to sleep in and one for me, if that's the way you want it."

At least he wasn't hiding the hope that she'd sleep with him. "Sounds lovely."

"Is that a yes?"

Sunday, the day after tomorrow.

"Yes, Sophie?" Michael repeated softly. "Please?"

"Yes, I'd like to come very much."

His hoot made her wince and hold the phone away from her ear. It also made her relax slightly. Then she remembered Abby. Abby had said there was no reason she couldn't take a trip with Michael and be away overnight. She felt vaguely embarrassed.

"...early. Can you be ready?"

Michael had been talking and he hadn't heard. "Michael, did you...what did you say to Abby?"

He laughed, and in her mind she could see his blue eyes glitter. "You are one old-fashioned lady. Does it make any difference what I told her? What happens between us is up to us. Abby wants me to be happy, and I believe she's decided being with you makes me happy. And it seems she thinks the same about you. If Nick's reaction worries you, too, don't let it. He wants the same things Abby wants. He just has a different way of showing his feelings."

She wasn't convinced, not about Nick anyway, but Michael was right about their decisions being their own to make. "What time did you say you wanted to leave on Sunday?" she asked.

"That's the girl. I'd like to pick you up at seven so we can get the delivery out of the way and still make a full day of it. Any problem?"

"No problem," she assured him and didn't fail to notice the rapid way he dispatched the rest of their conversation, as if he were afraid she'd change her mind.

"CAN YOU FLY A PLANE like this anywhere you want to?"

Michael flipped an overhead switch. "What do you mean?" They were taxiing across Friday Harbor, heading east.

"Well, just that I wondered if there were some places you couldn't take a seaplane."

"Gets a bit touchy without water." He grinned, ducking his head to scan commercial fishing boats moored at pilings.

Sophie laughed. "I asked for that. I meant is a seaplane able to land on any kind of water, anywhere?"

They accelerated, the nose of the plane lifting slightly. Spume knifed out on either side of the pontoons, shattering the sun-dappled surface of emerald-green water.

Michael checked gauges, so many gauges Sophie wondered how he remembered what they were all for, and slid levers. Then he was pulling back on the stick, and they were airborne, sweeping upward until tiny puffs of cloud, misting past the windshield, gave Sophie the feeling of increased speed that had surprised her after their first takeoff.

"Okay?" He glanced at her.

"Yes. I like it. I'd like to fly one of these." The right wing dipped, and her stomach rolled. Sky and cloud and water swung, tipped, then seemed to slow as Michael straightened out the plane. Sophie breathed through her mouth. "At least, I think I'd like to fly one," she added faintly.

"I'll teach you."

She looked at him disbelievingly, expecting to see a smirk, but his serious face suggested his offer was genuine. "Maybe one day," she said hastily. Given his persistence, all she'd have to do was suggest real interest and she'd be in pilot training.

He spoke over the radio, giving coordinates Sophie assumed, and a voice crackled in response.

"Sit back and relax," Michael said to her when the radio transmission was over, "this won't take long. What were you asking me?"

"About the plane's limitations."

"Mmmm." He nodded. "High water's out if you have a choice. These babies aren't built for landing and takeoff in rough stuff. But we can put down about anywhere as long as the weather's moderate to good. Not that we don't handle the other sometimes, but it's not a good idea."

That answered one of her main questions. Sophie rested her head back and watched the sky. She smiled, satisfied. Last night she'd spent time with the travel brochures. The De Havilland's range and capabilities were the one element that had still worried her when she'd finished her research. She wasn't worried anymore.

"Which island did you say we're going to?" She turned to Michael.

"Blakely. John's place is on the south shore, behind Armitage Island. Armitage protects the coast of Blakely nicely there."

He looked so good this morning, very young, very... sexy? She averted her eyes. Had she ever consciously considered whether or not a man was sexy? Jack had been a handsome boy, then a handsome man, and she saw only him, wanted only him, from when she was little more than a kid. Yes, he'd been a virile, exciting man—until the bottle and strangers had become his lovers. And she'd always taken what he was for granted. But she was looking at Michael Harris with new eyes, the speculative eyes of a woman whose mind and body were responding to desire for the first time in more years than she wanted to count.

"Are you sleepy?"

She jumped. "A little."

"Nap, then. You were up early this morning."

"So were you."

"Yes. I'll nap, too."

"My eyes are wide open." Sophie swiveled in her seat until she could almost face him. "Don't you dare close yours."

He tipped up his head in a silent laugh. "Scared, I knew it."

She didn't respond. *Scared.* She was scared all right, but not of his ability to pilot this plane. It was her own emotion that made her flesh tremble. What happened between them in the next twenty-four hours would be mostly up to her. And what happened could also decide whether or not they were ever together again like this. Sophie wanted to be with Michael. She glanced from his powerful hands and arms to his throat, his mouth . . . then met his eyes.

"I'm getting another of your royal once-overs, huh, Sophie? Will you know me the next time you see me, do you think?" he asked without inflection.

"I'll know you. I'm making sure of that right now."

"No kidding. You should be able to see me with your eyes shut in future. What d'you think? Do I pass?"

She could already see him with her eyes shut. "You're fishing," she said.

He shook his head slowly. "Never. Just curious. Will I get to stare at you later and decide what I like best, those brown eyes, your hair? It's soft. I get off on that, and the shape of your nose and chin, and mouth, and neck and—"

"Thank you," she said hastily and laughed, a nervous laugh. They would make love tonight. When she swallowed her throat hurt and her mouth was instantly dry. Whether she was ready for sex with Michael was a question she couldn't answer for sure yet, but deciding might take a long time, too long. He probably wouldn't wait around for her to make up her mind much longer. And why should she be afraid, make such a big deal out of something that was normal and could be so special? Surely, lovemaking with Michael would be special.

"That's Blakely." He pointed straight ahead. "Pretty?"

"Pretty," she agreed, peering over the nose of the plane, then craning sideways to see the densely forested island below. The ocean was shiny from here, more blue than green, navy where there must be deeper shelves beneath.

"We're going in. There's a dock. We can swim off that, too, as well as the boat. Fish, if we like."

He was happy, expectant. And he was glad to be with her. Sophie put her hands under her thighs, bracing for the slipping sensation that came when the pontoons touched down. She'd make sure Michael stayed happy. But why couldn't she surrender to the excitement? Why couldn't it become as much a mental as a physical anticipation that moved her?

He hadn't lied about the cove. It was idyllic, a small perfect bite out of the land, edged with yellow sand, touched by gentle froth-tipped waves and wrapped about with a backdrop of tall evergreens.

The plane settled comfortably on its floats, and Sophie admired the ease with which Michael maneuvered the craft across the tiny bay and alongside a wooden dock. He climbed out and secured mooring lines before hopping back onto the wing and offering Sophie his hand. Holding her steady, he jumped down again and lifted her in front of him, resting his hands lightly at her waist.

She looked at a button on his cotton shirt, at the dark hair where it veed together.

"Thank you for coming," he said so softly the breeze almost took his words.

"Thank you for asking me." She stepped away and walked to the other side of the dock where a glistening white powerboat bobbed and thudded against rubber bumpers.

She half expected Michael to follow, but when she glanced over her shoulder he was taking their bags and several boxes of supplies from the cabin of the plane.

Silently, she retraced her steps and picked up her bag and one of the boxes. She hadn't thought about the need for food and basic necessities. Michael had. Her box contained fruit and bread, and two bottles of wine. She realized she was clenching her teeth and relaxed the muscles in her jaw. She was young and free and so was Michael. They wanted each other, and there was nothing standing in their way.

She started toward the shore, and Michael fell into step beside her. "I'll come back for the rest of the stuff," he said. "You can get settled. The cabin is great if you like rustic." He stopped abruptly, and Sophie paused, short of breath from the weight of the box. "You don't hate rustic things do you?" he asked, a vaguely alarmed look in his eyes.

"I'm crazy about rustic," she assured him, setting off again. "Let's get there and dump all this. You brought enough for an army." She bowed her head but continued to walk. "Thanks for bringing everything, Michael. I didn't even think about food."

If he heard her he gave no sign. He passed her, leading the way to the larger of two log cabins, more a house than a cabin, Sophie decided, built on a grassed slope above a broad bar of fine shale that separated grass from beach.

"Are you still tired?" Michael asked. He stepped onto a wide porch and dumped his boxes on a rickety bamboo table. "I thought we could head right out on the boat if you feel up to it."

"Absolutely. Let's go." The cabin daunted her, the prospect of being alone with him in a confined space. She put down the box and her bag. "Let's just go now."

The pause before he answered felt endless. Sophie made herself look directly at his face. He was taking her measure, briefly, before he smiled and said, "I think we should at least go inside, don't you? Put away the food, look around, find our swimsuits, maybe?"

She had to glance away. He could see her uncertainty and must know its cause. "Of course," she said, striving for coolness. "But I'll help you get the rest of the supplies first."

"There's only my bag. You go on in." He stooped and took a key from beneath a piece of driftwood.

"Your friend leaves all this—" she indicated the cabins, the boat "—with a key where anyone can find it?"

Michael unlocked the door. "After you." He waved her inside. "This place is pretty inaccessible unless you're a very determined hiker or come by boat, or the way we did. It certainly wouldn't be very easy to rip off the microwave if you had to carry it through the woods, and the average boater around here doesn't need a second microwave."

"Microwave?" Sophie followed him directly into a long living room with a rough stone fireplace at one end. "Rustic, huh? You do love to tease, don't you, Michael?"

"A bit, I guess. What do you think?"

"I think 'Wow' covers it." Dark wood floors gleamed almost red. Bentwood furniture—couch, love seat and two chairs—was grouped close to the fireplace, billowy earth-toned cushions a soft contrast to deep-piled creamy-colored rugs. Sophie glanced about the room and to the kitchen visible beyond a dividing counter. "What does this John do, mine diamonds? This isn't quite my idea of rustic. If it were mine I'd have an armed guard posted. What *isn't* here?"

"You tell me." He sounded amused but smug. "John's an art dealer. Antiques, too. Very successful."

"Figures. Doesn't he know most people don't put Danish teak dining furniture and fabulous batik hangings in their cabins in the woods? And look at the kitchen." She skirted a row of tall stools by the counter and began an inventory of the fittings. "You could live in this place permanently." While she opened drawers and cupboards, Michael lounged in the archway from the living room. "Just what I always wanted." She pried a gadget from a slot in a wall rack. "Know what this is?"

Michael shook his head.

"Electric ice cream scoop. Kitchen tool for the cook with everything."

"You're kidding."

"Nope. My mother-in-law had one—in her permanent home in Des Moines, not in a woodsy cabin. It's electric. Plug it in and the Teflon surface gets warm so the ice cream doesn't stick."

"Fascinating." Michael's tone suggested he was anything but fascinated. He hadn't come to Blakely Island to discuss kitchen implements.

Sophie put back the scoop and dithered, winding up the cord with clumsy fingers, almost paralyzed by awkwardness.

"Do you keep in touch with your in-laws?"

His question didn't immediately compute. Sophie turned to look at him. "I'm sorry?"

"You mentioned your mother-in-law. I wondered if you were still close."

"I like her. My father-in-law died when Jack was quite young. Mrs. Peters is very capable. She ran a successful business for years until Jack was ready to take over, then she retired and left him in charge." She hesitated, remembering. Maybe Jack had had too much responsibility too soon. A wife, then a business and such high expectations from his mother. "She was good to me. We keep in touch."

She noticed Michael had become quiet. He moved into the living room and outside to carry in boxes. She frowned. He'd been the one to ask questions about her family, yet she suspected he really didn't want any answers. That was fine. She'd rather avoid the subject. "Give me that," she said, meeting him halfway across the living room and taking the top box from him. "And put the other one down. You go for your bag, and I'll find places for all this. You must be planning to work up an appetite, or not go home for a week."

"I wouldn't mind not going home at all."

She stopped, bracing the box on one knee. Michael regarded her steadily, somberly, and she didn't doubt he meant what he said, and not simply because he wanted to be with her. To Michael this hideaway was a place to escape all the problems back in Seattle.

"Get your things," she said reflectively. "It's time we had that swim you've been dreaming about for days. I'll put away the food that needs to go in the refrigerator and get changed."

At the door, Michael turned back. "The bedroom's up there." He pointed and Sophie poked her head from the kitchen to see. For the first time she noticed a railing below the vaulted ceiling. "The whole loft is bedroom and bathroom," Michael added, "and it's not too hard on the eye, either."

After he left she moved rapidly about the kitchen, stowing coffee and crackers, milk and cheese. The fruit she put in a basket and placed on the counter. Then she swept up her overnight bag and ran up spiral stairs from a corner of the dining area to the loft.

Without more than a cursory look around the bedroom, open to the lower floor and furnished in similar colors and style, she found her swimsuit and cover-up and went into the bathroom. Michael was taking a long time to get one bag—

deliberately, no doubt, and she appreciated his consideration.

Don't think. Her T-shirt and jeans hit the floor in quick succession, and her bra and panties. The one-piece swimsuit was peach-colored and shiny, cut high at the legs and low in the back—low between her breasts, too, but still conservative by today's standards. Quickly she put on the white gauze cover-up and belted it securely around her waist. Hardly pausing, she gathered her clothes, left the bathroom and stuffed everything in her bag before returning to the living room.

She saw Michael's well-worn flight bag before she saw the man. He must have been wearing his swimsuit under his jeans. The jeans and his shirt lay over the arm of the couch, beneath his feet, which were propped up and bare. His long body took up the length of the couch even with his head resting on top of his hands on the arm at the other end. His eyes were closed.

"Michael," she whispered and remembered the last time she'd thought he was asleep. He wouldn't catch her twice. "Up and at 'em, Harris. Time to hit the surf."

He opened one eye, lifted his head and surveyed her over the back of the couch. "Mmm. You look good." He swung his feet down and stood, tall, lean, muscles in his torso and long legs tensile and well shaped. He wore a brief yellow suit, a pencil line of pale skin below his navel intensifying the darkness of his tan. "Yes, Sophie Peters, you are very lovely. In fact, I suggest you hotfoot it out of here before I change my mind about going anywhere."

She laughed, thrilled by the languorous way his gaze swept over her, the appreciation she couldn't miss. Her anxiety had ebbed, and she didn't analyze why before she jogged toward the open door. "I'll beat you to the boat," she threatened him.

Michael overtook her before she made it off the bottom step from the porch. He ruffled her hair as he went, making her stumble, then ran ahead, a cooler bag swinging from one hand. "Hurry up, slow poke. You're all talk in this fitness drivel you keep giving me." He leaped in sideways steps, then ran backward until he almost fell. "Aargh," he yelled, flailing his free arm. "Come on, come on, Sophie."

She scrambled after him, held back by the sliding shale, then hampered by sand in her thongs. By the time she pounded down the dock Michael was aboard the boat and stowing the cooler bag in a locker beneath the port gunwale in the cockpit. He grinned when she approached and every inch of her body glowed. His smile, the welcome in his eyes, let her know this was as special a day for him as it was for her.

"Here, my lady, let me help you."

"Thank you." But the hand he offered didn't remain a steady support to allow her to step gracefully aboard. Instead, he waited for her first foot to reach the boat's side before he pulled her toward him and clamped her to his naked chest.

"Michael," she squeaked, her breath gone. "You play the dirtiest tricks."

"I know," he chortled.

His arms circled her tightly, and the hair on his chest tickled her skin where the cover-up had slipped awry. She was intensely aware of her breasts so lightly covered by the smooth fabric of her suit and pressed to hard, flexed muscle. Her toes barely made contact with the deck.

The palm of his hand passed fleetingly over her cheek and hair, and he kissed the hollow above her collarbone. "Mmmm," he said against her skin, "I don't care how much you beg for more, I insist we get under way—and I'm the skipper, right?"

She felt vaguely disoriented, then bereft as he released her and, after one more long stare, climbed the ladder to the fly bridge. "Right," she agreed, although he probably didn't hear.

Michael Harris was the skipper all right, of this boat and probably anything . . . or anyone else he decided to control.

Chapter Eleven

"We're going to jump off the boat and swim?" Sophie shivered a little inside her cover-up. Michael had taken the boat much farther out than she'd expected.

He cut the engines. "Jump?" he echoed. "Oh, my funny Sophie. You've never swum off a boat, I forgot. You'll love it. The water is so deep out here you hardly have to do a thing."

"How deep is it?"

He laughed. "You sound like the straight man on a late night TV show. But it is deep, my dear," he said, lowering his voice, "very, very deep... and murky. And we must be on the watch for pointy fins at all times."

"Michael," she began, but he was already loping down the steps from the fly bridge to the cockpit.

"Michael, wait." Sophie hurried after him. She waited until he dropped anchor, then pulled him around to face her. "Look, I don't want you to think I'm a chicken, but I think I'll just watch you swim."

With one finger he made a line down the side of her neck. "This is what they go for, beautiful pale skin. But I'll protect you."

She pushed his hand away. "I don't need protection. And I'm not afraid of some nonexistent sharks." Two canvas chairs stood against the stern, and Sophie dropped into one. "But I'm not coming in."

"Sure, sure." He smirked and climbed nimbly to straddle the side. "You won't be able to resist for long."

With his weight supported by locked arms, the muscles in his chest and shoulders stood out, golden and shiny. The moment before he swung his second leg over the water and dropped from sight, Sophie wondered how many other women he'd swum with in this cove, whether he took a different companion to some sunny spot every time he got a day off—a tan like his wasn't perfected in a few hours. And then she remembered that she probably saw more of him than anyone but Nick, and she felt mean and suspicious. His coloring was the kind that always looked good.

"Sophie!" His call reached her amid the squalling of gulls.

She got up and went to peer down at him. Water glistened in his hair. The sun, shining from behind him, shadowed his face, and she couldn't see his eyes.

"Come on in," he called.

"Is it cold?" She looked at the reflection of the boat on the gently rippling surface.

"Only at first. It's wonderful."

Sophie wasn't convinced. "Are there . . . are there a lot of fish out here?"

"I'm coming to get you." Michael made a move toward the ladder at the stern.

"No, no," Sophie insisted, pulling off her cover-up and swinging quickly to sit with her legs suspended over the water. "Give me a few minutes to get ready."

"To work up the courage, you mean?"

It was deep, very deep, and she wasn't a wonderful swimmer, not that she'd admit as much to Michael. "Michael," she said, dismayed at the way her voice skated upward, "I'm not afraid, honestly, but *is* it dangerous to swim out here?"

He came close to the boat's side, and she could see his face now, his smile, the glimmer of white teeth, his blue eyes. "Sophie," he said, and she heard laughter in his voice, "the most dangerous thing in this cove is me. Now—" he shrugged elaborately, one hand braced on the boat's side, the other sweeping wide "—if I scare you, I understand. I'm a terrifying brute."

Sophie pinched her nose between finger and thumb and launched herself, feet thrashing, into the sea. Humming pressure swelled up around her. Down, down she went, and then she was struggling for the surface, the water swirling before her eyes and about her, surprisingly clear but so green, greener than any she'd seen.

She broke into blinding sunlight, scrubbing at her face and eyes, pushing back streaming strands of hair.

Michael bobbed a foot away. "Great, isn't it?" He smiled.

"It's freezing," Sophie said through chattering teeth.

"You'll get used to it. I'll help you." He came so close she saw the darker flecks in his eyes. "Relax," he ordered and swam behind her, circling her waist with one arm and pulling her on top of him as he sidestroked easily away from the boat.

The coldness faded, turned into a rising heat. Michael moved beneath her, his body, his powerful legs buoying her. All around them the water slipped, soothing, lulling. She closed her eyes.

"Sophie." His mouth touched her ear. "Put your head back, rest it on my shoulder."

His voice seemed a long way away. She took several deliberate, calming breaths through her mouth before she spoke. "Aren't we supposed to be getting exercise?"

He pulled her head to his neck. "This is exercise."

"Not enough. Let's swim." Sophie rolled away, kicking, putting distance between them. Without waiting for Michael's response she broke into her best crawl stroke, a slapping effort she knew looked as clumsy as it felt. She'd never learned to breathe properly and preferred to keep her head above the water.

The sensation of something slithering beneath her thighs brought a scream to her throat. She kept her mouth shut, swallowing the noise and tried to change course, striking out to make a circle around the boat. *The boat.* She longed for the feel of that wonderful safe deck beneath her feet.

Michael must have gone the other way, she couldn't see him.

The thing touched her legs again, and this time she did yell, and kick ferociously...until her hips were gripped, then her waist, hand over hand, as Michael worked his way to the surface using her body as a float and popped his face out inches from hers.

"Hi," he said cheerfully, and she felt his breath on her skin. "Wanna play with me?"

His hands spanned her ribs. Sophie pried them loose, placed a fist on top of his head and pushed him under.

Seconds later he surfaced again, sputtering, shaking his head sharply and sending droplets flying in all directions. "Dirty trick, Sophie, my love. Always make sure you choose adversaries in your own league, or you may end up drowned!"

She evaded his grabbing fingers. "Typical. Boys are always like that. You want to play, and then you get nasty when someone plays better than you do." Her breath came in throaty pants.

Michael stayed in place, stroking slowly, suddenly serious. His lashes were so thick, sparkly with water and his eyes, stunning eyes. "I'm not a boy, and I don't think I want to play anymore," he said.

Muscles inside Sophie contracted. She skimmed a hand over her face and rotated, staring unseeingly toward the island.

She felt Michael coming before he slid an arm around her waist. He splayed the fingers of his other hand over her stomach. They held place, treading water, their bodies clamped together.

"We've played long enough, haven't we, Sophie?"

She was hot now, trembling inside. There was no smart comeback to diffuse the moment. The sexuality between them wouldn't go away.

He moved his hands carefully upward until he covered her breasts and she arched backward, the heat within her burning now. The water made of their skins slippery, incredibly sensitive stuff.

Michael kissed the side of her jaw. "I want you, Sophie." Then he laughed, and the noise rumbled against her neck before the laugh became an indrawn sigh. "I guess you'd call that a redundant comment." And his fingers parted the deep vee at the top of her suit, pulling the supple fabric aside until he held her naked breasts in his hands, and the heat in her became fire and fueled a weakness that made her limp.

From some old comment, she wouldn't think from whom, came the thought that she was too small. It always came. "I'm skinny, aren't I?" she said, a rush of embarrassment engulfing her.

Michael passed his palms slowly back and forth over her nipples as he spoke. "You are perfect as far as I'm concerned. Of course—" he chuckled low in his throat "—I'm probably the only one who thinks so, so you'd better stick close to me."

He couldn't know how fragile her concept was of herself as a woman. She made herself laugh. "I'll remember what you say."

"I'll make sure you do." His thighs, pushing against the backs of Sophie's, thrust her upward until she floated on top of him. Straps slipped easily from her shoulders and her arms were free.

"Kiss me," Michael said, and his voice cracked.

Sophie moved under his hands, revolved, ran her fingers around his neck and held him tightly. She bowed her head, resting her temple on his cheek. The sight of her flesh bonded to his brought a rage of desire that tightened her grip on him convulsively.

And she kissed him, hard, parting his lips, carried along by her own sense of power in this moment. Michael let her move his face with her lips, kept his hands on her back while she nuzzled his jaw up to reach his throat. A hint of beard stubble grazed her face, and she stroked his cheek with the tips of her fingers.

Abruptly, he caught her wrists and held her away. Even in the water she saw the rapid rise and fall of his chest. With more strength than she knew she possessed, she forced herself close once more, their arms still joined. He looked into her eyes, then at her mouth, before he delivered his own kiss, first searingly soft, then desperate and carrying the message of his need. His legs snaked around her, drawing her close. His pelvis, jutting against Sophie's, turned everything within her white-hot. Michael was aroused to a height where no man could continue to keep control.

"Let's go back aboard," he whispered hoarsely.

He held her hand and towed her back to the ladder, climbed swiftly up and helped her over the side.

A warm breeze caressed her breasts, and she became uncomfortably aware of her near-nakedness. Michael paused, looking at her, slowly taking in her body, and he touched her lightly, running his fingers up her ribs, hesitating, rubbing his knuckles gently over the sides of her breasts. Her own gaze passed from his shoulders over the wet hair on his chest, the slender dark line that continued down his flat abdomen and disappeared beneath his trunks.

"Come with me, Sophie," he said softly and took her hand again.

She went with him into the cabin, sank down with him on one of the couches lining the bulkhead.

"Take this off." Michael worked her swimsuit lower over her hips.

Sophie opened her mouth to speak, but no sound came.

"Lean toward me." A hard, insistent hand urged her closer.

"No."

"Mmmm. Help me."

Cold coursed into her. His face was different, set, his eyes almost unseeing. She gripped his forearms until he looked up.

"What is it?" Irritation. It was there, the early signs of the anger that followed any reluctance, any drawing back from sex. "Sophie, what's the matter?" He took her by the shoulders, and his fingers dug into her flesh.

She would not cry. Crying only made it worse, sometimes brought... But this was Michael, not Jack. Michael wasn't violent. "I—I'm not sure I'm ready. It's just that I guess I wasn't really prepared...." She faltered, felt a violent blush throb to her cheeks.

For seconds that felt like hours, Michael stared at her, then he smiled and shook his head. "You mean you aren't on the pill? Oh, sweetheart, don't worry. We'll take care of things."

Her scalp prickled and sickness overwhelmed her. Wordlessly, she struggled back into her swimsuit. Michael reached for her, but she shrugged away and walked unsteadily through the sliding door from the cabin to the cockpit. He was at her side before she could put on the cover-up.

"Stop it, Sophie." His fingers grabbed her by the elbow, and he jerked her around. "Stop right there and tell me what's wrong."

"Drop it." The corners of her mouth quivered. "I want to go back."

"Oh, we're going back. Fear not. But first you're going to tell me why you turned off on me."

"That's something you're not used to, isn't it, Michael? A woman who doesn't go along with whatever you want."

His fingers dug even deeper. "You were going along pretty well as far as I could tell, lady. You weren't exactly a shrinking violet in the water. What are you, a tease? Do you get your kicks out of turning men on, then leaving them hanging?"

"Don't!" She could hardly breathe. "Don't," she repeated softly. "I'm not a tease. I wouldn't know how to be. I changed my mind, that's all."

"Because of something I said?"

She lifted her chin. "That's part of it."

"The pill? Wasn't I supposed to be an adult and talk about birth control?"

The sensation in her throat sent goose bumps over her arms and legs. "All your other women would be on the pill, wouldn't they, Michael? You wouldn't want to risk an inconvenience like a pregnancy. Sex is purely an activity for you, isn't it, gratification?"

He released her and put his hands on his hips. "I don't believe this. Are you saying having children is the only reason for sex? This isn't the Middle Ages."

"I'm not saying that. It's just that—"

He waved a dismissive hand. "You were married for seven years. If that's what you thought, how come you don't have half a dozen kids?"

Tears sprang to her eyes, and she didn't look away in time to hide them. "I don't know why we didn't have children," she said simply and bent to retrieve the cover-up. "This was always a bad idea, Michael. I thought it was and now I'm sure. My life is set now. I've got what I want, and I won't jeopardize it by having a failed affair with . . . with . . ."

"You don't have to say any more." Michael's voice was tight. "And I'm sorry for the crack about children. That was a low blow. Just chalk it up to me being as insensitive as you think I am.''

He was angry, too angry to temper his reactions. Sophie wished she could say the right things, save the situation and have them both walk away without rancor. But it was too late for that.

She watched him take a step backward, turn and climb to the fly bridge. Soon the engine turned over, once, twice, and set up a steady rumble.

When they reached the dock, Michael stuck his head out of the bridge housing. "Want to start tying her up?"

Sophie nodded, grateful for something to do. She tossed the bowline ashore, balanced on the boat's side and leaped to the dock. Minutes later, she returned and gathered up another coil.

"Can you manage?" Michael called.

Her answer was to sling the nylon mooring line through the sun-glittered air of late afternoon. This time she stayed ashore, uncertain what to do next.

Michael had cut the engines and was closing the bridge door. He gained the cockpit in two strides, found the cooler bag they'd never used and joined her.

"It's too late to start back to Seattle now. Sorry. You'll be comfortable enough. I'll just get my bag and a few supplies and leave you alone."

He strode ahead with Sophie following slowly. Why couldn't she have gone along? Damn it all, why couldn't she forget the past? Sure, the matter-of-fact reference to birth control had been the final turnoff, but she'd been pulling away inside before that.

By the time Sophie entered the main cabin, Michael was putting a bottle of wine into a brown paper sack. He would go off on his own and drink. She took a jerky breath and wound her fingers together to stop them from shaking. Because of her he would drink to forget his frustrations.

"Michael," she began and cleared her throat, "Michael, let me cook you something. It's about time for dinner, and you didn't even have lunch."

"Don't worry about me. I'm a big boy." With the brown sack tucked under his arm, jeans and shirt held in one hand, his bag in the other, he left.

HE'D BEHAVED LIKE A JERK, said things only a jerk would say. But damn it, she'd given him all the right signs, then shut down cold.

Michael looked at the half-empty bottle of wine on the table by the window. No answers there. Drinking had never been any good for him. He picked up the cork, pushed it into the bottle neck and slammed it home with his fist.

The sky was dark now. No moon. Shadows of tall trees around the cabin were something he felt more than saw. And he heard boughs scrape and brush on wooden shakes and log walls.

Sophie was alone up there. He automatically turned his head in the direction of the big cabin. She shouldn't be alone in a strange place. The least he could do was go and make sure she was okay. He could forget himself for once and offer to sleep on the couch.

Who was he kidding? Every time he heard her move in the bedroom he'd go nuts. And she wouldn't want him there anyway.

What *had* made her make a one-hundred-eighty-degree turn? She wasn't any more interested in starting a pregnancy than he was, was she? She couldn't be. That wasn't it. He'd done something else to scuttle everything when they seemed on the same track.

He didn't like her being alone.

Hell. "Sophie, Sophie," he muttered and went out onto the narrow porch. The air in the cabin was still and musty.

She was lovely. "God." He lowered himself heavily to sit on the top step. Since when had he thought of women as lovely? Sexy, a turn-on, stacked . . . but lovely? Sophie *was* different for him, but he wasn't ready to look too closely at all the reasons why. Or to tackle the question of a possible future with her. There were enough problems in his life without that.

Crickets set up their clacking song in a clump of bushes beside the steps. Michael leaned his head on a post and stared up into blackness. The sky had texture, a thickness that closed him in. An unfamiliar sensation in his eyes made him blink. Must be allergic to something out here. He could count the number of times he'd cried since he was a kid. He'd cried after his father died, when he was finally alone, late in the night. And he'd wished then that he'd told his father how much he had meant to him, told him more often that he loved him, respected him for being real and uncomplicated.

That time he'd promised himself he'd let the people he cared for know how he felt. He drew in a great, uncomfortable breath and closed out the memory of all the tears he'd cried for Dallas, all the things he still wished he'd said to the man. Tomorrow he'd let Sophie know he thought she was a special woman, that he wanted them to go on being friends. Please let it be possible for him to keep things light around her. Let him be able to make her feel okay about today. *Why* had he made that crack about her not having children?

A breeze, light but welcome and carrying the tangy scent of salt, ruffled his hair and cooled his face. Maybe he'd sleep with the door open. If he could sleep at all.

He held the porch railing and hauled himself upright. Tomorrow he'd try to patch things up with Sophie.

The breeze came again, and he sniffed it before turning to the door.

There was the slightest rustle nearby, a footfall, and he didn't jump at the soft laying of a hand on his back.

"Will you walk on the beach with me, Michael? I can't sleep."

Chapter Twelve

The night seethed, the breeze fuller now, almost a wind and laced with salt and damp mist off a roiling surf that turned a pale and glowing green in the darkness.

Michael walked barefoot, jeans rolled up, hands in pockets, scuffing through the running wake of the incoming waves. The same eerie light that touched the water made of his body a dark outline inside the billowing white of his unbuttoned shirt. Sophie kept up, barefoot too, her hair loose now but still damp.

"I'm sorry," Michael said.

The sound of his voice surprised her as much as what he said. They'd been walking in silence for several minutes. She didn't answer, didn't know how to answer.

He stopped and faced the ocean. "I've always had a problem with my mouth," he said. "It seems to have a mind of its own sometimes."

"You haven't said anything you shouldn't," Sophie commented, standing behind him and a short distance apart.

His shoulders hunched and the shirt flapped wide. "Yeah, I did. Why you and your husband didn't have children isn't my business. I hurt you. And I am sorry."

She blessed the darkness that would mask the start of more tears. "You didn't mean to hurt. You were lashing out, and I don't blame you. That was my fault. Can we forget it, Michael?''

"Back there—" he inclined his head in the direction they'd come "—I was thinking I wanted to tell you you're something special and I respect you, I like you. We're going to see each other, probably almost every day, and I don't want there to be awkwardness between us. They say men and women can't just be friends, but I don't believe that. We could be if we worked at it.''

Sophie knew what she was going to do. She'd come to him knowing. Now she took a step that brought her close to him, the first step toward what she was sure she wanted and hoped he still wanted. Slowly, she raised her hands and laid them flat on his shoulder blades. He tensed but said nothing. Through the thin cotton his skin was warm. She stroked downward, pushed her arms under his to circle his bare waist and rested her cheek on his back.

Beneath her face a deep sigh moved him. He took his hands from his pockets and covered hers, crossed them to wrap her more tightly against him.

"I need a friend, Michael. A real friend.''

"We all do," he said hoarsely. "It's part of being human, the best part maybe.''

"I think..." Her mouth was dry and she swallowed. "No, I don't think, I know. I need a real friend who's also a lover.'' She closed her eyes tightly, not sorry to have told him but still surprised she had.

Michael pulled her in front of him. He lifted her hands to his lips and kissed each fingertip so slowly she wondered if he would ever reply.

He flattened her palms to his chest and covered them again. "I want to believe you're saying I'm the one you need. Am I, or am I just a dreamer?''

"Nobody's *just* a dreamer, Michael. The dreamers have it all. But yes, I need you. And I've wanted you for a long time, only I have trouble letting go. But you know that, don't you?''

"Yeah, I know. I keep hoping you'll tell me why one day.''

One day she would, Sophie thought; she'd tell him everything as soon as she could sort out all the feelings clearly enough to make sense.

Michael smoothed her hair back. "Are you going to let me in there, Sophie?'' He tapped her forehead.

"I guess I am. But can I have a little more time, Michael? I'm not really so complicated, just a bit mixed up about a few things that shouldn't matter anymore.''

"And you're not ready to sort them out yet?''

"I don't think so.'' She leaned against him. "Right now I just want to be with you.''

"You're with me, Sophie. Thank God. Damn.'' He laughed. "My heart's about ready to jump out of my chest.''

"I know,'' she said and kissed the spot where she felt the heavy beat. "Mine, too.'' And she loosened the belt of her cover-up, letting it fall open. "Feel.''

Even in the gloom she saw Michael's eyes lower, heard his sharp intake of breath before he bent his head to kiss her naked breast gently, lingeringly. "I feel it,'' he whispered and rubbed shaky palms the length of her, down her sides, around her waist until he spread his fingers over her bottom and urged her to him. "Is this real, Sophie? You aren't offering yourself to me out of pity?''

"I'm asking you to make love with me, Michael, because it's what I want.'' And she wanted to touch every part of him, to feel him cover her. "Is that okay? Is it wrong for me to say? I came to you knowing what I intended to ask you.''

He laughed again, mirthlessly. "Oh, it's okay, love. It's the best thing that ever happened to me.'' His lips came down on hers, and while he opened her mouth he slipped the cover-up from her shoulders. Warm moist air fanned her

bare skin but didn't cool. Michael's stroking caresses drew
her senses away from her mind until she was afraid the two
would disconnect before she did for Michael what she was
determined to do: make him forget, even if only for a little
while, that anyone existed in the world but the two of them.

Without warning, he stooped and swept her into his arms.
"Do you want to go inside?" he asked.

"No," Sophie said. "Here. Let's stay here where we can
hear the wind in the trees and the sea."

He asked her nothing more, but carried her back from the
ocean's edge, across the shale to the grassy bank. He set her
down. Then, standing before her, he took off the shirt and
dropped it with her cover-up, unsnapped his jeans and slid
them down his hips.

Sophie kept quiet, wondering if it were possible that he
didn't hear her heart now. Her only regret was that she
couldn't see him more clearly. In the darkness he was big, a
solid outline against a sky of dull silver, beautiful in his
power, but she'd like to look into his eyes.

"You're sure?" His hand cupped her shoulder as he
asked, and Sophie said "Yes" very softly and turned her
face to kiss his thumb. She was so sure. Tremors passed
through her again and again in dark, burning waves.

"Come here."

She came, stopping scant inches from him to make her
own touch map of his body. Even in his mounting passion
he considered her, worried in case she wasn't totally with
him.

"I didn't think this was going to happen," Michael said
and rested his hands on the swell of her hips. "This afternoon I thought I'd blown it with you for good."

"Don't say anything, Michael. You don't have to." He
was still unsure of her. How could she ever have compared
him with Jack, who never really seemed to care how she
felt? She shut her eyes for an instant, and her mind filled
with images of Michael laughing, his eyes, sometimes

shadowed and serious, sometimes glittering with mirth. Love. She stiffened for an instant and looked at him again. She was falling in love, had probably fallen in love with this man a long time ago, and she didn't want to fight that anymore.

He kissed her slowly, ran his tongue along her lower lip, nuzzled her face up to his, before he leaned away, massaging wide circles over her shoulders.

His skin gleamed, and Sophie lightly traced the shapes she could make out. With two fingers on each hand she drew his neck, his shoulders, the solid muscles in his upper arms. His chest, the roughness of hair there, made her tremble and sent an achy heaviness into her belly. His flat stomach, the lean hips, his unyielding buttocks, Sophie missed no spot. And when she dropped to her knees and placed her mouth on each inch her fingers explored, she heard him moan and wrapped her arms around his thighs. Triumph soared through her. She could please him, wanted only to please him, and his hands digging into her flesh, the incoherent sounds he made, told her she had the power to do that.

She glanced up and saw the tipped-up angle of his jaw, the hint of white where his teeth were clenched. She paused an instant before covering and caressing the most intimate parts of him and her breath caught in her throat at the shudder that shook him. Wordlessly, he pulled her into his arms as he slid to the ground and rolled onto his back with her clamped on top of him. He eased her up and kissed her breasts, took first one and then the other nipple carefully with his teeth. Sophie felt a cry rise up within her but never heard its sound. A direct, tightly drawn line of exquisite pleasure seemed to form between her breasts, the moistness of Michael's mouth there, and her womb. She could be what he wanted her to be. The message sang out in the silent places of her mind, and she reveled in the sense of power.

He rolled again, leaning over her with an elbow braced at each side of her shoulders. His next kiss was deeper than any that went before, stretching her mouth wide, his tongue searching. Sophie wriggled, arching her back, seeking, until he ran his lips downward to take a nipple into his mouth once more. The heat within her was suffocating now, the night airless. On he moved with his mouth, over her stomach, clasping her hips, nuzzling his face into her. She heard herself groan. Her thoughts were fractured now. She felt her body tense in waiting, open for the rush of sensation that must come. As if he felt it, too, Michael paused, just long enough for Sophie to urge him close again, and then she cried out, breathless, throbbing, and tried to do what she couldn't, to lift him away. He lay against her stomach for seconds while their labored breathing drowned out the wind and the ocean, then he slipped upward until his face rested against her neck.

"Michael" was all she said, and he lifted his face to look at her, his eyes catching their shine from the moon. The rest of her life, all of it before now, didn't matter, would never mean as much again. He rose above her, placed his thighs between Sophie's and entered her. And she drew him in deeper, willing their total joining.

There was no hesitation then, no holding back. They moved with all the strength that was in them, jarring little sounds from their throats, holding, urging, thrusting until the climax came and with it an abandoned cry that was made of their two voices. Then there was only stillness but for the sound of air rasping past their throats. His weight was leaden and wonderful, and Sophie held him so fiercely her arms ached. He had given himself completely, without reserve and without a selfish thought for his own pleasure unless he was sure his needs and wants were also hers.

He shifted to lie half over her, his legs wound with hers, an arm surrounding her body, lifting her near.

She couldn't speak. A fresh breeze dusted their sweat-dampened skins with the misty salt spray from the ocean. Tiredness swept into her muscles, and she relaxed heavily in his arms, let her head snuggle into the hollow of his shoulder. Peace, overwhelming, ecstatic peace, lulled her.

Michael lay back, too, not slackening his hold on her, and the ragged rise and fall of his chest calmed. He was quiet for so long she thought he slept.

"Sophie, are you awake?" he said at last and in a hushed voice.

She didn't want to intrude on this time, she wanted only to lie pressed to him forever, but she said, "Mmmm," and kissed his arm.

"I feel wonderful."

Exhilaration made her blood pound. "So do I."

"I don't seem to remember back before you came along. You're insidious, you know that?"

She thought a moment. "I don't think I do know that. I'm not sure I know what insidious means when applied to people."

He chuckled and brushed the backs of his fingers down her spine until Sophie wiggled and poked his belly hard. "What does it mean?" she prompted.

"I'm not sure. That you sneak up on a man without him realizing it, and then when you're there, he can't imagine you not being there? Yeah, I guess that's it."

"I see." Her throat tightened, and she lay very still. Was he saying he would always want her to be a part of his life? She sighed. The biggest mistake she'd ever made was to believe a man had wanted her and only her as his partner. Afterward, when it was too late and she was committed, a commitment she refused to break, she had found out she was second-best, the one Jack thought of as useful only when his first choice of the moment wasn't around.

"You're very quiet. Are you okay?"

She made herself smile against him and hug him tightly. "I'm fantastic. Can't you tell?" What she must remind herself, over and over again, was that Michael was very different from Jack. "I've never felt more okay than I do now, Michael."

He made a satisfied sound and rubbed his cheek on her hair.

She had to believe Michael was a man she could trust. Her next sigh drained her. What if things didn't work out between them? So little in life was certain. If his feelings for her changed, would she be able to laugh and brush off what they'd shared as simply a good time? The possible answer didn't have to be reached, or even thought about now. Tonight was perfect, and she would choose to accept what it had brought without reservation.

"Are you getting cold, my love?" Michael asked. "Want to go inside?"

Sophie stirred and sat up. "No," she responded simply. "It's lovely here."

Michael rummaged through their clothes and found her cover-up. He draped it around her shoulders and wrapped his arms around her. "Remember what we were talking about earlier?"

She tried to see his face, but caught only the glimmer of moonlight in his eyes. "When?" Again she was afraid the moment would break apart.

"We were talking about needing a friend. How everyone needs a friend."

"Yes," Sophie agreed softly. She kissed his neck. "Someone to share things with. I remember. I guess I've been more alone than I realized until tonight." Each word, every tiny admission that weakened the defenses she'd built, frightened her, yet also gave her new hope. "How about you?" She knew he had hidden facets, but would he admit them—ever?

"I've been alone for a long time, Sophie. Most of that time I've done such a good job of burying what I feel that I believed I was fine. I'm not, not really."

She held her breath, waiting for him to go on. He didn't.

"We make quite a pair," she said and laughed tightly. "The great pretenders. Stick with me, friend. You'll always be sure of a kindred phony spirit."

"You're not phony. Just scared, like I am. But I intend to stick with you. I've got a feeling we'll help each other in the end."

In the end. He made them sound like a permanent item. Sophie prayed she wasn't reading too much into his words. "Maybe you're right," she said. "And maybe it is time to go in. I'm finally getting cold."

Michael got to his feet, gathered their clothes and lifted Sophie into his arms.

"I'm too heavy, Michael, and you're tired. Put me down."

"You're not too heavy." He started uphill but paused to look down into her eyes. "You're never going to be too heavy, my friend."

"You awake?"

"Mmmm." Sophie snuggled deeper into the bed and pulled the pillow over her head. Soft music played somewhere, and there was a good smell, a morning smell. Sunshine and fresh air. But she didn't want to wake up yet.

"Sophie." A hand rocked her gently to and fro, then removed the pillow.

"I'm asleep," she muttered. "Sleep." The hand brushed her tangled hair from her face, and bright light hit her closed lids. "Ugh. Turn it off."

Michael laughed and kissed her shoulder.

Michael.

Sophie sat up, blinking. "Michael? What time is it? We've got to get back." Then she realized she was naked and clutched the sheet around her.

He laughed again. "It's eight o'clock, and we've got the rest of the day to get home." He wore jeans but no shirt.

Sheer drapes billowed in the breeze from two long windows beside the bed. Patches of brilliance painted the floor. "How late is it? How long have you been up?"

"Hours," he said airily. "An hour. Well, maybe twenty minutes. I want to get my stuff from the other cabin. And I started breakfast, too."

Sophie attempted to look suitably impressed. "An early bird. And efficient, too." The music she heard drifted up from the living room. She looked around the room, locating her own bag. "Um . . . you can shower first if you like." That would give her time to put something on and try to comb her hair.

"Bathe you mean."

"If you want." Whatever he preferred as long as she could collect herself while he did it.

"No, I mean there's no shower up here, only a bath. John's got a thing about people not taking time to enjoy life, and he says showers are part of an evil plot to eliminate one more simple luxury."

"He sounds eccentric."

"He is. But you'd like him."

Sophie grunted. "Anyway, you go ahead."

Michael sat in a wicker chair and hefted his feet onto a green marble stool shaped like a frog with a beige fur pillow on its head. "You first," he said with a hint of a smile. "Always ladies first."

She regarded him with narrowed eyes, wrapped the sheet more securely around her and made no attempt to leave the bed.

"Bashful?" His smile was villainous.

"I'll go when I'm ready."

"Want some help?" He swung his feet to the floor.

Sophie hastily wiggled her swathed body to sit on the edge of the bed. "I don't need help, thank you." His help was likely to land them back in bed, and much as the idea appealed, they did have to get home sometime.

"I could scrub your back," he offered hopefully.

"You could make coffee to wake a poor woman up. And give her a chance to make herself human." She rose, with as much dignity as she could muster, and shuffled across the room, the sheet trailing behind. At the bathroom door she remembered she needed her bag and reversed her path, twisting the makeshift drape so tight she was forced to shuffle her feet.

Michael's laugh was more a howl. Sophie paused to glower, then struggled on until she was finally back at the bathroom door with bag in hand.

"I'll make the bed, too, if you like," he said, still slouched in the chair.

"You do that."

"I need the other sheet."

She couldn't help smiling. "Right." Inside the bathroom she unwound the sheet and tossed it out. As she closed the door she heard him say, "Chicken," then the sound of his footsteps on the stairs.

Despite the temptation to linger in the legendary John's sunken gold-toned tub with its mirrored backdrop and tantalizing selection of perfumed bubble concoctions, Sophie didn't dally. In less than fifteen minutes she was dressed in shorts and T-shirt, her hair swathed in a towel. She scoured the tub rapidly and rinsed away the suds.

When she opened the door her heart shot into her throat. "Michael Harris, you almost gave me a heart attack!" He stood just outside, leaning against the wall. "You said you were making coffee. And the bed, you said you'd make the bed." The sheet lay where she'd thrown it.

"Coffee's perking," he said. "And we don't have to make the bed. When John comes in he brings a maid. She's the one who uses the other cabin, and she's a Tartar. Doesn't like anyone messing with the housework around here."

"The maid, huh?" She swept past him. "Some maid, I'll bet."

"Honest." Michael raised a hand. "Marge is about ninety and wears a lace cap."

"Sure she does. I'll go finish the breakfast. Please make it fast with the bath, Michael. I'm anxious to get back to Justin and Maren."

He muttered something unintelligible.

"What did you say?"

"Oh, nothing, nothing. I'll be out in a jiffy."

She studied his innocent face, then shrugged and went down to the kitchen. One glance showed her how much progress Michael hadn't made toward breakfast. He'd started the coffee and set a box of pancake mix on the counter. "Men," she muttered and picked up the box to read its instructions. Seconds later, after a thorough reconnaissance of the refrigerator and cupboards, she put the mix back into one of the cardboard boxes Michael had brought. Organized he might be, but without eggs, which this mix needed, or syrup, or even lemon juice and powered sugar, this was one dish they'd have to forgo.

Yesterday they'd had no lunch and no dinner. Early in the morning after Michael had awakened her with a caress that ended in sweet languorous lovemaking, they'd eaten cheese and crackers as hungrily as lumberjacks, but that had been too long ago. Sophie was starving again. Well, cereal and fruit would have to do, but first the coffee.

Half an hour later two places were set at the counter. Linen napkins of a Hawaiian tapa design flanked neatly scalloped grapefruit with a cherry in each center and frosty glasses of orange juice. Sophie poured the cereal and filled a pitcher with milk, then sat down, satisfied, and looked toward the loft. Not a sound.

She went outside and took several deep breaths. From the porch the ocean looked like a blanket of morning stars, their points poking each other. She squinted against the glare. Daisies grew in clumps along a narrow border, and she picked a handful before going back inside.

After deliberately slamming the door and glancing toward the silent loft, she grimaced and went to put the flowers in water. "There," she said, setting the vase on the counter. Still no sound came from the loft. She set about cleaning the kitchen. The work had to be done, and she did want to get back to Seattle in good time.

Fifteen minutes later Sophie left an immaculate kitchen and went to stand, undecided, in the middle of the living room. Was Michael all right? She never left the children alone in the bath for an instant.

Ridiculous. Michael wasn't a child. He was a thirty-four-year-old man who'd lived alone for years. She wasn't *his* nanny.

Ten more minutes. Damn it, she'd chewed one of her fingernails. She made up her mind.

With a mug of coffee presented before her like a shield, Sophie climbed slowly up the spiral staircase and peered over the top step, half expecting to see Michael on the bed, waiting. The room was empty.

Her heart made a slow revolution, and her stomach followed. On tiptoe, she approached the bathroom and tapped lightly. "Michael," she said softly, "Michael, are you okay?"

Nothing.

Sweat broke out on her brow and upper lip. She felt sick. "Michael!" she almost yelled. "Say something. Are you all right?"

The bathroom door wasn't quite closed. Slowly, she pushed it open, the heavy thud of her heart making her feel weak.

Moisture hung in the air, and Michael's special, clean smell, but that and another wet towel were the only evidence of his having been there.

Sophie thundered down the stairs, spilling coffee as she went. He must have gone outside while she was working in the kitchen. Her scalp tightened. He wanted to be alone, to get away from her for a while. What other reason could there be for him to sneak out of the cabin?

On the porch she hesitated, then went back inside and poured a second cup of coffee. Keep it light, she warned herself. Everything was okay, it had to be. She was just looking for problems.

She saw him as soon as she went outside again. Scuffing sand, his hands sunk in the pockets of his jeans, he wandered along the shoreline, alternating his attention between the horizon and his feet.

A lump of pure apprehension formed in her throat, but she walked resolutely toward him and shouted, "Hey, there, Michael. Breakfast's ready."

He waved and came up the beach, leaning into the incline and taking long steps. He was smiling.

"How did you get out here without me seeing you?" Sophie asked when he was close enough for her to hand over one mug.

"You were busy," he said. "And I needed to think for a while, I needed to be on my own."

Sophie swallowed with difficulty. "Sure. I know how that is." Her voice must be steady, nonthreatening. Any show of emotion could be a mistake now.

"Do you?" He bowed his head. "I hope you need thinking time now, and for the same reasons I do."

He was trying to tell her something, something he didn't expect her to take well. Sophie hunched her shoulders and said, "What are you thinking, Michael? Or aren't I supposed to ask?"

"You can ask. And I'm ready to tell you. I'm falling in love with you, Sophie, or I'm pretty sure that's what's happening. It never happened before so I don't have anything to compare it with."

His broad shoulders flexed. Sophie watched the muscles move. He... No. She breathed through her mouth, long calming breaths. Yes, he had said he was falling in love with her. She'd hoped, dreamed that he'd feel something more than physical desire for her, but she hadn't expected this, not yet.

"Didn't you want me to say that, Sophie?" He looked at her, his face intensely solemn. "Aren't you ready? Is there still something holding you back, or am I moving too fast?"

"I'm . . . I didn't expect it, that's all."

"And you don't feel the same about me," he said flatly.

"I didn't say that. It's just that this is a special place, Michael, a dream place. Sometimes we say and do things in dreams, then wake up and find out they weren't real." She rested a hand on his arm. "Oh, Michael, *is* this real?"

He craned his head toward the ocean. "I need you." His eyes found hers again. "I think we're good together. We don't have to do anything different from what we're doing now except spend more time together, alone. You have your days and nights when you're free, and where you spend them is your business."

The skin on her face prickled. "Meaning?"

"I'd like you to. . .I'd like you to live with me as much as you can."

She should have known. Sophie closed her eyes. If she were less vulnerable she might even be able to laugh. She had believed his idea of love and the responsibilities it brought with it were the same as her own. He *thought* he loved her? He'd like her to live with him whenever she wasn't working. And for a few seconds she'd been fool enough to think he might be talking about marriage. Blood rose in her cheeks, and she turned away quickly.

"I'm going in. We'd better eat and get back."

"Sophie," Michael said, but she was already on her way toward the cabin. Her nerves jumped, and the ache in her womb was there again. She'd gotten too far in, too fast, and now she'd have to face all the problems that were bound to come.

"Will you stop!" Michael's fingers on her elbow checked Sophie's flight. He held her fast until she met his eyes. "I'm not hungry, Sophie, and I don't think you are, either. Please, will you come and sit with me?"

To their right, a short distance from the house, a group of wooden pilings had been driven into the ground. Sophie let Michael take her hand and lead her to sit atop one of the thick poles. Her feet swung several inches above the grass.

"Now we're going to talk some more." Without waiting for her answer, Michael sat beside her, still holding his coffee. "I guess you didn't like what I said to you just now. I'm not known for my eloquence."

"I'd rather not talk about it. We both need a lot more time to think."

"I don't."

"That's what you want to believe, but you're wrong."

He took a long swallow from his mug. "Whatever you say. You're the expert on relationships."

She looked up into his face but couldn't tell if he was being sarcastic.

"Like I told you, the past few years haven't been so easy for me," he said distantly. "You help me forget some of that. Is that a sin, to want more of something that makes you feel good?"

"No. Of course not." He was unhappy. For all the light-hearted banter, the playfulness, the wonderful loving, Michael Harris was a disturbed man reaching out for escape. "There's something I want to talk to you about," she said. Maybe the moment had come for her to let go of a little of her protective reserve and give him at least a hint of how she'd become the woman she was today, why she couldn't be the casual lover he wanted. And maybe by revealing more of herself, she'd encourage him to be open.

He moved her hair behind her shoulder and seemed to relax slightly. "Talk, Sophie. I love to hear you talk."

"Thank you." She gave him a quick smile. Her hands felt unsteady, and she tightened her grasp on the mug. "The story isn't original. It's definitely not very interesting, unless you're one of the people who were involved like I was."

He rested his forearms on his knees. "If it involves you I'm going to be interested."

"Okay. This is the short version. I married a man who hadn't grown up yet. He was handsome, intelligent, and everyone expected great things of him. The pressure was too much and he cracked. But the cracking took a while." She scrubbed at her eyes with one hand and felt Michael take the mug from her.

"You don't have to go on, Sophie. Please, don't push if it's too much." He rubbed her back rhythmically.

"I want to say this. You need to know. Michael, Jack fell apart bit by bit, and he tried to take me apart with him. No, I don't mean that. He didn't do it deliberately, but he couldn't help himself. He was sick, and he took a lot of it out on me, and that left me pretty scared about getting involved again. Do you understand that?" She looked at him, and he stared back, her own pain mirrored in his eyes. "I'm gun-shy, I guess you'd say."

"I don't blame you. Did he... was he abusive?"

The old shutter started to come down. "No! He was a good man." She breathed slowly, gathering calm. "Anyway, I thought you should know."

"Thank you for trusting me."

He must guess she'd only scratched the surface of the truth, but he also knew she was trying for openness. It was a start. An unfamiliar lightness came to her. She'd taken a step toward burying the past by having the guts to at least talk about some of it. Now if Michael would just risk letting her inside the private segments of his world, the ones he'd alluded to but continued to hide, they might really get somewhere.

"Michael," she began diffidently, "you've got a lot on your mind, too, haven't you?"

For a split second she felt him draw away. Then he held her shoulder and said, "I don't think I've made much of a secret about that."

He wasn't going to make this easy. "I wondered...well, is it just the business that's on your mind? Or is there something else?"

With one toe he made angular patterns in the sand between clumps of scrub grass. "There's nothing else really."

She wasn't convinced, but she couldn't make him confide in her. "I've been wondering...I did some checking around...." She faltered, then rushed on. "I might be able to help a bit with the business." Immediately she wished she could pull the words back.

Michael looked at her, one brow raised.

"I told you Jack and I had a business." Getting this out quickly was the only way she could do it. "Well, it was a travel agency. When Jack took it over from his mother I helped him. We learned together. He was really a good businessman." She paused to swallow. "But then he...he couldn't manage like he used to, so I had to do more."

"You were both pretty young to take on something like that, weren't you?"

"My mother-in-law was there for as long as we needed her. And Jack was really good—"

"So you said."

He definitely didn't like references to Jack. She couldn't help that. Jack was a part of the sum of her life and if Michael was interested in her at all he'd have to accept that Jack had existed. "Anyway, while I was in the business I learned a lot about figuring out what people wanted most in a vacation. Of course, different people have different tastes. Some are traditional—solid hotel, room service, escorted bus tours, that sort of thing. But there are plenty who are always on the lookout for something different."

Michael made a polite noise as if he were only partly listening.

"Islands Unlimited could get in on something like that." As soon as she said it she paused, lips parted, expecting a barrage of questions.

Michael's "How? We're just island-hoppers" sent her enthusiasm plummeting. This would be even harder than she'd envisioned.

"Listen." She pulled up her knees before continuing earnestly. "All these moods you have, the uncertainty, the flare-ups with Nick. They come from worry about the business, and something right has to happen, for all of you."

"How do you know so much about what we need?"

"You've as good as told me, and so have Abby and Nick."

"If you say so."

"Why couldn't you look into laying on tours, include accommodations and unusual activities? Hiking in places like this?" She waved toward the forest. "And night cookouts on the beach and tie-ups with boat trips for deep-sea fishing? The possibilities are there and they're endless. The business would turn around, I know it would."

"Hmm," he said thoughtfully, then was silent.

"Is that all? Hmmm?"

"It's an interesting idea, but it won't work."

"Why not?" She craned her neck to see him. "How can you just say it won't work without even thinking about it?"

"Because I know it won't, that's all."

"You're not being fair, to you or to me. I'm not a fool. I understand the pitfalls, but it could work with enough planning."

"And a hell of a lot of capital."

"No—"

"Yes." He cut her off gently and smiled. "Yes, Sophie. Thanks anyway, but don't worry about it anymore. Nick and I have everything under control, and we'll make it.

Now, we've got a couple of hours before we have to leave.
How about another swim?''

That smile was sad and it didn't fool her. However much
he protested, she knew he was worried.

"I don't think I'll swim," she said, "but you go ahead."

Michael stood up in front of her, looking toward the
ocean. "Not without you."

Sophie stifled a gasp. Why hadn't she noticed the scar on
his back? The reason came immediately. Last night it had
been too dark, and this morning he'd never turned his back
on her. The raised, webbed welt that slashed the center of his
spine was discolored even under his tan. She started forward to touch it but pulled her hand back.

"Michael," she said tentatively, "what happened to your
back?"

The force with which he swung around startled her. His
lips were pulled back from gritted teeth.

He realized a moment too late that he was overreacting.
Carefully, he let his face relax and fashioned a smile. The
damn scar, he forgot it sometimes. "Old war wound," he
said and knew he sounded as uptight as he felt.

"From the crash?"

The color of her eyes deepened when she was serious, and
she was serious now. She'd misunderstood his quiet times,
his references to difficult years. She thought they were
purely a product of business worries, but she'd have no way
of knowing about Dallas. He'd asked her to become a part
of his life. She'd shared so much of herself, and he knew it
hadn't been easy on her. He owed it to her to explain the true
nature of the ghosts he still hadn't banished. With Sophie he
was sure he could learn to forget.

"Is that how you were burned? In the plane accident? It
is a burn, isn't it?"

"Yeah." He looked away and back at her. "The plane
caught fire."

He saw her turn pale and felt ashamed. This was no good. The horror was something he shouldn't share, not with someone as gentle as Sophie.

"What happened, then?"

"Nothing. You don't want to hear."

She reached to hold his hands. "I do want to hear, and you want to talk about it, don't you?"

Prickling behind his eyelids horrified him. "I thought I'd never want to talk about it again. But I do want to tell you, Sophie. It won't help, but I do want to. See, I killed him." The choking noise in his throat shamed him.

She stood and slid her fingers around him to draw him close. "Sit on the grass with me, Michael. Come on, tell me what happened." She urged him down, making coaxing noises while his legs responded slowly to the messages from his brain.

Sophie didn't say any more, didn't prompt or dig, but she sat facing him and pulled his head onto her shoulder.

"He was my buddy. Dallas was my friend, and because of me he died. He was jammed under the panel, and I should have got him out first, but I thought I had time, so I went to help get the passengers out. Then the fire started. I couldn't even get back in there."

"But you tried and you got burned."

"Big deal. I tried. I should have got him first."

"Was there an inquiry?"

His eyelids pulsed and his palms were clammy. "Sure. And I'm a hero, y'know. Hero Michael Harris who managed to get himself burned and knocked out before he could save his friend." A laugh congealed in his throat. "Some hero."

She was rocking him. "Why did they say you were a hero?"

His nose was running. He wiped at it with the back of a hand. "Bravery, my dear. Saved a bunch of passengers et cetera, et cetera."

"How many passengers died?"

He couldn't even see through the tears. "None."

"Because you got them out."

"Partly. The flight attendant helped."

"How many passengers were there?"

"Twenty-two." The pictures started again. Red flames, screams he couldn't hear anymore, clutching hands he no longer felt. Red blood. Everywhere, blood.

"Michael." Gently she lifted his face, brushed the moisture from his cheeks, kissed the corner of his mouth, his brow. "You did what you had to, and you were right. You had to go and get those people out. You must have tried to help Dallas as soon as you crashed."

"I couldn't budge him. He was jammed."

"Was he conscious?"

He stared at her, trying to make himself think about her question. "No, I don't think so. He was bleeding and he wouldn't answer me."

"They must have said something about his death afterward. What did they say?"

He rested his brow on hers. "That he was killed by the impact."

"Then why won't you believe it?"

"Because they don't know. And now I'll never know."

"Think, Michael." She shook him. "If you let yourself think you'll know they were right. Dallas was already dead, and you had to save the living. What is it really? Is it that you feel guilty for being alive when he's dead?"

Oh, God, she knew. Stricken, he looked at her through hazy eyes. "Wouldn't you feel guilty?"

"For a while maybe. But then I'd have to let go and get on with living."

"The way his wife let him go? Yeah, I guess you're right." He longed to hold her again, make love to her again, to forget.

Sophie kissed Michael's cheek and ran her fingers into his hair. She made little soothing noises while her thoughts scrambled. This Dallas was the man whose wife she'd met the night Michael had taken her to dinner.

She hugged him until her arms hurt. "It's going to be okay, Michael. Believe me. It can take a long time, but it'll be all right." She should be giving herself this lecture. What did they say? Physician, heal thyself. "Michael, why don't we pack up and go home now? I think it's time. We've come a long way, but we should move carefully from here on, be sure we know what's right . . . for both of us."

"You're right for me."

"If I am, there's plenty of time to find out."

He shook his head but let her pull him to his feet. "We never know how much time there is, Sophie."

She stroked his jaw and smiled up at him. "Be patient, Michael."

"Do I have any choice?"

"No. Neither do I." She had no choice about loving him either.

Chapter Thirteen

"To your right, ladies and gentlemen, is Orcas Island. It's kind of horseshoe shaped, and the body of water scooping inward in the middle is East Sound."

Michael spoke mechanically, spewing forth the travelogue he'd given a thousand times before. Sometimes he wondered if the passengers even listened. Today he didn't care. A few more hours and he'd make his last run of the day. He could return to Seattle and make an excuse to go to Nick and Abby's and try to see Sophie.

"Orcas has the largest park in the islands, Moran State Park. The view from the top of Mount Constitution is something."

"That in the park?"

A question from a passenger still surprised him. "Yes," he said. "Bike's the best way to the top if you've got the stamina. The real hardy souls hike up. I go by car."

A smattering of laughter greeted the comment, and Michael smiled up into his cabin viewing mirror.

Sophie wasn't trying to make things easier for him. If he didn't know in his gut that what happened last weekend had meant as much to her as it did to him, he'd think she'd rather not see him at all. In the three days since they got back, she'd managed to be busy every time he tried to reach her on the phone. And when he made sure they walked into each other, she smiled that gentle smile of hers and made some excuse not to talk.

"The island you see closest to you, off the coast of Orcas, is Shaw. Population about a hundred. General store, post office, gas station and that's about it. The University of Washington has a biological preserve down there. The water birds are supposed to be worth seeing."

Sophie was holding back, protecting herself. And she'd been hurt much more than she'd confessed. Her little story about what happened with her husband had to be a pretty brief synopsis, and he'd ferret out the whole thing if it took him the rest of his life. His scalp tightened. *The rest of his life?* He was smitten. And he had pretty solid proof that she felt the same about him and that she needed him. He started to whistle, then cleared his throat and realized he was grinning.

"Okay, folks, we're coming to the big time—Friday Harbor, the metropolis of the San Juans. Shops, restaurants, art galleries. See the best whale museum in the world. Go see killer whales offshore if you're lucky, and porpoises. And the harbor's full of more jellyfish, sea anemones and duster worms than you've ever seen anywhere. And crabs."

He made radio contact with the port and circled to come in for a landing.

Abby could know more about Sophie than she'd already told him. She hadn't really told him anything. Yeah, he'd talk to Abby when he got back. He straightened his arms and took in a deep breath. Sophie needed him. He felt like a new man. He'd never spent much time thinking about what a woman needed from him. Was that why he didn't die in that crash, because Sophie was going to need him? Boy, he'd be in analysis next, or writing poetry or something. She was driving him nuts. He blinked and saw her in his mind, standing on the beach, telling him to feel how hard her heart was beating. The quickening in his body was instant, and he expelled a long sigh as he leaned on the stick.

"Going in, folks. Make sure those seat belts are snug."

ABBY WALKED SLOWLY between rows of peas. "Give me another one."

Michael handed her a piece of string, and she deftly tied a vine to a bamboo stake. "When do you leave for Omaha, Ab?"

"Friday night. I don't want to miss too much work."

"How long is it since you saw Nick's folks?"

Abby considered. "Over a year. Maren was still a baby. The Dorsets have been making disgruntled noises for ages."

"I'm glad you're going. You'll enjoy seeing Janet and Crete, too. I think Nick misses his sister a lot."

"He talks to Janet on the phone pretty regularly, but I know you're right. Life just kind of gets away from you sometimes."

"I like Janet," he said, one eye on the house, watching for Sophie. "She's a lot like Nick."

"Mmmm. Another one, please." She took more string. "They were always close. People thought they were twins when they were growing up. It'll be good to see her, and Crete and Penny and the new baby, of course."

"Are you sure Nick can't go with you?"

Abby straightened and looked at him somberly. "You know the answer to that. If his mother wasn't making such a song and dance about how we haven't seen Janet and Crete's new baby *I* wouldn't be going. We shouldn't spend the money. I just hope Mrs. Dorset will be too busy crowing over Justin and Maren to make a fuss about Nick not going with us this time."

"It'll be okay."

Abby took the strings from his hands and ran them absently through her fingers. "Are you going to be okay, Michael?"

He looked at her sharply. "Is that a code, sister dear?"

"No, a straightforward question. You're more than just casually interested in Sophie, aren't you?"

Michael looked away. "Is it that obvious?"

"Yes. And I'm glad."

"Doesn't seem to be doing me much good. Not as much as I'd hoped, anyway."

She rubbed his forearm. "Walk down to the lake with me. I think it's time we had one of those talks we used to have, the ones where you told me how to run my life—only I'll tell you this time." She smiled, and he saw what he so often forgot, how very beautiful his gray-eyed sister was.

"Lead on, guru. I'm fresh out of ideas, so if you've got some I'm all ears. Where is she, by the way?"

Her laugh was husky. "That's why you hotfooted it over here this afternoon, isn't it, to see Sophie?"

"Would it do any good to deny it?"

"No. She's at the library with Justin and Maren. She's really marvelous with the children, Michael. I think she genuinely loves them. Do you know Justin can write the whole alphabet and his own name? And he's beginning to read?"

"Doesn't surprise me. Whatever she does she does well." He squinted toward a bright sail ballooning above a small yacht. Sophie did everything more than well, including tying him in knots.

They walked slowly down the flights of steps leading to the lake and sat on a log near the boat house.

"Shoot," Abby said, folding her hands in her lap. "Let it all hang out as you would say."

"Just like that?" He raised his brows. "What am I supposed to say?"

"How you really feel about Sophie. What you want to happen between you. And if it's not happening, why you think it's not."

"Yes, *ma'am*." He gave a mock salute. "Anything else?"

"That'll do for a start."

He bent over and dragged up a blade of coarse grass growing from the sand. "In order. One: I'm probably falling in love with the woman."

Abby leaned against his shoulder. "That's a good start."

"Two: what do I want to have happen with her? I guess that's the biggie. When we were away I kind of suggested we should spend more time together, and I think that put her off."

"Kind of suggested? Did you or didn't you? How'd you put it?"

He chewed the grass, then kept it between his teeth. "You always were direct. Actually, I said something like why didn't she live with me on the days when she wasn't needed here."

"Oh, Michael." Abby punched his arm lightly. "You old romantic you."

He turned to look at her. "Do I sense a little sarcasm in that remark?"

"You sure do, brother. Couldn't you just have gone for spending more time together before you came in with the big guns?"

"Okay, okay. I already figured out I messed up—as usual. I should have asked Nick what to say first, only I wasn't sure how things would go."

"Nick?" She craned around to look into his face. "What do you mean you should have asked Nick?"

He blushed and put a hand over his face to try to hide it. "He helps me out with . . . with . . . oh, hell."

"With? Come on." Her fingers beckoned the rest out of him.

"Nick helps me out with lines, I guess you'd call it. He's much better with women than I am. I mean, he knows what to say—I mean—damn. Don't tell him I told you that. He'll kill me."

She turned a laugh into a cough. "Let me get this straight. Nick is your consultant in matters of the heart. He tells you the appropriate comments for given situations."

He nodded miserably.

"That I would love to hear. Boy, am I going to be listening for some of the right lines from him in future."

"Can we forget it, Ab? Please."

"I'll think about it. Apart from your less than charming approach, is there something else standing in the way of this romantic success story? Like she can't stand the sight of you?"

His stomach fell sickeningly. "Did she say that?"

"Oh, Michael, you idiot. Of course she didn't. I'm just trying to get a handle on why you two aren't making more headway."

"I thought you might know something about that."

"Me?" She looked puzzled.

"What do you know about her marriage? She's told me bits and pieces about her husband. I know she had a rough time with him. But she still defends the guy. I get the feeling she went through a lot more with Jackie boy than she told me."

Abby slid to sit on the sand and rested her back on the log. "Funny," she said thoughtfully, "but I've had that feeling, too. That she's covering up. Not because she's said anything direct, more for the same reasons as you, because she's . . . yes, she's defensive of him. And she looked funny when she talked about his dying. Not sad like you'd expect, but kind of closed." She looked up at him. "Why do you think it matters?"

Michael shook his head. "She said he got sick and couldn't cope, made her life tough. But that doesn't really explain why she's so shy sometimes, almost timid. So I'm searching for a reason, and the previous husband still seems the most likely place to look."

"*Previous* husband? You mean only husband, don't you? Or are you thinking more ahead than you're saying?"

Color flooded his face again. *Like some pimply high school kid.* "Don't jump the gun, Abby."

"If you say so, Michael. But for what it's worth, I think she's crazy about you."

Slowly he lowered the blade of grass. "You do?"

"I do. All it takes is for Nick or me to mention your name, and she seems to forget what she's doing. And she watches for you, Michael, I know she does."

His lungs expanded hugely and he felt warm. "So why has she started running away whenever we come face-to-face? And why isn't she ever available to talk to me on the phone?"

"Frightened, maybe. Have you thought of that?"

"Frightened of me?"

"Of herself was more what I had in mind. Of being hurt again."

"Yeah," he said slowly. "She already said as much. But I wouldn't ever hurt Sophie."

"Oh, Michael, I know you wouldn't." Abby squeezed his hand quickly. "I also have a hunch she doesn't quite believe how indispensable she is to us. She seems to think she has to fall over backward to please in case we're dissatisfied. That would make her insecure and jumpy, too. And I blame our mother for that. I know she keeps looking for ways to undermine Sophie. She isn't very subtle about it, but she worries Sophie anyway, I know she does."

"I can't believe that's what's bothering Sophie. But it brings up another question. Do you think Sophie's cooling it with me because she doesn't want to jeopardize her job with you and Nick?"

Abby made circles in the sand with a stick before she spoke. "Yes. But I do everything I can to let her know her private life is her own and that I want her to have one. Michael, can I give you an idea, the start of a whole script rather than a few lines?''

"I wish you would."

"I won't shock you?"

He eased her chin up until she raised her eyes. "Try, Abby. You've got my full attention."

Now she was a little pink. "Well, as we know, I'm taking the kids out of town for a couple of days. Why don't you invite Sophie over to your place? She hasn't even been there yet, has she?''

He made a negative noise.

"Tell her you're going to cook her dinner. That you won't take no for an answer. Then when you get her there, woo her, seduce her, Michael. Don't make the mistake of talking about her living with you in her spare time like she's something you can take or leave. Just seduce the woman and worry about what comes next afterward."

In the silence that followed, little waves bubbled and sucked at the shore. Michael looked at his sister and wondered if he'd ever truly seen her before. "Abby Harris Dorset," he whispered, then grinned broadly, "you're brilliant. Nick just lost a consulting job."

HE DITHERED, half in and half out the door from his dining room to the deck. Was eating outside such a good idea? Would the evening turn cold too soon and break the mood?

Better not risk it. "Ouch. Hell!" He stubbed his toe on the bottom track of the door and stumbled onto the deck. Hopping, he started gathering silverware, then changed his mind and set it down again. It wouldn't cool off for hours.

The anthurium he'd paid a fortune for stuck out of its vase at all the wrong angles. He should have had the florist arrange and deliver them. Greenery. That's what was missing, leaves.

Galloping with an uneven gate he went down the steps to the yard and scouted around until he found some rhododendron leaves that weren't wilted. Elegantly rolled ti leaves were what he needed, but these would have to do.

Back on the deck he poked the leaves between the flowers' long bare stems and stood back to survey his efforts. Not great but better.

A buzzer sounded from the kitchen. The beef Wellington couldn't be done already. Sophie wasn't due for another hour. He checked his watch. Good Lord, half an hour was all he had left, and he was still barefoot and in jeans.

The pastry crust around the beef wasn't brown yet, and he glanced heavenward with a prayer of thanks as he reset the oven timer and made for his bedroom. He wished Sophie hadn't insisted on driving herself over, but at least she'd eventually agreed to come. Accomplishing that much had been no mean feat. He'd told Abby about it, and she'd given him one of her pitying looks while she explained that Sophie was simply hedging her bets by making sure of her own transportation. Michael wasn't sure he knew what Abby meant by that, but he'd stopped badgering Sophie to let him pick her up.

Twenty minutes later he was pacing the living room dressed in black tie and dinner jacket and white tucked shirt and roasting to death. This wasn't going to come off. She'd laugh at his formality, and then he'd feel a fool.

The town house looked great, though, he thought with satisfaction. His home for six years, it felt just right, a perfect fit for him. He still found himself admiring the great cathedral ceiling from time to time and congratulating his own taste in keeping the walls stark white between vertical oak beams. The floors were also oak and reflected the soft blues and greens of the silk rugs he'd picked up in Pakistan.

Dolly, the woman who cleaned for him once a week, did a first-class job. His rosewood dining table glistened, and she always made sure his magazines were left where he liked them, on the circular coffee table with its glass insert.

He'd change quickly before Sophie arrived. Wear something casual instead. The thought had barely formed when the doorbell rang and he froze, a hand shoved into his hair.

The ring came again, and he pushed his shoulders back. This was it.

He picked up the box containing the green orchid corsage and walked with measured steps to the door. When he threw it open Sophie was about to go back down the steps to the driveway.

"Hey," he said brightly. "Changed your mind?"

She looked at him over her shoulder, and Michael kept his smile in place with difficulty. Her eyes were huge, and she wasn't smiling. "I thought I must have the wrong night," she said, turning toward him. She held a small white purse to her breast with one hand, in the other she carried a bottle of wine, which she thrust abruptly at him.

He took it from her. "You didn't have to bring anything." She wore the pink sundress she'd worn the night he took her to Ray's Downtown for dinner, and he was as crazy about it tonight as then. "Come in," he said with a rush, "come in, Sophie. Dinner's almost ready. Do you like Beef Wellington? The crust's out of a package, but Dolly said— Dolly's my cleaning lady—Dolly said packaged pastry's fine. Come on. You need a drink." He laughed and the pitch sounded high. "*I* need a drink." The stiff double vodka martini he'd had while he made dinner was a dim memory, and his nerves were jiggling again.

She came, smiling tentatively, looking around, walking almost on tiptoe in her high-heeled white sandals that showed off the slight tan she'd gotten on her legs last weekend.

"This is beautiful, Michael. Lovely. I love blues and greens together, and with the water and the trees around here they make the outside come inside."

He hurried to set the wine on an end table and returned, taking the orchid from its box as he came. "Do you like orchids? I do."

"So do I." She looked down as he concentrated hard on pinning it to the strap of her dress. "Thank you. I didn't expect anything like this. You look marvelous, Michael. Like a *GQ* model. But you didn't have to dress up for me."

"Yes, I did." He finished fastening the flower and looked at her mouth, his hands hovering inches from her shoulders. "You look wonderful yourself, sweetheart." With jerky palms, he caressed her arms from shoulder to elbow and back before turning away and going to a drinks tray on the coffee table.

Sophie was right behind him. "I'm sorry I don't have something more glamorous to wear. I always think about buying a new outfit when it's time to get ready to go out."

He straightened, an empty glass held in one hand. "That's my favorite dress." His voice did something funny again, and he cleared his throat. "I order you to wear it at least twice a week from now on."

She laughed and he joined in.

"What will you have to drink?" The quick sliding away of her eyes unnerved him. "Scotch, Sophie? A martini?"

"Ah, no, no. In fact, if you've got a soft drink that's what I'd like most. I'm thirsty."

"I could open some wine."

"No, thank you. Coke would be great."

"Right." He bowed from the waist and went to the refrigerator. "One Coke coming up."

She accepted the glass he brought her, laughed at the cherry and piece of mint and the wedge of pineapple he'd used to garnish the drink.

"I thought we'd eat outside. It's warm and the sun isn't quite down. We can eat and watch it set. Unless you'd rather eat inside. You'd probably prefer—"

Her fingers, softly pressed to his lips, quieted him but did nothing for the thunderous condition of his heart. "Outside will be lovely," she said. What was with him? he wondered. He could think of at least a dozen men, and probably twice as many women, who would go into hysterical laughter if they could see him now.

He did make himself another martini, and it went down as smoothly as the first. By the time they'd eaten the stuffed mushroom caps he'd made, also to Dolly's specifications, he felt good. Things were going exactly as he'd hoped.

"You did all this yourself," Sophie said when he ushered her onto the deck and carried out the entrée, held aloft on a steel platter and surrounded with tiny red potatoes, buttered baby carrots and celery hearts.

"Every little thing," he said and went back for the rolls. A shell dish heaped with seafood salad already sat at each of their places.

"This is too much." Sophie sat in the chair he held for her. "You have hidden talents, darling." She glanced at him and hastily away.

Darling. He smiled smugly into the early evening glow. Abby was brilliant, and he wasn't doing so badly himself.

The rosé wine she'd brought wasn't as suitable as the Pinot Noir he'd chosen, but they'd drink it first anyway. Sophie was delightful. She ate well, complimenting him with almost every bite she took, and although she didn't seem to care for wine a flush came to her cheeks with what little she did drink. Michael finished the rosé and opened the Pinot Noir.

"No," Sophie said when he offered her some, "I don't want any, thanks."

He pushed the bowl of fresh fruit he'd bought for dessert toward her, but she shook her head. "You aren't much of a drinker, are you?" he asked lightly.

She stared at the last blood-red remnants of the setting sun. "I'm not a drinker at all, Michael. It's getting late. I should get home."

"Nonsense. As they say, the night is young and so are we." He caught the table with his elbow as he stood and grabbed a glass the instant before it would have tipped over. "How about those reflexes? Pretty good, huh?"

He couldn't understand why she looked so strained. Probably better go pretty slowly for a while yet.

"What's your favorite music?" he asked when they were in the living room. Sophie stood in the middle of a rug, her hands clasped in front of her. She must be as nervous as he'd been earlier. "Name something. I've probably got it," he persisted.

"Billy Joel singing something. Anything really."

"You got it, babe. Sit down."

He smiled at her until she sat on the edge of the couch. She looked surprised as she sank into deep cushions and scooted back a few inches. "Comfortable, huh?" he said.

She nodded.

The cassettes were in a muddle, but he found the requested selection and snapped it in.

On the way to sit beside her he collected the glass he'd brought in from the deck and put it on the coffee table. He could smell that light perfume she wore. Her face was turned up to his, and her hair, worn loose the way he liked it, fell away from her shoulders. Her breasts rose and fell rapidly. Muscles in his thighs tightened. The way she looked naked was a clear picture in his mind.

"Sophie," he said and sat close beside her, "I've missed you."

She bowed her head. "I've missed you, too."

When he pulled her into his arms she made a small noise, and he smiled against her neck. "I was afraid you wouldn't come tonight." He bent to kiss the soft flesh at the tops of her breasts.

"I shouldn't have."

"My sweet, Sophie—" He closed his eyes, registered what she'd said and lifted his mouth from her skin. "Why? Why shouldn't you have come?"

Sophie inched along the couch and stood. "We aren't right for each other. I can't be what you want."

Michael got slowly to his feet. "Since when? What is it with you? What was it for you when we made love last weekend, some sort of penance?"

The visible shudder that passed the length of her turned his stomach.

"You're afraid of me, damn it. Aren't you?" He advanced on her, and she backed away until she slammed into the wall. He skinned a hand over his eyes. His head suddenly ached. "Aren't you? But how can you be, after everything was so good between us?"

"You're drunk."

"What?" A pain throbbed behind his eyes now. Sure, he had several drinks and some wine, but so what? He put a hand on the wall at each side of her head. "I've had a few drinks but I'm not drunk. Most men like a few drinks."

He held her shoulder and shook her.

"Don't. Please don't." She flinched, craning her face to the side and crossing her arms over her head.

Michael's insides fell away. His blood seemed to turn to water. "What the hell's the matter with you?" He tried to pull her arms away, but she hunched over and slid down the wall. "My God," he muttered, standing over her, "say something to me."

"Don't," she cried again. "Don't hit me. Let me go."

His mind cleared, icy clear, cold. "I'm not going to touch you," he said with difficulty. But she must have been touched before, hurt before, and that was what she was so careful to hide. He stepped back. Trying to help her up would be the worst thing he could do now. "It's okay, Sophie. You're okay."

Minutes passed before she uncovered her face and stared up at him. She looked haunted and ill.

"I'm not drunk," Michael said quietly. "And if I were I wouldn't hurt you."

"I'm sorry." She was crying. She took the hand he offered and stood. "I'm so sorry. I don't know what made me do that."

"Don't you know, sweetheart?" he asked, sure that he knew very well. "I think you do."

"Well, I guess I do." The soft brown eyes took on a darting quality. "Once I knew someone who used to drink too much and get...angry. For a moment I thought you were like that. Stupid of me. Forgive me, please."

"There's nothing to forgive. Why don't I make us some coffee?"

Sophie leaned sideways to pick up her purse from a chair. "Not for me, thank you, Michael. I'm going home. I've already ruined the beautiful evening you offered me." Tears welled in her eyes again, and he fought against trying to hold her. "I have a way of ruining everything I touch—the things I really care about. Forgive me."

"Don't go, Sophie. Stay and—"

The breeze from the open front door and the faintest hint of her perfume swept in before he'd finished speaking. He knew better than to follow. Tonight he'd let her go, and tomorrow and for as long as it took to figure out if he wanted her badly enough to help her face what had made her treat him like an attacking animal.

Tires spewed gravel and he heard her drive away. Could Saint Jack have been even less holy than he'd thought? Could he have been the someone who used to drink too much and get angry? And if he was, how much permanent damage had he done to Sophie?

Michael picked up his glass from the coffee table. He looked at it until the wine inside became a dark blur, then, with the power of a fury that almost choked him, he hurled it against the stone hearth.

Chapter Fourteen

Granny says. Granny says. If she didn't know better, Sophie would think Justin knew that comparing her way of doing things to his grandmother's was the key to ruining a perfectly good day.

"I'm sure your grandmother would agree with me on this, Justin," she said carefully, keeping her voice level. Justin, his feet planted apart, his hands behind his back, stood in the middle of his father's study looking like a small version of Nick in an intractable mood. Sophie tried again. "I know your father would want you to call him at the office if there was an emergency. And I know he would never get angry with you even if you called when there *wasn't* an emergency. But he's very, very busy, Justin. And he probably isn't there, anyway."

"Why can't I try? Granny says moms and dads should always be...be..." He screwed up his face, searching for whatever Wilma had told him before he puffed and said, "Granny says I can call her if I want to ask something and you and Mommy and Daddy are too busy."

One morning with Wilma, four hours designed, Wilma had said sweetly, to give Sophie some time to herself, and Justin was impossible again. "I'm not too busy," she said patiently. "And your parents are working, which means they're busy for a while, but they'll be home later, and I know they'll be glad to talk to you then.''

His little old man stance dissolved, and his frown, and he sniffed. Two great tears rolled slowly down his cheeks. "You won't let me go out in Markus's boat. And when Mommy and Daddy come home it'll be too late," he wailed. "I want to go on Markus's boat."

"Shh, Justin, shh." Sophie dropped to her knees and gathered him into her arms. "You'll wake Maren. And she's only just started her nap."

The wail rose several pitches. "You like Maren best. Everyone likes Maren best 'cept Granny. I always have to be quiet because Maren's sleepin' or something. And I don't get to go out with Daddy 'cause he's always busy. And Mommy's always busy. Markus's daddy takes him lots of places, and they use their boat all the time, and..." He buried his face in Sophie's shoulder and sobbed.

If only she didn't know there was some truth in a few of the things the boy said. Justin wasn't the underprivileged sufferer he felt at the moment, but his parents, particularly Nick, seemed less and less available to the children. And clearly Wilma wasn't helping the situation. She must be using her times alone with Justin to impress him with how sympathetic and accommodating she could be. A sickening wave of anger rose in her throat. Wilma hadn't given up her plans to take Sophie's place, only changed tactics.

"Justin," she said gently, "we all love you and Maren just the same. And you have to remember that when you're in my care, which is a lot of the time, I have to make decisions the way I think is right. It's very nice of Markus's family to invite you out on their boat, but I don't feel it would be right for me to give permission. Maybe when you learn to swim better, I won't be so worried. I know Nick and Abby would agree with me. And there will be lots of times for you to go on the lake. Daddy and...and Uncle Michael are very busy."

"You said that."

"Listen to me, Justin," she said sharply. "Don't be rude." Her temper was slipping. "Your parents work hard to give you nice things. They aren't always having a good time, my boy. Do you know that in the last ten days I don't think I've seen your daddy for more than a few minutes? And that was when he was coming in to go to bed or leaving in the morning." And she hadn't seen Michael at all. She squeezed her eyes tightly shut for a second. She missed Michael, but she'd better get used to that.

"Don't care." Justin gulped and pulled away. "He's never going to be not busy. I wish I lived with Granny."

The end. She was fed up to the teeth with Granny. "Stop it, Justin," she ordered. "Stop it right now. You sound like a spoiled brat." Immediately she closed her mouth and got up. She turned away, afraid he'd see the tears in her eyes.

"You're not s'posed to talk like that," he said between great gulps. "Granny says you get mad too much. She says we don't know what you were before."

Sophie faced him slowly. What she was before? What would make Wilma say such a thing? Michael. This must be something to do with what happened with Michael. She'd behaved like a madwoman. He'd been shocked and she didn't blame him. He'd asked what was wrong with her and suggested there was something she wasn't saying about herself. Would Michael have told Wilma about that awful night? If he had the woman would have new ammunition: *Sophie's unbalanced. Oh, God.* Surely Michael wouldn't talk about her, to anyone.

"Justin," she said with as much calm as possible, "we're not going to talk about this anymore. You're not being a very nice little boy, and I want you to go to your room. When you've decided what you should say to me about this afternoon, you may come back down and apologize. Then we'll forget all about it."

"But—"

"No buts. Run along. And, Justin—" she held both of his hands until he looked directly at her "—I think the best thing we can do is have a family discussion, don't you? A talk with your mommy and daddy so we all know what's going on?"

"S'pose so." He sniffled.

"I know so. We all love you very, very much. You know that, don't you?"

"S'pose so." Tears overflowed again, and he leaned his damp face against her leg.

Sophie swallowed hard, but she knew she mustn't allow herself to crumble entirely. She ruffled his hair and kissed the top of his head. "Okay, sport. Off you go now. Maybe you should sleep awhile, too."

"Maybe," he said and left the room with his head down.

Sophie waited until she was sure he'd had enough time to go upstairs and returned to the kitchen. Unfortunately, Justin did have good grounds for some of his complaints. Nick was close to being an infrequent visitor in his own home, and since Abby had returned from Omaha she'd become more and more withdrawn. They were both worried, and Sophie had never felt so helpless. If only Michael had taken her seriously when she'd tried to suggest a new direction for Islands Unlimited. The familiar nasty ache clamped down in her throat. Michael couldn't stay out of this house forever. How would she cope even with the sight of him?

Keep busy and don't think. That would work—until she saw him. She gathered the ingredients to make a fresh batch of play dough for the children.

There must be some changes made for Justin. Enrolling him in a preschool for the fall would be a start. School opened in the first week of September, only six weeks away. All good programs would be filled soon, if they weren't already. Twice she'd mentioned it to Abby, who had hardly seemed to listen.

The room was stuffy. Sophie slid open the patio door and breathed deeply. Outside, roses, heavy and drooping in the midafternoon sun, bobbed tiredly on their stems. Later she'd cut a few and put them in the library where Abby sometimes sat alone in the evenings.

She was pouring flour into a big mixing bowl when Wilma's familiar "It's only me" rang from the hall, and the woman bustled into the kitchen.

"Hello, Wilma," Sophie said, guardedly pleasant. "Still pretty warm out there?"

"Whew, I would say so." She plopped a large box on the table and went to the refrigerator. "Oh, no iced tea? Well, maybe orange . . . no? Never mind, they say water's the best thing for you." And she got a glass and filled it. "You have so much to do, Sophie. I don't know how you get through it all. No wonder you forget a few things. I probably would, too."

Sophie bit the inside of her cheek and added more salt and water to the mixture in the bowl. "Give me a minute to finish this, and I'll make some iced tea," she said levelly. "That sounds good to me, too. I don't think you can beat iced tea on a day like this, do you?" She should get a medal for control.

"Mmm." Wilma sat down and stretched out her legs beneath her floral dress. "I brought this over." She patted the box on the table. "An extra potty chair one of my neighbors was getting rid of."

Chunks of tacky dough gummed Sophie's fingers together. Slowly, she scraped the mess off. "We've already got a potty chair, Wilma."

"Oh, I know. But I thought it would help if you could have one upstairs as well as downstairs. Make it easier to catch Maren at the right moment. You know what I mean?"

Sophie thought she was beginning to know exactly what Wilma was intimating. "I suppose so."

"Maren's over two now." Wilma made the statement and let it hang.

"Twenty-six months," Sophie supplied tonelessly.

"Girls usually train faster than boys."

"I don't think you can generalize. But I have heard that said."

"Of course, I realize you haven't had children of your own so..." The sentence trailed off.

Sophie didn't trust herself to look at her. "I have been a nanny for some years, Wilma. And I've trained a number of children. I don't believe in pushing. If you turn the process into a trial the child dreads, you only make it harder. Maren will train when she's ready. She's already dry at night. It won't be long now."

"Oh, I'm sure you're right," Wilma agreed comfortably.

The phone rang. Sophie picked it up carefully with a gummy finger and thumb, and Nick told her, more shortly than usual, that he wouldn't be home for dinner and would appreciate her letting Abby know.

When she hung up, Wilma was watching her with bright eyes. "He's working too hard, Sophie. Abby, too. I know these young people are ambitious these days. They want to get ahead. But sometimes I wonder if it's worth it." She drank some of her water. "And it's harder on you than it should be. You know... Why didn't I think of it before? I must be too tied up with myself these days. Why don't *I* see what I can do with Maren?"

Sophie stared at her for a moment. "I'm sorry, Wilma, but I don't know what you mean."

"Why don't I take Maren to my house for a week or two and train her? She is late, Sophie. And they say that's often a sign of a child looking for extra attention. You're too busy to do nothing but run around after one child, but I could just give her the time she needs and make it easier for you."

Counting to ten had never worked to calm her, and she doubted it would now, but Sophie tried the system while she washed and dried her hands punctiliously.

"What do you think?" Wilma persisted.

"I think it would be an imposition on you," she said. Could you get cramp in your face? She deliberately slackened her jaw. "I have lots of time to give Maren attention, really, Wilma. All the time in the world. Looking after Justin and Maren is my job. And I do know what I'm doing."

"Yes, but—"

"Thank you, but I can't let you do it."

"I'll mention it to Abby," Wilma went on stubbornly. She got up and smoothed her dress. "Justin's been a bit naughty lately, too. Those two need more individual time. You know what I mean? Not that I'm saying you don't do your best, but, well..." She looked at Sophie and smiled, a sudden sympathetic, conspiratorial smile. "Oh, I've said too much and upset you, haven't I? I didn't mean to, Sophie, dear. I'm sure you know best, and I won't say anything to Abby now. But you let me know if you change your mind. I'm only a phone call away as they say, and I can be here in a jiffy, anytime, day or night. There's nothing that's likely to divide my attention if I'm needed."

Sophie's hands trembled. She watched, speechless, as Wilma gathered her purse and patted her hair. She heard the woman say goodbye, but the kitchen door had already closed by the time she mumbled a reply. The click of those sturdy sandals Wilma wore all summer echoed on wood, and then the solid thud of the front door jarred Sophie.

Damn, damn, damn. She brought her fists down on the table. *Granny says you get mad too much. Granny says we don't know what you were before.* Relentlessly, Wilma Harris was working on Justin, probably hoping he'd repeat what she said to Nick and Abby. And now she'd come into the open with Sophie. Wilma wouldn't say anything to Abby. But she'd be watching and waiting. Nothing was likely to divide *her* attention. The way an almost-affair with Michael was dividing Sophie's? She sat and pressed her face onto crossed arms atop the table. She couldn't, wouldn't believe Michael had told his mother the details of what had passed between them. Wilma had simply made remarks that seemed to fit. Damn, now she really was getting paranoid.

The afternoon dragged, and the early evening. Justin had appeared with Maren in time for their snack, and the boy looked so wan that Sophie didn't have the heart to remind him of their earlier disagreement. Abby came home late. She'd spoken to Nick from the store, and the preoccupied, slightly sad set of her face made Sophie glad the children were already in bed. This was certainly no time to discuss preschool for Justin, or any of her other concerns. At nine she said good-night to Abby and returned to the boat house.

She felt like a slug. For days she'd done nothing but work, then read until she could fall into blessed, mindless sleep. Exercise was what she needed. Instead of running the bath she longed for, she put on leotard and tights and snapped in a Jane Fonda exercise video.

Within minutes, sweat drizzled between her shoulder blades and her braid thumped uncomfortably on her back. When the phone rang, she picked it up, jogging in place, and panted a weak "Hi." Abby must have forgotten to tell her something.

"Sophie?" Michael asked.

She stopped trotting. Her pulse roared in her ears. "Yes, Michael."

"Nick asked me to call you."

"Oh." She looked at her feet. The little muscles at the corners of her mouth jerked.

"How've you been?"

Jane Fonda's image blurred on the television screen. "Not great." Good old honest Sophie, one polite question and she let him know how miserable she'd been.

"I'm sorry."

How've you been? I'm sorry. Polite, yes, a polite stranger.
"Nick thought I should give you a call."
She gripped the phone with both hands. Why did he keep talking about Nick? "What does Nick want you to say to me, Michael?"
"Sophie, I really am sorry."
"Nick asked you to tell me you're sorry?"
"Don't make this any harder." He let out a slow breath. "Have you thought about . . . about . . . Can we talk?"
"I don't think talking would help."
He sighed again. "Have it your way, but I'm going to talk anyway. I just got off the phone with Nick. He'd been talking to Abby, and evidently she's having a rough time with Justin. The kid can't sleep or something and—"
"I'll go over right now. He wasn't sick when—"
"Will you listen, Sophie?" he interrupted. "Justin isn't sick now. But he woke up in a sweat and said a lot of stuff about not being loved. You know he's not Nick's son by birth. His father left Abby while she was pregnant with Justin, then dropped out of sight completely right after Nick and Abby were married. The guy was no good, a creep who was having an affair with Abby's best friend before he even left. Justin's better off without him, but Nick always feels he has to compensate. He's afraid Justin will think he's second-best to Maren if he doesn't keep showing the kid just how important he is."
Sophie absorbed what he had said. "I didn't know what a rotten time they'd really had," she said slowly. "It makes me sick to think about it. But I understand where Nick's coming from. Because he's been too busy to spend much time with the children he's on a guilt trip, huh?"
"You've got it. Anyway, Nick's stressed out. He wanted to get right home and talk to Justin, but he can't. He's got to make a night flight to Friday Harbor and see some guys first thing in the morning about a contract to carry medical supplies. I'd go for him, but he's the one who's made all the

contacts so it would look funny, and we don't want to risk losing the business.''

Sophie carried the phone across the room and switched off the television. The sound of Michael's voice brought sweet sad longing. "So what does Nick want me to do about Justin?'' And why hadn't Nick called her himself?

"He thinks it would be a great idea for you to come along tomorrow when I take the boy hiking.''

She put a hand over her eyes. "I don't understand. Why would you take Justin hiking? He's not old enough. And Nick doesn't like you being with me.''

"Sophie, Nick's happy for us to be together. He was just touchy that one day, that's all. He was glad we—'' He coughed and cleared his throat. "He was glad when we went away together.''

Uncomfortable heat throbbed into her face and neck. "Justin's not old enough for hiking.''

"He's not going alone, we'll be with him. It'll do him good, and Nick's all for it. I had to think of something to make him quit worrying, at least for the immediate future. He's walking a fine line emotionally, and so is Abby. I just want to help.''

All day she'd been worrying about Justin. He needed more time with men, and he was crazy about Michael. "Justin loves you," she said and swallowed. "Take care of him, Michael. He's just a little guy.''

"You can make sure I do, Sophie.''

"I'll have to stay with Maren.'' She should say something about the other evening, apologize.

"My mother's taking Maren. It's all set.''

Wilma again. Sophie gritted her teeth. More evidence to prove her attention was divided. Another chance for Wilma to show how easily she could take over complete care of the children.

"Sophie? We'll leave at ten, okay?''

"I don't think so—''

"Well, I do. No more argument. Nick and Abby and I have it all worked out. Ten. Good night, Sophie."

"Michael, I—" A click let her know he'd hung up the phone.

PATCHES OF SNOW, webbed with gray rime, undulated between rock outcroppings like giant organisms made of crystal soap bubbles. Sophie paused, hands on hips, and looked back the way they'd come. They were above the tree line now and the Cascade Mountain Range stretched away, massive blue-gray peaks reaching into a cloudless sky. Here and there a brighter blue glittered where a high lake caught the sun. Below, dense forests, woolly green masses flattened by the angle of her vision, cloaked the foothills and rose up the mountainsides.

"Oodly, oodly, ooh-ooh!"

She laughed and shaded her eyes to spot Justin above her, doing his imitation of Michael's yodeling attempts. He was tethered to Michael's waist by a long rope that Michael had assured him seriously all mountaineers wore. The trail had been gentle in most places, but this, Michael had told Justin, was training for the big time. One day they'd climb Mount Rainier. And at that Michael had made owl eyes at Sophie over the boy's head. This man should have sons and daughters of his own, she thought, but the idea of him with the woman who would bear his children made her want to cry.

"Wait up, leader," she yelled, falsely cheerful. "Had to stop to adjust my clamp-ons."

By the time she reached the two of them, the air she breathed seared her throat. "Wait," she gasped. "Please. Need to sharpen my ice pick, too."

Justin eyed her curiously. "You tired, Sophie?"

"Uh-uh, no way," she said, then twisted and flopped against a bank, "only dead. See?" She opened and closed one eye.

Michael and Justin laughed, and Justin poked her tummy, but she kept her eyes closed.

"Well, Justin," Michael said with a sigh, "I guess we'll have to leave her here and go have our rations alone. Gee, it'll be tough having to eat three people's lunches, but we'll just tough it out."

Justin giggled.

Sophie opened her other eye and scowled. "How much longer before we can sit down—for a long time?"

"Up there." Michael pointed. "On top of that flat rock. We can sun ourselves and even snooze if we want to. Have you ever slept in the sun on a rock that's the last thing between heaven and earth?"

"No, but it sounds wonderful." She sat up and stared at him. His jaw was a sharp angle against the sky as he studied the rock. A thoughtful man. A dear, special man and she loved him. Sophie hung her hands between her knees and watched a chipmunk scurry across the trail. Her lungs expanded with the scent of dried pine needles and clean earth under the sun. She did love Michael. All the way up this mountainside he'd talked to her gently, kindly, in between patiently answering Justin's chattered questions, putting her at ease, making her feel this day would have been less for him without her. He'd steadied her frequently, taking her hand in his with an unconscious familiarity that made her never want to let go.

He let out another of his piercing, wobbly mock yodels and grinned down at her. Wincing, Sophie put a finger in each ear.

Justin pulled her arms down and yanked at her. "I want my rations, Sophie. Billy beef and hardtack, right, Uncle Mike?"

"Bully beef, Justin. And I think your uncle could just be a bit mixed up in his types of rations. Or are you a seafaring man, too, Mr. Harris? Hardtack and all?" She got wearily to her feet, groaning at her resisting muscles.

Michael gave her a withering glare and turned to Justin. "You'll notice as you get older, Justin, that women ask too many questions, unlike we men who know how to get into the action. Follow me, lieutenant."

"I get it," Sophie puffed, scrambling after them and wishing someone would tie a rope around her and pull, "this is training for the Swiss Alpine Corps, right? We're pretending to be ski troops only without skis."

"Skis come later," Michael called over his shoulder. Then he stopped and came back. "You are a bit beat, aren't you? Hang on to me." And he offered her his hand again.

Grateful, Sophie did hang on and smiled at his broad shoulders while he hauled her up. Soon he'd picked Justin up in his other arm, and despite the pack on his back, he still climbed effortlessly. His strong legs flexed inside worn jeans, muscles straining from time to time when he gave her an extra heft. She'd never get tired of watching him.

The top of the rock was as he'd described it, an island poking from a sea of rubble and scrub, the last land before sky.

They made what Michael referred to as their base camp: strategically placed pieces of log to act as backrests, a pile of pebbles to lodge the thermoses upright. Justin trotted happily back and forth carrying out orders. Sophie watched the two of them with a deep sense of peace and pleasure. For these few hours she'd let the rest of her world go away.

"Ahh," Michael said complacently when they'd eaten and safely stowed empty bags and boxes in the backpack. "This, dear Sophie, is what heaven must be like. A full stomach, a gorgeous place to sack out in and your favorite person beside you."

Every muscle and nerve in her body jumped. She looked quickly at Justin, but he'd moved away and was playing happily, talking to an imaginary companion about their next "great big climb."

Michael glanced at the boy. "He's not listening," he said.

"It's lovely up here," Sophie said unevenly. "Lovely being with you. Thanks for bringing me." Without looking at him, she untied the nylon windbreaker from her waist and made a pillow.

"Comfortable?" he asked when she'd stretched out and adjusted the jacket beneath her head.

"Yes." She hardly trusted herself to speak.

"I love you, Sophie."

She opened her eyes slowly. Trembling started, first in her hands, then spread throughout her body.

Michael leaned over her, turned his face to study her carefully and planted a solid kiss on her lips. "I love you," he repeated and shaded her face from the sun with his hand, a hand that shook. "Say something to me, will you? I never told a woman I loved her before."

Sophie lay still. "Yes, you did."

"I did what?"

"You told a woman you loved her before... or sort of, anyway."

He pulled her over until she stared up at him. "I did not tell a woman that before."

Slowly, she sat up. "Michael, remember... Blakely Island?"

"Oh, vaguely, I guess. Wasn't that the place—"

She kissed him into silence, pushed her fingers into his hair, opened his lips with hers and heard the catch of breath in his throat. "Yes, that was the place," she said, kissing him again, and then again, lightly while she smoothed the arch of his brows with her thumbs. "And there was a moment there when you told me you thought you loved me. But of course you've forgotten, and I understand."

He pulled her arms down and wrapped both of her wrists in one hand. "Very funny. I remember the moment, lady. I've been remembering it in living color every day and every night since. And I'm thinking we should do something about a repeat performance of that weekend before this man goes completely off his rocker."

Sophie leaned against him and nestled her head on his shoulder. "There are a lot of things we need to talk about, Michael."

"No, there aren't. We want to be with each other. That's it."

"It's not it. Not all of it. There are...things I still haven't told you about me."

"Oh, no!" He held her away. "You're leading a double life. You're a closet gambler...a nymphomaniac, maybe." He rolled his eyes. "I should be so lucky."

She smiled faintly. "I'm not a gambler."

"You're not?" He bared his teeth in a parody of a leer. "But there is hope for the other?"

How did you tell a man you wanted desperately to let go and love, but that you were afraid the dream would dissolve, the way another dream with another man had dissolved? How did she tell Michael that coming to him that first time had cost her more in struggle than he'd ever know? The struggle had faded with the passion and his gentleness, but the anxiety she felt now was as fresh as it had been when she'd turned on him aboard the boat. And she couldn't forget that, though she'd known he was gentle, his coming toward her in anger at his town house had produced the old fear.

"Sophie," he said quietly. "What are you thinking?"

She smoothed the collar of his shirt. Could she tell him the truth about Jack? All of it? "I was thinking that this is a special time and place, and I'll never forget it." Over his shoulder, mountains and sky took on a shimmery haze.

"Neither will I," Michael whispered and kissed her again.

Sophie heard the scream while their mouths were still pressed together. For a second neither of them moved. Then Michael was scrambling up, dragging her with him and they held each other, searching the area.

The scream came again. From below.

"Justin," Sophie breathed. "Oh, my God, Michael. He's fallen."

Where Justin had been playing lay a scatter of sticks and little rocks. The rope he and Michael had used to play mountaineer snaked across the ground and hung over the edge of the plateau. The broken stump of a scraggly alpine sapling told the story, that and the closed noose at the end of the rope.

"Keep calm," Michael said, a white line around his tight lips. "And stay here. Sit down."

"Like hell." Sophie shot across the uneven area and threw herself down to peer over the spot where the rope disappeared. She snatched the line and met no resistance; it whipped up easily. "Justin!" she called, stifling the scream that rose in her own throat. "It's all right, Justin." She couldn't see him.

Michael dropped to his stomach beside her, one arm over her back. "Cool it, Sophie. We'll get him."

"Get him?" she breathed. "I can't even see him. Why isn't he making any more noise? He's dead, Michael. Michael!" She grabbed his shirt. "He's dead. We let him play here all on his own, and he's dead. He's—"

"Stop it! Listen!"

She shook uncontrollably, but she held her breath, straining to catch any noise.

"Can you hear that?" Michael narrowed his eyes.

A soft whimper filtered on the breeze.

"Lie still a minute." He inched forward, angling his body over the edge until she couldn't see his head and shoulders.

Sophie automatically hooked both hands into his belt and held on tightly.

He moved back, digging the toes of his boots, one by one, into the layer of debris on the surface of the big rock. More and more of his torso appeared again until he paused, braced, and with a grunt, lifted Justin over the edge and sat up with the boy clutched to his chest.

"Justin, Justin. Oh, Justin." Sophie knelt close and pulled him into her arms. She stroked back his hair, examining his pale face, felt his arms and legs, turned his palms and found bloody scratches. "Where do you hurt, darling?"

A big jerky sob broke from him. "Nowhere, Sophie, 'cept my hands. I was practicing for the mountain climb like Uncle Mike said, and the rope broke."

She glanced at Michael who held his bottom lip in his teeth and shook his head.

"Sure you were," she said to Justin. "Never mind. As long as you're all right there's nothing to be sorry about. We'll go home now. We'll just go home, and I'll make sure nothing happens to hurt you again."

"He slipped right underneath the rock lip," Michael broke in. "He was just sitting under there, poor little guy."

Sophie held Justin's wrists and dug in the pack to find antiseptic spray and dressings for his hands.

"Everything's okay, Sophie," Michael said. He put a hand on her shoulder, but she shrugged away. "You need to sit down and take some deep breaths," he continued.

"We're going back," she said. Panicky tremors made her legs weak. "I want to get Maren and go home now."

Michael didn't answer. She looked at him over her shoulder. His face was pallid beneath the tan, his skin streaked with dust. He spread his hands in a helpless motion. "You're overreacting, Sophie. Take it easy, please. The boy's okay."

"We're going home," she repeated. She finished cleaning Justin's hands and set off downhill with the little boy clamped firmly to her side.

Within seconds, Michael caught up. In the two hours it took to reach the trailhead, they barely spoke, pausing only for Justin to drink water. When Michael insisted on carrying Justin, Sophie felt again the panicky sense of separation, but she pursed her lips and strode on. She'd made a bad mistake, but it wouldn't be repeated. In future she'd do what she'd undertaken to do and concentrate on the two children who had been placed in her care.

Michael had hardly driven out of the trail parking lot when Justin curled up in the back seat and fell asleep. Silence closed in around Sophie, and dread, and deep confusion.

"Ready to discuss it?" Michael said when the sound of Justin's steady breathing let them know how solidly he slept.

"We have to forget about each other as anything but acquaintances."

His laugh was short and mirthless. "Really? How are we going to do that? And why in God's name should we?"

"I've made up my mind, that's why. Everything in my life hasn't been roses, Michael. I won't bore you with more of the details. There's no reason for you to know." She almost added "now," but turned her head away instead. "What I've got with Nick and Abby means a lot to me. I'm safe there, and happy. I won't risk that."

"I don't understand you. A little mishap that could have happened regardless of who was along, and you're ready to throw away what we have."

"You don't understand, Michael. I will not risk my job for something that could go away tomorrow. And there are some things happening right here and now that you don't know about." He opened his mouth to speak, but she waved him to silence. "I like your mother, or at least I try to like her, but she doesn't want me around. For months she's been trying to prove I'm not right for the job, and the kind of thing that happened today, if she found out, would be just the proof she needs to present to Nick and Abby."

Michael turned the wheel too sharply, and Sophie gripped the edges of her seat. He was angry but she knew she was making the only decision that made sense.

"Have you ever thought," Michael began loudly, then glanced over his shoulder at Justin and continued more softly, "that it is time you quit and had your own home and family? Maybe if you had your own husband and children you wouldn't be so paranoid about hanging on to someone else's."

"What do you mean by that crack?" The wretched shakes wouldn't go away. "I'm not normal, is that it? Just because I'm not ready to go look for a serious relationship, I'm only part normal woman, I suppose."

She heard him breathe out heavily. "Sophie," he said in a voice that was icy in its intensity, "you're already *in* a serious relationship, aren't you?"

There was no right answer, nothing she could say that would make him understand that she wasn't ready to accept what he seemed determined to offer—himself for as long as he remained interested in her.

"Will you do something for me?" she asked quietly.

"I'll try." There was a brittleness there, a fury he barely held in.

"Will you promise not to tell Abby what I said about Wilma? I want to stay where I am, and I want to stay because they trust me, not because of anything I've said about Wilma. And I don't want to turn Abby against her mother— or influence you, Michael."

"And that's all you want from me?"

She lowered her eyes to hide the start of tears. "Yes, please."

"Right. You've got it."

He didn't speak again until he greeted his mother when they arrived at Wilma's north Seattle home.

"Thank you for having Maren," Sophie said, hurrying inside the front door, praying she'd make it through the rest of the journey back to Leshi without breaking down.

"You could have left her overnight," Wilma said, helping to collect Maren's toys and bag. "She would have been company for me." A plaintive note entered her voice, and Sophie saw the baleful look she aimed at Michael.

Michael stood by, unspeaking, his face a set mask.

"Granny, Granny, where are you?" A sleepy Justin came into the chintz-papered living room and walked to his grandmother's open arms. "We practiced mountain climbing."

"You can tell Granny tomorrow, Justin," Sophie said quickly. "We're all tired now."

"Granny," Justin went on, undeterred, "I had a 'venture. Uncle Mike and Sophie were busy so I played by myself."

Wilma looked from Sophie to Michael. "Busy on a hike? You didn't leave him alone, did you?"

Sophie felt a rare flash of fury. "Of course we didn't leave him alone. Come on, Justin, let's go."

"We were on a big rock," Justin said. "And Uncle Mike and Sophie were kissin' so I practiced climbing and I fell off." He paused, his eyes huge as he nodded at Wilma. "I fell off the rock into a hole, and they didn't find me for *ages*. But I was very brave. I didn't even cry much."

Chapter Fifteen

Sophie went slowly downstairs, a basket of laundry dragging heavily on her arms. Her legs still ached from yesterday's hike. Probably meant she'd better double up on her exercise efforts.

The house was silent. By late morning, Nick had returned from his early appointment in Friday Harbor and immediately announced he was taking the children back to the office at Lake Union. He'd talked about how much they would enjoy watching the action outside while he worked. And Sophie had felt sorry for him, hearing in his voice both resolution and a quiet desperation. She hoped he would manage to concentrate despite the continual stream of questions she knew the children would keep up.

At the laundry room door she turned her shoulder to push and jumped violently. Abby had stepped from the little library off the hall, her face somber.

Sophie set the basket down. "I didn't hear you come home, Abby. You scared me."

"Come in here, please, Sophie. I want to talk to you." She stood aside, waiting, while Sophie walked slowly to sit in a straight-backed chair.

Abby hesitated, then began to pace back and forth across the champagne-colored carpet. She wore the slim-fitting black pants and loose shirt that were almost her uniform for climbing ladders to build the spectacular store displays she created as much as supervised. Sophie's throat squeezed together. Nick had come to take the children away, and now Abby was here. There could only be one reason.

"This is about yesterday?" she asked, pressing her feet firmly to the floor to stop her legs from shaking. "I'm sorry, Abby, really sorry."

"It can't go on, Sophie." She paused in front of her. "Something has to change, you see that, don't you?"

Grown women didn't cry when they were confronted, not when they'd known this must happen. Sophie bowed her head and rubbed her palms slowly back and forth on her thighs. "We only took—*I* only took my eyes off Justin for a little while. This was nothing to do with Michael, Abby. One minute Justin was there, playing and talking to himself, the next he'd slipped off the rock. Oh, Abby, I don't blame Wilma for telling you. He could have been killed." And now she did cry, the tears dropping silently from unseeing eyes. "I don't want to go, Abby, but I understand how you feel."

She heard Abby's soft footfalls on the rug, then Abby sat on the floor at Sophie's feet and offered one of the two small brandy snifters she held. "Drink this. I think we both need something." A dash of golden cognac rocked in the bottom of each glass.

Obediently, Sophie took a sip and suppressed a grimace as the liquor burned her throat.

"Abby," Sophie blinked rapidly to stem the tears, "if you give me another chance, I promise I'll never let anything happen to the children again. Wilma had a perfect right to tell you about...about what we were doing when Justin fell. That's all over with."

"My mother didn't tell me anything," Abby said quietly. "But Michael did. He came to the store this morning, something he's never done before, and he told me everything."

Everything? "He promised." Sophie took a deep swallow of brandy and coughed. "He promised he wouldn't tell you what's been happening with Wilma. He promised me."

Abby placed a cool hand on Sophie's arm. "He didn't tell me anything about Mother. I already know how she feels and what she wants. I've always known, but that's my problem, not yours."

"I don't want to make things difficult between you. She's lonely, Abby, and she loves you all."

"And she's been choosing all the wrong ways to show it. Michael had a long talk with her this morning. We're going to figure things out with Mother. The main thing is that she won't be bothering you anymore."

Sophie slid back in the chair. Her head felt light. "So Michael did tell you about Wilma. I didn't want him to do that."

"You aren't listening, Sophie. No, he didn't tell me about that. He didn't have to. He explained about yesterday with Justin and said you were upset. *I* said I thought Mother was making you jumpy. She had talked to me about wanting to take over training Maren and a few other things. When I explained all that to Michael this morning, he took off for our poor mother's house again, and she's probably still smarting. But he did what had to be done. Next we have to figure out a solution to keep her from being so lonely she does this kind of thing."

"Didn't you come home to ask me to leave?" Sophie had a sensation of drifting and folded her hands carefully around the glass. "Because of what happened—"

"Justin's all right," Abby broke in, "thank God. Now let's put it behind us and talk about what I'm here to talk about—you and Michael."

Sophie hunched over. "There isn't anything to talk about anymore. I promise you I won't let personal things interfere with my job again. It was a mistake." Air only reached the tops of her lungs. She wouldn't allow herself to think about Michael.

"That isn't the answer," Abby said softly. "Michael needs you. I don't know exactly what he has in mind, but I do know you're very important to him and he's desperate not to lose you now."

"Now?" Sophie echoed. What about next week or next year? How long would she remain important to Michael? "I'm wrong for him, Abby. He's so... he's every woman's dream, and I'm ordinary. Oh, I don't mean I've got a plain-Jane-poor-me complex. But I'm not glamorous enough to keep a man like Michael interested for very long."

Abby stared at her blankly. "Why would you say a thing like that? You're lovely and bright."

"If it can happen once it can happen again." She covered her mouth at the slip.

"What happened to you?" Abby said very quietly. "You were hurt the first time around, weren't you?"

She shook her head.

"Okay, it's none of my business, but just remember I've been there. I was married to a man who had an affair with a woman I thought was my best friend, while I was pregnant with his child. Within days of my telling him about the baby he said he wanted a divorce. He couldn't stand to touch me. How do you think that made me feel?"

"Oh, Abby." Sophie reached for Abby's hand and immediately felt the pressure of strong fingers surrounding her own.

"I thought I was the most unattractive woman on earth. I thought I would spend my life bringing up a child alone. After a while I became so defensive I actually believed that's what I wanted, to be alone with my baby and to hell with the rest of the world."

"Then you met Nick."

"Then I met Nick and—" Her eyes filled. "Sophie, I couldn't imagine that a man like Nick would be interested in an ungainly woman carrying another man's child. But he loved me, he's never stopped loving me, and although we haven't had the easiest time lately, I know Nick's love isn't something I'll ever have to question.''

They were silent for a long time, holding hands, and Sophie felt a bond she'd never felt with another woman.

''But Michael isn't Nick,'' she said at last.

''He's a wonderful man, Sophie.''

''I know, but I'm afraid, and the fear is something I have to work through...if I decide I want to.''

Abby let out a long sigh. ''You have had a bad time, haven't you?''

Sophie smiled faintly. ''It started out so beautifully with my husband, Abby. I loved him, and I'll always be convinced he loved me in the beginning. But by the time he died he hated me.''

''No, Sophie, no.'' Abby shook their hands, leaned forward. ''He couldn't have hated you.''

''Maybe not. But it felt that way.'' She got up and took Abby's glass. ''Will you forgive me if we don't talk about it anymore now? I think I'd like to get on with some work and take time to think. And Abby—'' she paused in the entrance to the hall ''—thank you for caring about me. Michael will be all right, you know. So will I.''

She wasn't all right. A week later, climbing the steps to the boat house after another day that had been a blur of routine with the children, Sophie wondered if staying here would be more than she could bear. Every day, sometimes twice a day, before and after his scheduled flights, Michael came to the house. Always he found a reason to cross her path, to talk, or try to talk. And he looked strained and pale. She told herself the business was responsible for the lines of fatigue on his face, that and maybe some vestiges of the old nightmares about his dead friend, but he definitely wanted to see her, and the guilt she felt at adding to his unhappiness weighed heavily.

Before she could close the front door she heard hurrying footsteps and looked out to see Abby at the top of the stairs.

"Sorry, Sophie," Abby said, puffing slightly. "I've got to talk to you. And you'll have to listen, please."

Not now. "I'm pretty tired, Abby. Can't it wait?"

"I'm worried. I'd go to Nick but he's got enough to think about, and anyway, he can't help. Only you can."

Sophie didn't hesitate. "Come in." She held wide the door. "What is it, Abby? What's happened?"

"It's Michael."

Sophie turned away.

"No, no. I don't mean—Well, in a way I do mean... This is a mess. He's worried sick about the flight service, much more so than I've ever seen him. Even Nick is more optimistic than Michael. Nick feels that with the increased cargo loads they're getting the revenue is okay, but all Michael can see is winter coming and a big drop-off in passengers. He's convinced they'll go under."

"I'm sorry," Sophie said helplessly, "but I don't know how I can help him." Her brain switched back to her earlier thoughts about how she might have helped, but Abby hadn't come to her expecting concrete suggestions in that area.

"Neither do I." Abby went to stare through the window at the lake. "It's just that I don't know where to turn, and I'm worried about him. He doesn't look good."

"I know." Sophie joined her, freshly aware of Abby's elegant height, her delicate bone structure. "Maybe he should take a break."

Abby laughed bitterly. "That's the last thing he'll do. Sophie, couldn't you spare some time for him?" She flushed and looked away. "I don't have the right to ask you that when I know you're having your own battles. And I do know you're troubled, I can see it. But maybe if you and Michael were together again, both of you would be happier."

"I don't think so," Sophie said slowly. She wanted to say yes, but if she was ever going to heal she must be strong. "But I do wonder if I couldn't help in some other way."

Abby raised a brow. "How?"

"Can you sit down for a while? I'd like to show you some things I worked on a few weeks ago, and, well, can you stay?"

Abby stayed. Hours later her face was pink with animation, and she strode about the living room, waving brochures and pieces of paper Sophie had used to make notes.

"Why didn't you tell me you knew so much about the travel business? And keeping books? You must have laughed watching me trying to make sense of the figures. You're brilliant, Sophie."

Sophie sprawled full-length on the couch, tired but happy. "Not brilliant, just practical. What do you think of the time-share tie-in? I only came up with that a few days ago, and I know it would work."

"It will work. It will definitely work. You're going to organize it, and the rest of this stuff."

"Oh, no." Sophie leaped to her feet. "I bequeath my brain waves to you. I've got a job and I love it. You can explain all this to Nick and Michael. They'll listen to you, and then Michael will be too busy to imagine he needs me."

Abby spread her hands on her hips and glared. "I begin to see what my brother means. You, Sophie Peters, are an infuriating woman."

"Infuriating?" Sophie laughed despite herself. "I must remember to thank him for the compliment sometime. But I'm not changing my mind about this."

She returned Abby's parting hug shyly and slept better than she had since before the hike.

In the morning she walked into the main house and was immediately confronted by Abby, Nick and Michael. They sat at the kitchen table, drinking coffee. Michael jumped up the instant Sophie walked in.

"Coffee, Sophie?" he asked. She could feel him as tangibly as if he'd put his arms around her. His blue eyes were so soft. She smiled at him. "Thanks, Michael. Such service."

"We've been waiting for you," Nick said. She noticed his hair stood on end in front as it usually did when he'd been doing paperwork or worrying about something.

"Am I late?" She checked her watch. "The children aren't up yet, are they?" Part of her job was to arrive before Abby left and in time to dress Maren and make breakfast.

"You're early," Abby put in. "We were hoping you would be. Justin and Maren can play upstairs for a while if they wake up before we're finished."

Sophie was instantly apprehensive. "Finished? Is something wrong?"

"Sit down, sweetheart." Michael put a mug of coffee on the table and held a chair until she sat.

Sophie glanced uncomfortably at Nick and Abby, certain they must have noticed Michael's unconscious term of endearment. The two of them were too engrossed in each other to show any reaction to the comment.

"Now," Michael said, pulling his chair close to hers, "Abby held a summit meeting in the middle of the night and told us about the things you've been working on. Sophie, we think some of them could just work."

"I know they can," she said simply. "The first thing that would happen would be an increased cash flow, and if you can show a lender that you have solid prospects, deposits, prepayments and so on, you can also get an interim loan if you want the added financial cushion."

Michael stared at her with open admiration. "I never had any idea you understood any of this."

"I did try to give you some ideas, Michael, but you wouldn't listen. Not that I blame you. I'm not an expert."

"You are as far as I'm concerned," Nick said. He slowly rubbed Abby's forearm. "As I see it, with your ideas in operation, we'd become a sort of specialized travel agency as well as a carrier."

"Right." She leaned forward. "Exactly. When's the last time you took a trip—I mean a vacation trip, with transportation, accommodation and so on?"

Nick turned up his palms, thinking. "Before Maren was born, I guess. Why?"

"After you made your reservations, didn't you have to pay at least the transportation in advance, with a penalty for changes or cancellation, and a deposit on your hotel or whatever?"

"Yes," he agreed slowly.

"Yes," Sophie repeated, "and in many instances, the entire sum for the accommodation is also due in advance. If Islands Unlimited sets up package vacations and sells them all-inclusive, you can realize extensive revenue in deposits alone. There'll be a lot of work—and expense—in advertising and plugging into the right travel channels, but it can be done. I know it can because I've done it."

She went on to explain her ideas for a unique service for time-share vacationers, those who couldn't take advantage of the particular block of space they paid for on an annual basis. So many of these people, Sophie explained, lost out completely when they were unable to take advantage of the time allotted them and not flexible enough to swap with another owner at any specific time. Islands Unlimited could offer an attractive alternative, she assured them enthusiastically. They could give the time-share accommodation owner the opportunity to choose, at a reduced fee, a package vacation in the San Juans in exchange for the trip they couldn't take. One of the big appeals would be the possibility of leaving on short notice, another the wide variety of activities and locations. Then Islands Unlimited would tie into several established travel agencies and sell the vacant spaces they inherited from their customers.

"How would we tie into other agencies?" Abby asked.

Michael and Sophie spoke at the same time, then Michael deferred to Sophie. "Computer," she said. "We wouldn't need the extensive equipment a more diverse agency needs. We won't be dealing with airlines or land carriers, although we can if we're asked, even with minimum outlay."

"You really do know this stuff, don't you, Sophie?" Nick said, smiling. "I guess the first step will be to research facilities in the islands."

"That and selling our service to the customer via other agencies and—I think this is most important—through direct advertising. I'd suggest pretty heavy newspaper ads and even radio spots. Who knows—" she laughed "—maybe even television in time."

"Well, that's it, then." Nick smacked his hands on the table. "We get started right now. And you'll be our, what will you be? Manager? Manager-consultant? Name your title, kiddo, and if fate smiles you'll be able to name your salary before too long."

"Before too long she's going to need more staff," Abby said seriously. "I've got a hunch our main problem may be coping fast enough with the extra work expansion will bring."

Sophie drank coffee, peering down into the mug. She should have foreseen this.

"You're quiet," Nick said, leaning toward her. "Planning the empire already?"

She set down the mug. "I can't become involved in this the way you're suggesting."

Silence was short-lived but uncomfortable before Michael covered her hand and shook it until she looked at him. "Why would you say you don't want to be part of what you've designed yourself? It wouldn't even get off the ground without you.''

"Yes, it will." Slowly, she pulled her hand away and stood up. "All I've done is push you into looking at alternatives. Every one of you is capable of putting the thing in motion. Then you'll hire an expert to do whatever else you need."

"We've already got the expert." Michael stood, so close she had to choose between stepping back, staring at the middle of his chest or craning her neck to meet his eyes. She looked at his chest.

"Sophie, you've got to do it," Abby said.

"I've got a job," she reminded them, "and it's what I want. Justin and Maren need me, and I need them."

Michael swallowed a retort. He balled his fists at his sides. If he didn't keep a tight hold on himself, this situation, together with too little sleep for too long and the nearness of this woman, were going to make him do something that would embarrass them all.

"Sophie—" Abby began.

"I'd like to talk to Sophie alone," he interrupted. "Is that all right with you, Abby? Nick?"

"Of course," Abby said immediately. She made a move to get up, but Michael said, "Stay please, Abby. Could we use your study, Nick?"

Without waiting for Nick's response, he held Sophie's elbow and propelled her firmly from the room.

Her arm trembled in his hand. He glanced at the top of her shining blond hair, the thick lashes that hid her brown eyes. She was fragile, not just in build but somewhere deep inside and firmly guarded from scrutiny.

"The children will be getting up," she said as he closed the office door behind them.

"Will you stop making an excuse out of the children, Sophie. I'm starting to get very sick of you hiding behind your duty to a couple of little kids."

She paled. "That's nasty. I don't know why you say things like that. And I do have responsibilities."

"Whatever you say. But for now, Abby and Nick will look after your responsibilities. We need you, Sophie. *I* need you."

"It wouldn't work." She stood in the middle of the rug, her head bowed. Against the light from the window, a glistening halo hovered around her hair.

Longing and frustration threatened to close his throat. She'd presented them all with a way to avert professional disaster, and he wanted her beside him, working...and loving. He sat in the closest chair.

"Justin's going into preschool in a few weeks."

Sophie looked at him sharply, then smiled. "When did that happen? I've been trying to get Abby to think about arranging for him to go. He's a dear, Michael, he really is, but he's bored and that makes him naughty sometimes. He needs other children. Oh, I'm so glad."

She did love the children. He breathed deeply through his nose. It was time she had a baby of her own. "If we arranged for my mother to look after Maren in the mornings while Justin's at school, you could be free to work with us."

The lashes lowered, camouflaging the instant reading she must know her eyes gave when she was troubled. "I don't want to give up—"

"The children," he finished. If he didn't hold on he'd lose it, and he already knew what any display of temper did to Sophie. "You could still spend afternoons with them, and some evenings, if you want to. It could work, Sophie."

She locked her slender hands together. "I don't think Nick and Abby would be interested in a part-time nanny. And they probably wouldn't go for unsettling Justin and Maren too much."

Wavering, she was definitely wavering, he decided and felt guardedly triumphant. "Nick and Abby came up with the idea in the first place."

"I don't know." She did look at him now, and his stomach turned. "I'd probably have to be involved in researching resorts at the beginning and...and I like it here. I've never had the kind of security I've got here." A brilliant blush rose in her cheeks, and she sucked in her bottom lip. "You don't want to know about that, but the children—"

"Damn it all," he exploded before he could stop himself. "If you can't handle it, just say so. But so help me, if you say 'children' to me again I'm going to blow my stack."

"You already have," Sophie muttered and sank to sit on the edge of a magazine table, "but maybe I can't handle it."

He went to her side then, shoving his hands in his pockets, certain if he didn't, there would be no stopping himself from touching her. "You can handle it. As far as I'm concerned, nobody does anything better than you. And nobody could do what we need as well as you."

"I don't know—"

"Will you do it, Sophie? Will you at least give it a trial? It won't mean you aren't primarily responsible for Justin and Maren in Nick and Abby's absence for as long as you want to be."

She tugged her braid forward over one shoulder while she looked uncertainly into his eyes. God, if he could just have time with her, enough time.

"Yes," she said. "Okay, I will try. I want to."

Chapter Sixteen

"Everything's going so well." Michael slid a box of files under the sofa table in Sophie's living room, put her suitcase by the bedroom door and unzipped his flight jacket. "I think what we got in the past few days could be gold mine material."

Sophie closed the door and dropped her briefcase by the wall. "We aren't totally out of the woods yet, but it sure looks like we're on our way."

"You're starting to get pretty cramped in here. You need a desk." He nodded toward the mass of papers on the dining table and the overflow atop the closest kitchen counter. "Maybe it'd be even better if we looked into getting bigger quarters at Lake Union and moved you into an office there."

"I don't know." She watched him walk about the apartment. A striking, vibrant man, he carried with him an aura of power she'd never be able to ignore, no woman would be able to ignore.

In the last four weeks, since they'd put their plans into action, Michael had spent at least a part of every day with her. And when they traveled to inspect a prospective resort, as they had for the past three days, they were together all the time. The cautious first steps they'd taken as business associates had quickly become confident strides, side by side, showing how well they worked as a team. She lifted her hair off her neck, looking at Michael, seeing him the way she always saw him now, as a wonderful and gentle man she never wanted to be without: a man whose sexuality was as unstudied as it was magnetic. She missed their intimacy, but he'd evidently made up his mind to do as she had asked and back off. The next step would probably have to be hers. She would get to it, Sophie thought, meeting his blue eyes and smiling. Soon she'd find the courage to tell Michael how totally important he'd become to her.

He smiled back and took off his coat, draping it over the back of a dining chair. "Think about it, Sophie. Good idea? The office, I mean?"

"Hmmm? Oh, I'm comfortable here, Michael. I don't want to take the time to find another apartment." She wished she never had to move from this place. Wilma was taking more and more responsibility for Justin and Maren, but at least living here, close to the Dorsets, meant Sophie could keep in contact with the children.

"Why would you need another apartment? I wouldn't want you to move...at least...I only meant that you should have more work space. You belong with—" He looked at her and smiled, that disarming smile that never failed to turn her heart over. "What should I say, I wonder? You belong with us? Yeah, I guess that's it, kiddo, you're a member of the team now."

You belong with us. What had he almost said? That she belonged with him? Was now the time to tell him she loved him, something she'd never done even when he'd told her his feelings for her?

Sophie took off her jacket. In the last three weeks they'd grown steadily closer and being with Michael almost constantly had proved what she'd tried not to admit before: that she wanted him, permanently. And that was the one thing Michael had never declared, a desire to throw in his lot with Sophie's for good.

"Would you like a drink, Michael?" She'd managed to break through at least one barrier. She no longer panicked when someone around her had a drink or two, and Michael liked to relax with a Scotch when they sat at her place to talk strategy. He nodded without looking up from the computer printout he'd picked up, and she poured him the drink. They often spent evenings like this, hashing out figures, drawing up plans, looking over some of the advertising material Abby had been preparing so competently.

Sophie got herself a Coke and set the two drinks on the dining table. "How does it look?" she asked, indicating the printout.

"Loads of interest in Lopez Island," Michael said. "Nick was sure there would be. Funny, I never thought much about it, but the place does have a lot to offer. Not too big, but not a total backwater, either."

"What did you think of Hotel de Haro?" They'd just returned from the beautiful old hotel at Roche Harbor on San Juan Island, and Sophie thought it could become one of their biggest draws.

"I was crazy about it." Michael pushed the paper on top of a stack and lifted his drink, clinking ice cubes together. He considered carefully what to say next. Sophie was letting go with him, had let go almost completely if he was reading the signals she was giving accurately. He made up his mind. *Now*. They were right for each other, and now was the time to push for what he was sure they both wanted.

"By the look on your face you'd think you hated the place," she said, wrinkling her nose. It had been too long since he kissed that nose, her mouth, too long since that one night when she'd brought him alive the way he'd once thought he never could be again.

There was a tightening in his body, a tensing. Sophie was smiling, waiting for him to speak. He felt as if a chasm were opening at his feet and if he didn't jump across they'd be permanently separated from each other.

"The hotel was perfect," he said finally. "Except for one thing."

She raised a brow. "What? You can hike for miles, or bike if you prefer. The woods are wonderful. And that lovely pebbly beach. A lot of people would go for the bungalows, but for me the rooms in the main hotel are the thing. Mine was fantastic. Tippy old floors and the biggest bed I ever saw. And how about the bathtub on clawed feet? And the restaurant? The food was outstanding; you said so, too. Did I miss something?"

"I guess you did."

"Spill it, Michael. We don't want to make any mistakes here."

"Oh, we won't, don't worry. But didn't you feel something was lacking?"

She appeared to consider, sipping at her Coke. "I suppose if you were a total civilization type you'd miss your hot tub off the terrace, but you don't go up there for—"

"That's not what I meant." He let an instant pass while he prayed his timing wasn't off. "I was thinking more along the lines of that great big bed you were talking about."

He saw her draw in a sharp breath and held his own. She wasn't a fool, and she'd proved coyness wasn't her style. Her response would be direct, the way everything in her life was direct—almost everything. Michael concentrated on her face, the darkening in her brown eyes. There was still time to sort out the rest of those things they'd continued to hold back about themselves.

Stillness, tension that was unmistakably sexual, brought sweat to his palms. "The bed was fine," she said at last, a faint flush rising in her cheeks. "Wasn't yours?" So she would fence a little, after all. She put down the Coke to straighten papers with fumbling fingers.

He'd knocked her off balance, and she was playing for time. Too much time to think could be bad, he decided. Forcing her to confront would give him the most accurate reading of her feelings for him. He closed his hand on her small wrist. "My bed was the same as yours," he said.

"Yes." She looked up at him, frowning slightly. He heard her swallow, saw the nervous way she passed her tongue over her lips.

"It was too damned big for one man, or one woman."

"What point are you making, Michael?"

"Isn't that obvious?"

She tried to pull away but he held her effortlessly. Her wrist trembled inside his fingers, and he took her hand instead, held it between both of his and stroked the knuckles lightly. "Do you know how long it is since we met, Sophie?"

"Not for sure. A few months," she said quietly.

Moisture glistened along her lashes. He hadn't been wrong about choosing this moment to challenge her. Her emotional pitch matched his own, he could feel it.

"Fifteen months. I first saw you the day Abby and Nick interviewed you. That was in July of last year. Now it's October again. How about the last time we kissed? Do you remember that? Or the time we made love, the only night we made love?"

Sophie's mouth had dried completely. Michael was working toward an ultimatum. He had to be. He was a man who needed a woman in his life, a lover, and if she wasn't prepared to fill that spot she couldn't expect him to keep on waiting.

He drank his Scotch in one gulp, never taking his eyes from hers. Vague color rose over his cheekbones.

"Don't you remember anything, Sophie? Or don't you want to remember about us?" He looked at the ceiling and gave a hard little laugh. "You know it's funny, but I thought it meant as much to you as it did to me. I thought you remembered what we had together as if it happened yesterday, the same as I do."

"I remember. I want to remember. You're... Michael, you're so important to me. But we can't forget we're business acquaintances, too, now and—"

"Acquaintances?" He released a hissing sigh. "Hell, Sophie. We are never going to be acquaintances. We've been lovers, sweetheart. It works to go from being friends to lovers but not the other way around, not for me, anyway. And not for you. I've been patient. I've waited for you to give me some sign that you're ready to even talk about what's between us, and there is a lot between us, Sophie. And I thought maybe we'd arrived at the right time to start over. But I guess I was wrong. You're doing a great job of hiding in this new job. I thought if I could once get you out from behind the shield of the children, we'd make some progress. But it isn't going to happen if I don't push, is it?"

"Oh, Michael, Michael." She pulled her hand away and turned her back. "I'm not hiding behind anything. Why do you always say things like that?"

"You drive me to it."

"I make you angry. Yes, I make you angry. I'd like to be the right one for you, Michael, but I'm not sure I can be."

She heard him pull out a chair. "Meaning what, Sophie? That you just want to be my business acquaintance from now on?"

"No, damn it." She swung to face him. He'd sat on the chair, his long legs stretched out in front of him, his hands pushed into his pockets. "You never give me a chance to tell you what I really want. You're too busy analyzing my psyche. And, whatever you think my psyche is just fine."

"Is it?" The chandelier above the table shot his hair with blue lights. His eyes bore into her with intensity.

"I'm not hiding behind this new job, Michael. I enjoy it, that's all. And it takes a lot of time. We both know it has to be given a lot of time if it's going to be successful." She paused for breath. "And I didn't hide behind the children, or not consciously, anyway. I really love Justin and Maren, and it means so much to me to stay close to them. Children have always been important to me, and Abby and Nick's are the first I've been able to impact for any length of time."

"Sit down," Michael said abruptly.

She hesitated, then went to the chair he hooked out with his toe.

"This is a good place to start, Sophie."

"I don't know what you mean."

"Okay, I'll spell it out. Instead of using up all that love you have to give on someone else's children, why don't you have some of your own?"

At first she wondered if she'd fully understood what he'd said. She should have her own children? *Her* children. Angry tears sprang to her eyes. Not *their* children, she noted, only hers. When? After she and Michael had finished with their grand affair?

"Thanks for the advice. I'll think about it," she said tightly. He wasn't going to see her cry, no matter how much it cost her to hold back the tears. "Michael, we shouldn't get into a personal discussion when we're so tired." And definitely not until she was ready to decide if she was prepared to become his lover again.

She started to get up, but he reached to grasp her shoulders. "I'm not tired, Sophie," he said. Was she imagining a sheen in his eyes? "I've been putting on a good show of having my act together, but I passed beyond being tired weeks ago. All I feel is frustration and the kind of exhaustion that turns your nerves raw. I want us to be together, Sophie. *Now.*"

The corners of his mouth turned down. He stood and offered her his hands. She slipped her fingers into his and let him help her up. "Sophie," he said, and his voice broke. "Sophie, I don't think I can go on like this much longer." He bent to kiss her jaw, and she smelled a trace of the Scotch he'd drunk.

"I'm sorry you've had a bad time," she said lamely. Her chest hurt, and her throat. "And I'm sorry if I've had something to do with causing it. Maybe what we need is a little time apart to decide what to do next."

"What I need is to stop lying awake at night and imagining I feel your body beside me. I reach out for you and there's nothing, Sophie. There's nothing in there for you, either." He nodded to her bedroom. "Don't you ever feel alone? Or do you like it that way?"

She bowed her head. "No. I hate it."

"Then why not come to me? What else do I have to say to make you come to me?"

He really didn't know. That she needed permanency in a relationship was something that hadn't crossed his mind. "I can't explain, Michael. If you don't know what's holding me back, I can't tell you."

"Try, damn it."

Her heart started a faster beat, pulsing in her throat. "We don't both want the same things. And we still haven't been as open with each other as we should, about who we really are and why. At least, I think you have, but I know I haven't."

"I thought that's what loving and being loved meant. That two people decide to get to know all there is to know about each other, then work their way into a total relationship, together."

She stared at him, her heart an erratic drumroll now. "Yes." Her voice seemed far away. "That's what I thought, too. Only—"

"Only nothing." Abruptly he kissed her brow, drew back to look into her eyes and rested his chin on top of her head. "You're the only one who managed to make me start looking at the way I feel about the crash...and Dallas. Nick understood with his mind, and he helped a lot, but he couldn't do anything about what's been going on in here." He pressed a fist to his chest. "You did, Sophie. It isn't going to disappear overnight, but it'll get easier, with you to help me."

The tears did threaten then, and she blinked rapidly. "It will get easier, Michael. I know it will."

"Won't you let me help you, too?" His voice was incredibly soft. "Whatever it is that's holding you back from me, we can work it out together."

Panic rushed in, and desperation. Why did she have to keep confronting the past? Why couldn't she just forget?

"Sophie," he pressed. "What else happened with Jack?"

"Nothing. There's nothing more. I told you everything that matters." She shook free and clutched the edge of the table. Her legs were weak. "The business is going so well, Michael. We're going to be fine, you'll see. If I can help you feel better I will. I'll talk to Nick about you being so tired. And I won't let him know we've had this discussion. He'll understand when I say I think you need to take better care of yourself."

"Damn it." Michael's voice rose. "I've got a mother. I don't need another one, or a nurse. And I've got a sister, too. I need a living, breathing woman. I need you. How many ways are there to say it?" He took a step toward her and Sophie backed away. "Are you afraid to be a woman?"

He matched her step for step, advancing as she retreated. "I'm not afraid of anything," she said, and her voice cracked.

"The hell you're not. Look at you." His hand closed on her shoulder. "I don't understand you. Why was it okay the time you decided to make love but not okay anytime I made an approach?"

She held on to his forearm, almost afraid she'd fall. She couldn't form a coherent thought.

"Answer me." His mouth became a grim line. "You wanted me that night. Why?"

"It wasn't easy," she whispered.

"Oh, really?" His laugh cut the last shred of her composure, and she closed her eyes. He laughed again, tilting up her chin until she looked at him. "You mean it wasn't any good for you?"

"No!" she shouted. "No, it was wonderful."

"Wonderful?" he echoed incredulously. "Then why have you avoided me like the plague ever since? Why are you turning me off now?"

The backs of her knees connected with the edge of the couch, and she fell to the seat. Michael stood looking down at her. "Stop it, please," she begged. "I can't explain, except . . . except . . ."

"Except?" He watched her mouth.

"You're angry now. You weren't angry then. Once I knew you'd be gentle, it was all right. But you get angry with me like . . . Jack," she finished and closed her eyes. Her body slowly went limp. She slumped against the back of the couch and turned her head away.

"Like Jack? Like your husband?" The cushions beneath her gave as she felt him sit beside her. "Look at me, Sophie."

She did as he asked, rolling her face toward him.

"Jack was the one who used to get angry, the one you talked about that night you came to my place for dinner?"

She nodded, pushing her hair away from her face. It was time to let go of the rest. A trace of peace crept into her mind. Telling Michael everything about Jack would feel so good, so right.

"And anytime I show any emotion, you think I could turn into the kind of a man Jack sometimes was and then you want to run?"

Sophie nodded again. He looked hurt and she'd done that. She'd caused this good man, a man with normal emotions and reactions, pain he didn't deserve. "I'm sorry, Michael. You don't need this. I've caused you nothing but trouble from the beginning, and there's no reason for you not to walk away from me. I wouldn't blame you."

"I would. I'd be a fool," he murmured. One large hand caressed the side of her face. "You're worth anything I have to go through—we have to go through—to be together. Sweetheart, the only thing you ever have to remind yourself when you feel threatened is that I'm not Jack. I'm nothing like Jack."

She covered his hand and moved it over her mouth. "I know. I've always known it inside here." She spread her fingers over her heart while she kissed his palm. "But Jack did...things to me. I don't know if I can stop what happens in my head sometimes when I think it's all going to happen again."

"I'm going to hold you, Sophie. If I don't I'm going to go nuts. Is that okay?"

"Michael, do you really want a woman who makes you feel you have to ask permission to hold her?"

His answer was to lift her onto his lap. "Can you tell the rest of it now? The parts about your marriage you left out? I think it all needs to be said, don't you?"

A rush of nausea made her breathe in deeply. Yes, it needed to be said. She wanted to tell him. "Jack wasn't always mean. And he wasn't mean anyway unless he was drunk."

"Ah, and that's something else, isn't it? You get uptight every time I take a drink?"

"Not so much anymore." She rested her cheek on Michael's chest. "And in time I will put it all in the past, what went on with Jack. He was sweet when we were first married. He changed, but I think that was partly my fault. Running the business and being married was too much responsibility for him. He didn't mean to hurt me."

"Tell me all of it, Sophie. We can't go on until you do." A knuckle beneath her chin raised her face to his. "You want us to go on, I know you do."

She played her fingers over his mouth. "You may just know me too well, Michael Harris. A woman likes a few secrets of her own."

He kissed her, a brushing, infinitely tender kiss that barely parted her waiting lips. They looked at each other for a long time, then Michael smiled a little, encouraging smile, and Sophie leaned her head against his shoulder.

Michael didn't speak. He understood her struggle and wouldn't push her to go faster than she was able.

"Jack got drunk and then he got mad," she began, and her voice cracked. "He'd blame me because he wasn't happy, and afterward he wanted to make love. I couldn't...I didn't want to."

Michael drove his teeth into his bottom lip, and she saw his nostrils flare. She was making him uncomfortable, but she wouldn't stop now.

"It was always the same. I tried to reason with him, pretend to be asleep when he came home, anything I could think of. But he'd start in, and when I refused he hit me."

Michael pulled her fiercely against him and cursed under his breath.

"And then we...he had intercourse with me."

When she finished speaking there was no sound but their breathing.

"It wasn't love anymore," she said after a while. "I was being assaulted. He destroyed something inside me. After he was dead I hoped I'd be able to feel again, at least try to make another start with someone else, but I only moved further into myself...until I met you. Michael, making love with you was new. Do you know what I mean?"

He was silent for an instant before he said, "Tell me."

"I'd never been made love to before. Not really. Jack just used my body. I don't think he meant it to be that way. He didn't know any better. But you loved me while we were together, and it was wonderful."

"I love you now," Michael said softly. "I've never stopped loving you."

The breath she might have taken was snatched away, and she wrapped her arms around his neck. "Thank you. I...I love you, Michael. It won't all come right for me immediately, but I do love you, and I'll work on it."

"We'll both have to work on it. From here on we'll have to help each other with the forgetting. Why didn't you leave Jack, Sophie? Why did you let him pound you so far down?"

"I'm not sure. I know I should have left him, but I'd loved him. We were together from when we were school kids, and I couldn't just go away."

"Someone should have killed the bastard," Michael ground out.

"Someone did. He killed himself. They called it an accident. He'd been out with a woman. He told me that. Jack had a lot of women, and he liked to talk about them. They didn't tie him down like I did, and they were exciting. I was just there, and he thought I should be prepared to be used when he wanted me. You asked once why we didn't have children. Jack didn't want any. He said he would one day, but he couldn't cope with any more pressures than he had then, and I think he was being honest when he admitted that."

Michael pushed his fingers into her hair. "How did he die?"

She'd never told anyone exactly what she believed about Jack's death. "The coroner said it was an interaction between drugs and alcohol and that it was an accident."

"But you don't believe that?"

"No. I think he wanted to die. Even when he drank enough to make most men pass out Jack was still wide-awake. He never slept unless he took pills. This time he took a lot of pills, and he took them with whiskey. He knew what he was doing. His life was a mess and he wanted to die."

"Poor guy," Michael muttered, and she looked at him sharply.

"I hate his guts for what he did to you, but he must have suffered."

"He did." Warmth seeped slowly back into her body, and she smiled at Michael. "Thank you for saying that. He was a part of me for so long, and I've learned to remember some of the good times. They say that happens when you lose someone you've loved, don't they? Even if there were a lot of bad times, too?"

"I guess they do." He took her hands from around his neck and held them. "I'm afraid to ask, but do you feel the same way I do? Do you think we should be together, work things out together, for both of us?"

Smarting in her eyes made Sophie blink. "I love you, Michael." She laughed self-consciously. "Now that I've started saying that, you may get tired of hearing it, but I do. I want to be with you more than I can even say."

A deep sigh moved Michael, and he cradled her cheek with one hand. "I'm looking forward, suddenly. It feels odd. I don't remember looking forward for a long time."

Sophie rested her forehead on his chin and smiled. "There is something I'd like to clear up, Michael."

"What?" She felt him stiffen.

"Those children of my own I'm supposed to have? The ones who will make me a well balanced human being with her mother instincts in the right place? Where exactly should I go to get them?"

Michael grunted and moved until he could see her face. "Is that supposed to be funny?"

"I just need an honest answer."

"Okay." He sniffed, his eyes focused on a point above her head. "It could probably be arranged—in time, you understand—for you to get them from me."

Sophie smiled. "Thank you very much."

"So, we have a deal then, Sophie?" Michael wasn't smiling anymore.

She nodded and extended one hand. "A deal."

50	73
	74
1	7
52	